D0586110

34 115 0028440217

Eye of the Raven

4

Eye of the Raven

KEN McCLURE

ARGYLL AND BUTE COUNCIL
LIBRARY SERVICE

First published in Great Britain in 2005 by
Allison & Busby Limited
Bon March Centre
241-251 Ferndale Road
London SW9 8BJ

http://www.allisonandbusby.com

Copyright © 2005 by Ken McClure

The moral right of the author has been asserted.

This book is sold subject to the conditions that it shall not,
by way of trade or otherwise, be lent, resold, hired out or
otherwise circulated without the publisher's prior
written consent in any form of binding or cover other than
that in which it is published and without a similar condition
being imposed upon the subsequent
purchaser.

A catalogue record for this book is available from
the British Library.

10 9 8 7 6 5 4 3 2 1

ISBN 0 7490 8334 4

Printed and bound in Wales by
Creative Print and Design, Ebbw Vale

Ken McClure was an award-winning research scientist with the Medical Research Council of Great Britain. His medical thrillers have been translated into twenty-one languages and all are international bestsellers. He lives and works in Edinburgh. *Eye of the Raven* is his seventeenth novel.

Other titles by Ken McClure

The Gulf Conspiracy
Wildcard
Deception
Tangled Web
Resurrection
Donor
Pandora's Helix
Trauma
Crisis
Fenton's Winter
The Scorpion's Advance
Chameleon
Requiem
Pestilence

'LOOK NOT FOR PITY IN THE EYE
OF THE RAVEN.'

JOHN LYLY

(1554 -1606)

The Rev Joseph Lawson took up stance at the door of his church to watch his congregation – all eight of them – depart at the end of the Sunday evening service. He could not help but feel – with what he thought was a brave attempt at humour – that what they lacked in numbers they made up for in years. He guessed at a combined age of something over six hundred.

Willie MacPhee, a long-retired bank employee and the last of the group to complete the walk along the overgrown path through a maze of vandalised headstones and neglected shrubbery, turned to close the gate behind him. His pronounced stoop and the fact that the sleeves of his beige rain jacket were too long made it difficult and his wife's body language exuded impatience as he continued to fumble with the mechanism. When he heard the rusty latch finally fall into place, Lawson raised his hand to wave farewell but there was no response. He reasoned that probably neither MacPhee nor his wife could see that far.

Lawson closed the heavy front door and rested his forehead against the wood for a moment. Somewhere in the distance he heard local youths bawling out some football anthem as they made their way to the wooden hut that comprised the local social club, intent on a second night of lager-fuelled oblivion in the aftermath of their team's Saturday victory. Lawson knew the words well enough; they had more to do with religious bigotry than football, not that the singers were religious by any stretch of the imagination: bigotry was just an easier option than agnosticism or atheism, which demanded some intellectual input.

'Morons,' Lawson murmured although this wasn't a sentiment you expressed too loudly here in the central belt of Scotland, especially the part known as 'Orange County' where seventeenth-century battles were stop-press news and King William of Orange still reigned supreme.

As he turned, he noted that the porch smelt of lavender and liniment. He sniffed again before smiling and murmuring,

'God be praised.'

There was no smell of stale urine this week. Old Mrs Ferguson had finally been taken into hospital where he supposed she would block a bed for what remained of her probably good but unremarkable life. Lawson silently wished her well and walked through into the main body of the church to gather up tattered hymnbooks before returning them to the sorry pile in the porch.

He paused to appraise the church notices giving times and locations of the various activities at St John's, thinking that they really needed renewing. They had faded badly, the corners curling over the drawing pins, but this only made him consider who was going to see them anyway? Bible class comprised of two insurance clerks and a librarian. Scouts were eight youngsters and a leader he was beginning to have doubts about and the Young Mothers Club – four girls, all under twenty-two, of whom only one was married and two had no idea who the father of their child was. 'God give me strength,' he murmured before turning away.

It wasn't that Lawson's faith was faltering but he did have the distinct impression that he was being tested – perhaps not in the way the martyrs had – for he had little in the way of pain and suffering to endure – no, for him, indifference and suspicions of irrelevance were the chosen instruments of examination. The telephone rang in the vestry and mercifully broke his train of thought.

'Reverend Lawson.'

'John Traynor, assistant governor at the State Hospital here, minister. Sorry to interrupt your Sunday but Hector Combe is asking to see you.'

'Can't it wait until Wednesday?' asked Lawson, seeing the threat to his planned evening in with a couple of drams of Ardbeg malt and Ian Rankin's latest Rebus book. Wednesday was his usual day for visiting The State Hospital at Carstairs and he found once a week more than enough. Carstairs was a secure establishment for the criminally insane – Scotland's equivalent of Broadmoor in England – and not the kind of place to offer comfort to those of low spirit or foster an unquestioning love of humanity.

'Fraid not, minister. Combe's very poorly. The doctor doesn't think he'll see out the night.'

'All right, give me an hour,' said Lawson, resigning himself to a forty-minute drive across bleak moorland in the dark when the weather forecast was for rain driving into central areas of the country, aided by strong westerly winds.

As he changed out of his robes in the vestry, Lawson couldn't ever recall the patient, Combe, expressing a desire to speak to him before. The more he thought about it, an unpleasant sneer was what he associated most with the man, a look on his face that suggested cynical superiority and an outlook that equated religious belief with weakness. This of course, was before the man's illness had destroyed his capacity to display any expression at all. Combe had been receiving treatment for cancer of the jaw, which had involved radical surgery to his face.

Combe was a dying man and that, as Lawson conceded, often changed things. Perhaps it wasn't too surprising at all that he was seeking some contact with the Church at this late stage. A great many tended towards repentance when the grim reaper was about to call...just in case.

As he'd feared, the rain started in earnest as he set out in his old Ford Escort for Carstairs and positively lashed down as he drove across the barren stretch of moorland between his Upgate manse and the State Hospital. At one point he had to slow down almost to a standstill when the wipers failed to cope with the sheer volume of water. The sound of the rain hitting the roof of the car was impeding his ability to think straight and his every instinct was to turn back but if this was to be Hector Combe's last night on earth he felt obliged to push on if at all possible. He felt guilty for hoping that the governor would be right in his prognosis of death for Combe. He really didn't want to be doing this for no reason. The rain slackened a little and he started to make better progress although it seemed as if every dip in the road harboured a small lake, which threw up a bow wave and threatened to swamp the car's electrics.

Lawson's thoughts turned to hoping that he could disguise his dislike of the prisoner, Combe, when he got there. Combe was a psychopath, a convicted murderer who had killed four people during his adult life without compunction or remorse. Lawson knew that it was incumbent upon him to seek out some saving grace in the man, particularly at a time when it was fashionable to believe that all people must have one, but Lawson found it hard to share this view. His dealings with the inmates at Carstairs had convinced him otherwise. There had been times in that benighted place when he had felt the presence of evil to be almost tangible. Some of the inmates seemed to exude it, an invisible miasma of malevolence that challenged the very concepts of civilised society.

The car emerged from the confines of a long avenue of trees and Lawson felt the familiar hollow feeling come to his stomach as the high perimeter fence of the prison – or hospital as they insisted on calling it – came into view. Floodlighting highlighted the barbed-wire rolls stretched out along the top against the night sky. All that was missing was The Ride of the Valkyries.

'It's not your day today is it minister?' asked the prison officer who looked into the car to check his credentials.

Lawson appreciated the ambiguity of the statement but knew well enough what the officer meant. 'I understand Hector Combe is dying,' he replied.

'And I'll dance at the party when he does,' replied the man without bothering to append an apology as he waved Lawson through to where he parked the car and completed the formalities of admission before being escorted to the assistant governor's office.

'Good of you to come at such short notice, minister,' said the assistant governor, John Traynor, when he saw Lawson appear in his doorway, brushing the rain from his shoulders. 'Hell of a night.'

The prison officer, who'd ushered Lawson in, closed the

door behind him as he left and Traynor motioned Lawson to sit with a wave of his hand.

'I have to say I was a bit surprised when I got your call,' said Lawson. 'I don't recall Combe and I ever having much to say to each other.'

Traynor nodded. 'I have to say I hadn't marked him down for deathbed repentance either,' he said. 'He's always struck me as being hard as nails and cold as ice. I suppose it only goes to show I never did discover the inner man.'

The comment had been tongue in cheek. Lawson knew Traynor to have little time for what he regarded as 'trendy psycho-babble' when it came to penal matters.

'How is he?'

'Lucid but fading fast.'

'Relatives?'

'None that care to call,' said Traynor.

'Best get on then,' said Lawson.

Traynor pressed a button and two prison officers appeared. 'Take Rev Lawson to see Combe, will you.'

As Lawson walked behind the leading officer he was aware of the sound of rain hammering against a metal section of the roof. He glanced upwards and the officer walking beside him said, 'Hell of a night.'

They passed through three locked sections before the leading man said, 'He's along here.'

Lawson knew this part of the establishment to be a hospital within a hospital, a sickbay for the already mentally ill when they went down with some more physical ailment. The smell changed from stale food and urine to sweat and disinfectant. The leading officer unlocked a heavy door and asked, 'Do you want us to stay, minister?'

Lawson shook his head. 'I'll be all right.'

'Have a care,' said the man. 'He looks as weak as a kitten but you can never be sure with that bastard. Be on your guard. He might just fancy taking you with him for the hell of it.'

A male nurse who stood well over six feet tall and looked more like a boxer than a nurse acknowledged Lawson's arrival with a nod and walked with him to Combe's bedside.

'The minister's here, Combe,' the nurse said in a surprisingly soft, lisping voice.

Hector Combe, his face pointlessly disfigured by surgery to combat a cancer which had subsequently spread throughout his entire body anyway, opened his eyes. Even at death's doorstep, they were still the compassionless glittering orbs that Lawson remembered. They always made him think of a bird of prey contemplating its next meal.

'You asked to see me, Combe,' said Lawson, sitting down on the chair that the male nurse had brought up behind him. It creaked loudly when he moved on it so he tried to remain still.

'Dying,' said Combe hoarsely and with difficulty as he twisted his lips in an effort to form the word.

'Comes to us all,' said Lawson, guiltily aware of the starkness of the comment but unwilling to soften it.

'Confession.'

'For an awkward moment Lawson thought that Combe might be Roman Catholic. He asked him.

'Not that kind…another one…another death…'

Lawson felt a chill run down his spine. He moved uncomfortably and the chair creaked. 'You want to confess to another murder?' he asked.

Combe's hand shot out and gripped Lawson's wrist, forcing him to think of the throats it had held, the cords, the knives… He had disembowelled one victim. He tried to pull his hand back but the white bony claw with its bulging blue veins held fast. 'Julie Summers…it was me.'

'Who?'

'Julie Summers…the babysitter…it was me. I killed her.'

It had been several years before but Lawson remembered the murder of a teenage girl in a village outside Edinburgh. 'The West Linton girl?' he asked tentatively.

Combe nodded and relaxed his grip on Lawson's wrist. 'Yeah.'

'But they got the man for that. I remember it well enough,' said Lawson.

Combe seemed amused as indicated by a slight wrinkling of his eyes for he was incapable of smiling. 'Stitched up...some poor bastard, they did... God knows why.'

'We can't be talking about the same case here,' said Lawson. 'The evidence against that man was overwhelming.'

'It was me, I tell you,' insisted Combe. He seemed annoyed at being doubted and Lawson could feel impatience and hostility emanating from him.

'Why?' asked Lawson, feeling bemused but also under obligation to ask something more.

Combe looked at him as if he were stupid, then he said sarcastically, 'Because...she was there...'

Lawson saw from the look in Combe's eyes that this had been intended as a joke. He was filled with horror at the very idea of anyone making such a comment and a chill ran down his spine at the unwelcome insight he'd been given into Combe's mind. 'What were you doing in West Linton?' he continued hoarsely.

'I was on my way...back to Manchester...been in Edinburgh on a job... There she was...wiggling her little arse...all on her ownsome at that time of night...bloody asking for it. Would have been a shame to waste a nice little peach like that,' he said. 'Don't you think?'

Lawson was appalled. He felt totally out of his depth but he was trapped in a situation that demanded he stay. Combe was confessing to a priest. He had to hear him out. 'Let me get this straight,' he murmured, pausing to swallow because his mouth had gone dry. 'You are saying that it was *you* who raped and killed Julie Summers?'

'No fucking *saying*...about it,' said Combe angrily. 'I did it! Want to know every little fucking detail, do you?... Fucking turn you on, will it?... Don't get much pussy in your line of work, right?'

Combe started to talk and Lawson felt his senses reel as he was subjected to hearing every detail of a rape and murder. Combe appeared to feed on his revulsion and seemed to gain strength from Lawson's every wince.

'Scratched me, so I broke the little cow's fingers... This little piggy went to market... Snap! This little piggy stayed at home... Snap! This little piggy...'

'Stop!' commanded Lawson as a wave of nausea enveloped him followed by the almost irresistible desire to strike Combe. With great difficulty he regained his composure and asked hoarsely, 'Why are you telling *me* this?' Why not the governor, the police, the authorities?'

Combe ignored Lawson and continued, 'Silly little bitch...didn't have to start screaming the place down...did she? I had to shut her up before she woke the whole fucking village.'

'Why *me*, Combe?' insisted Lawson, raising his voice.

The glittering eyes turned to Lawson betraying puzzlement. 'Need to square things with the Church ...before I meet my maker...don't I?' he said. 'Make sure...everything's in order like.'

Lawson couldn't quite believe his ears. Did Combe really think that that was all there was to it? 'In order?' he repeated.

'That's what you do...in't it? Make...a clean breast of...things. Confess and then the sheet's...wiped clean. Right?'

Lawson said like an automaton, 'You think that by telling me this you will automatically be accorded forgiveness for what you've done?'

'Yeah,' affirmed Combe, irritated at Lawson's continual questioning of what he clearly felt was obvious. 'That's how it works. You know it is. That's the deal. Salvation and all that...that's what you call it, right?'

'Wrong,' said Lawson, feeling a deep anger well up inside him and speaking as if pronouncing sentence. 'Hector Combe, if there is any justice, you...will undoubtedly burn in hell.'

'What the...fuck kind of a minister are you?' demanded Combe, making an angry but only partially successful effort to sit up before lapsing into a coughing fit as he fell back on to one elbow. The nurse reappeared and held a metal bowl up to Combe's face to receive what he was bringing up from his raddled lungs. Lawson was very aware that Combe's eyes never left his as he continued to hack up blood and phlegm. They were filled with hatred. Lawson wanted to look away but found himself mesmerised as if held in thrall to some strange animal he had absolutely no understanding of.

Combe finally pushed away the bowl. 'Fucking...tosser,' he managed to gasp. 'What kind of a f...'

Combe appeared to freeze in mid-sentence and Lawson, still transfixed by the strength of Combe's hatred, found himself part of a frozen tableau for a few moments before the look in Combe's eyes suddenly became quite neutral and, with a final gurgling sigh, he fell back on his pillow, dead.

'Not exactly Oscar Wilde when it came to last words, was he?' murmured the nurse who'd seen the distressed look on Lawson's face and come over to join them.

Lawson accepted the offer of a whisky in the assistant governor's office and took two large gulps before he could say anything, finding welcome if only momentary distraction in the burning sensation in his throat.

'Combe couldn't have done it,' said Traynor. 'The police got the right man for the Julie Summers murder. He's eight years into a life sentence in Barlinnie. It was thought at the time that he should have been sent here but the medical experts declared him perfectly sane.' Traynor snorted his derision and added, 'He rapes and murders a thirteen-year-old girl, and they don't even come up with a "personality disorder". Makes you bloody wonder.'

Lawson was only half-aware of what Traynor was saying. He was still thinking about his nightmare meeting with Combe. His hand was shaking as he raised the whisky glass to his mouth for a final gulp. 'Combe was adamant that he did it,' he said.

Traynor looked at him sympathetically and said, 'No way, minister, but I'll send in a report to the relevant police authority of course.'

'Why confess to something he didn't do?' persisted Lawson as the whisky finally started to have a calming effect and he got his wits back about him.

Traynor shrugged and said, 'I've long given up trying to work out what goes on inside a psycho's head. They don't think like you or I do. Don't dwell on it, minister.'

Lawson, who had just undergone what he felt was perhaps the worst experience of his life, looked questioningly at Traynor as if he were completely insensitive to what he'd gone through. Of course he was going to dwell on it! It was going to haunt him for the rest of his life. All that came out however, was, 'Oh dear God,' as looked down at the floor and shook his head.

Traynor still seemed insensitive to the extent of Lawson's trauma. 'About Combe's funeral, minister, would you want to officiate yourself?'

When Lawson responded with a blank look he continued, 'Perhaps in the circumstances you'd prefer me to ask someone else?'

'Definitely somebody else,' said Lawson.

Chapter Two

'Julie Summers?' exclaimed Detective Inspector Peter McClintock of Lothian and Borders Police, his red face showing disbelief. 'Combe confessed to killing Julie Summers?'

'That's what the report says,' confirmed his sergeant, Mark Ryman.

McClintock maintained his look of incredulity as he firmly shook his head and said, 'No way Jos , we put David Little away for that one eight years ago and the evidence against him was watertight.' After a few moments' thought he added, 'Why on earth would a nutter like Combe want to put his hands up for the Julie Summers killing? It doesn't make sense.'

Ryman shrugged and said, 'Apparently he confessed to some Church of Scotland minister who was on-call at Carstairs last night.

'Some guys get all the good jobs,' muttered McClintock.'

'His name's Joseph Lawson; he's the minister over at Upgate. The report suggests it was a deathbed confession,' said Rivers. 'Combe moved on to the great State Hospital in the sky shortly afterwards.'

'Not all bad news then,' muttered McClintock. 'Except for God, that is.' But his mind was already drifting elsewhere. He was running through the details of the Julie Summers murder in his head and it wasn't that difficult given it had been such a high profile case.

Although an arrest had been made and a conviction secured on irrefutable evidence, it had left a trail of damage in its wake, including several resignations from the force and the suicides of both the initial suspect, Bobby Mulvey, and his mother, Mary.

A missing schoolgirl was the kind of case that the press made a meal of and there had been massive public interest at the time. Before the body had been found, Bobby Mulvey, a seventeen-stone, six-foot-tall man with the mental age of an eight-year-old, had been brought in for routine questioning.

He had lived in the same street as Julie and had been seen talking to her on the day she had disappeared. Because of this he received a particularly rough ride from the tabloids.

Although they didn't actually accuse him in print, they did succeed in fuelling a whispering campaign against Mulvey, which spread like wildfire throughout the small community and beyond. To his added misfortune, Mulvey looked like everyone's idea of a suspect for that type of crime. He was swarthy, had long unkempt hair and seemed to have a permanent leer on his face. McClintock remembered the officer in charge of the investigation at the time, DI Bill Currie, saying that Bobby Mulvey was the only man he'd ever come across who actually looked like a photo-fit picture.

Mulvey didn't have a police record but he had more than once caused unease among the locals by throwing spectacular temper tantrums in public – usually after some of the local kids had been baiting him. This was something his mother insisted they did on purpose in order to provoke such a response.

As rumour and innuendo about Mulvey's involvement fermented into openly voiced suspicion, some of the locals had demonstrated their frustration at what they saw as police ineptitude by throwing bricks through the Mulveys' windows and daubing the walls of their small cottage with abusive slogans. His mother's insistence that Bobby had been particularly fond of Julie and would never have done anything to harm her only served to foster a general belief that he might have made sexual advances towards her and got angry when she had rejected him.

Julie's body was found some three days later after a massive search involving hundreds of public volunteers who'd responded to an appeal put out by the papers. Her naked, broken body had been discovered lying like a discarded doll in woodland about half a mile outside the village. She had been sexually assaulted and strangled with her own underwear.

Under terrific pressure from the media to make an arrest, Currie decided in his own mind that Mulvey must be guilty

and brought him in again. He attempted to break him by sub-
jecting him to what amounted to unceasing verbal abuse for
thirty-six hours interspersed with episodes of actual physical
violence.

Mulvey, desperate for sleep and in need of respite from the
angry men who constantly accused him, finally broke down
and confessed to the rape and murder of Julie. He probably
would have admitted to causing the downfall of the Roman
Empire and having complicity in the murder of John F
Kennedy had Currie and his team suggested this were so.

Mulvey's mother had complained bitterly when she was
finally allowed to visit her son and saw the bruising to his ribs
and his kidneys. She tried lodging an official complaint but
found the police surgeon, Dr George Hutton, less than helpful. Hutton hadn't been interested in tabulating or recording
her son's injuries. He shared the public's distaste for anyone
who could carry out such a crime and felt confident that the
tabloid-readers weren't going to be too concerned with a little
physical discomfort being meted out to little Julie's killer
should details leak out. Apart from anything else, Hutton
played golf with Currie and wanted the glare of publicity to be
off the force just as much as Currie so they could all get back
to normal. The public wanted Bobby Mulvey's head on a plate
and that was exactly what the force had given them – or so it
seemed.

Currie and his team could hardly believe it when DNA evidence from the forensic lab said that a mistake had been made
and that Mulvey was innocent of the crime. In an embarrassing *volte-face*, they were forced to release Mulvey and start the
hunt all over again. For Bobby Mulvey however, it was a case
of out of the frying pan into the fire. He was set upon that
same night by a mob who were unaware of the real reason for
his release and who had put it down to some legal loophole
being exploited by some clever-dick lawyer in an age when the
system always seemed to be on the side of the offender.

This had been due to Currie and his superior, Supt. George
Chisholm, being extremely reluctant to admit their mistake in

public and even less keen to explain the circumstances under which Mulvey's 'confession' had been obtained. They had issued a fudged press statement listing 'technical factors' as the reason for having let Mulvey go and carefully avoided using words like 'innocent' with reference to Mulvey or 'mistaken' with regard to themselves. They had removed the police guard on the Mulveys' home and it was only hours before Bobby Mulvey was dragged from it and beaten senseless. Not content with that, one of the mob had carved the words 'rapist' on his back with a Stanley knife while his mother looked on helplessly.

Bobby Mulvey spent three weeks in hospital recovering from his injuries during which time his mother decided that enough was enough. She recognised that she was getting too old to look after her son and that no one else would do it when she was gone – especially after seeing what the establishment in the shape of the police had put him through. Mary Mulvey had mixed a cocktail of every pill and sleeping tablet she could find in the house and added it to the cocoa that she and her son had every night before bed. She and Bobby ended their lives together on the carpet of their living room floor, the outside walls of their cottage daubed with obscenities and its broken windows letting in the winter rain.

Currie, now under almost intolerable pressure to find Julie's killer and make an arrest, could hardly believe his luck when the forensics lab came up with a DNA match for the crime. The suspect, David Little, a professional man living with his family in the same village as Julie, had given a DNA sample along with all the other males in the village at the outset of the murder investigation. He didn't have a police record but he had previously been reported to the police for being in possession of pornographic material found on his computer at work. He had subsequently been released without charge.

Little's DNA fingerprint proved to be an exact match for the semen found in the victim and it transpired that he knew Julie quite well. She had acted as a babysitter for him and his wife on several occasions in the recent past. Little had maintained his innocence throughout but the evidence against him was so overwhelming that he went down for life with a judge's recommendation that he spend at least twenty-five years in prison.

In the aftermath of the case the tabloid press, wishing to distance themselves from all blame and looking for a new angle to sell papers, decided to concentrate on the Mulveys' tragic suicide. They suddenly felt the need to 'expose' what they called 'the heavy-handed methods' used by the police in the investigation and cited this as the main reason for its tragic outcome for the Mulveys.

They openly accused the force of being responsible for the deaths of 'two of society's vulnerable people', charging them with the age-old tactic of picking up the 'local loony' as a quick fix whenever public interest was high in a case. In doing so they managed to broaden their remit by resurrecting doubts that had been expressed about several other cases over the years. The public at the time had been happy to jump on the press bandwagon, mainly to assuage their own guilt in the affair.

Currie had been forced to take early retirement from the force on health grounds, as had his superior officer, George Chisholm. George Hutton, the police surgeon who had failed to protect Mulvey and process the complaint lodged by his mother about the injuries he'd received at the hands of Currie and his team, was also put out to grass, as was the forensic pathologist involved in the case, Ronald Lee.

'So why the hell would Combe pull a stunt like that?' muttered McClintock, still sounding puzzled.

'No doubts at all?' ventured his sergeant.

'The DNA evidence was perfect,' said McClintock. 'It was a one hundred per cent match for Little. The odds against it being wrong were countless millions to one.'

'So maybe Combe just wanted to make trouble for the force by bringing up that Mulvey business all over again?'

'I think I like that idea better,' grunted McClintock. 'That would be entirely in the bastard's nature.'

'So we just forget it?'

'No, we do things by the book. We dig out the file on the
Julie Summers case; make sure there was no margin for error
– as indeed there wasn't – and then we'll forget it.'

An hour later, when he came back from a meeting with his
superintendent who had been telephoned personally by the
governor of The State Hospital about the confession,
McClintock found the Julie Summers file on his desk. The
first thing that struck him was a small sticker on the front
cover saying that a copy of any material added to the file after
the closing date of May 4th 1993 should be forwarded to the
Sci-Med Inspectorate at the Home Office in London without
delay.

'Wonder what their interest was...' murmured McClintock.
He knew that they were a small body concerned solely with
hi-tech crime in science and medicine. He supposed that the
so-called confession of Combe to the murder would have to
be appended to the Summers file...or would it? McClintock
toyed with the notion of burying it somewhere else but then
thought better of it. There was always a chance that the story
might leak out to the press. Half the bloody nation seemed to
be on the phone to the papers these days. No, he would play
this strictly by the book and forward a copy of the confession
to London. The chances were that Sci-Med would probably
just file it themselves after seeing it for what it was – the ramblings of a now dead psychopath.

John Macmillan, head of the Sci-Med Inspectorate, looked
thoughtful as he closed the Julie Summers file in front of him
and pushed the desk intercom button. 'Send Dunbar in, will
you, Miss Roberts.'

In the outside office Steven Dunbar smiled at Jean Roberts
as she indicated that he should go through. 'Don't let him
bully you,' she said conspiratorially.

'I'll try not to,' replied Steven in a stage whisper. In truth he
got on very well with John Macmillan and had done ever since
joining Sci-Med as one of their medical investigators.

The Sci-Med Inspectorate had been set up under the directorship of Macmillan as a small, specialised Home Office unit whose function it was to investigate possible wrongdoing in the world of science and medicine. These areas of modern life had become just too technical for the police to keep up with and, while they had specialised units to deal with fraud and crime in the art world, they were often very much at sea when it came to many areas of science and medical technology. Sci-Med's small team of specialist scientists and doctors filled the gap and carried out preliminary investigations to establish facts before – if necessary – handing over their findings to the police with their recommendations.

Although Steven had qualified as a doctor, he had never practised medicine in the conventional sense. He had joined the army straight after his registration year and had served with the Parachute Regiment and on attachment to Special Forces on assignments that had taken him all over the world. In the process, he had become a specialist in field medicine, having been called upon to apply his medical skills under a variety of trying and testing conditions ranging from surgery under the stars in Iraq to setting broken bones in the South American jungle.

He had known well enough when he left the forces in his early thirties that there would be no call for his particular medical skills in civilian life and also that it would be too late for him to train in any other field. The career bandwagon would have passed him by. He had been preparing himself with a heavy heart for life as an in-house physician with some large commercial concern or looking for some clinical post with a pharmaceutical firm when, to his great relief, he had been approached by the Sci-Med Inspectorate and offered something much more attractive and quite different.

Sci-Med had been looking to recruit a new medical investigator and they were looking for a physically fit, medically qualified man with a record of achievement and resourcefulness. Steven fitted the bill. He had been tested under conditions of extreme pressure and had come through with flying colours. Sci-Med understood that there was a world of difference between the team-building games of corporate enterprise and real life situations where the stakes were always so much higher. A couple of days abseiling and clay pigeon shooting was a universe away from coping in situations where real bullets flew and the margins between life and death grew alarmingly narrow. Steven had gone on to become one of Sci-Med's best investigators.

'Two days ago I received an update to a file from the Lothian and Borders Police in Edinburgh,' said Macmillan. 'They were updating it and found our sticker on it.'

'Something interesting?' asked Steven.

'I'm not sure,' replied Macmillan. 'I don't know if you remember the case but some eight years ago a man named David Little was convicted of the particularly brutal rape and murder of a thirteen-year-old schoolgirl in a village outside Edinburgh.'

'I remember,' said Steven. 'It was headline news at the time. The girl had been babysitting. Little was some kind of academic who lived locally. What was our interest in the case?'

'Little wasn't just any old academic,' said Macmillan. 'Dr David Little was a leading medical scientist, a leader in his field who had just been recruited from Harvard to set up a new research unit at a hospital in Edinburgh.'

'He's American then?'

'No, he's English, but he had been working in the States for the usual career reasons of better facilities, more money, greater academic freedom etc. He had however, been tempted back to the UK with a big money offer to set up his own unit here in the UK with joint funding from the Wellcome Trust and the Medical Research Council.'

'What exactly was his field?'

'Cell biology. He was an expert in stem cell technology. His aim was to make organ transplants a thing of the past and he reckoned he could do it in ten years. The idea was to persuade patients' own stem cells to repair damaged organs so there would be no need for the introduction of any foreign tissue and the problems of rejection that always brings.'

'The stuff Nobel prizes are made of,' said Steven.

'Quite so but instead he raped and strangled a schoolgirl and ended up in prison for the rest of his natural life.'

'From what I remember of the case, prison was too good for him,' said Steven.

'A view shared by many,' said Macmillan thoughtfully.

'So what was the update about?'

'A convicted killer who'd been serving life in Scotland's State Hospital at Carstairs for multiple murder, a psychopath named Hector Combe, confessed on his deathbed to a local clergyman that *he* carried out the crime.'

'But there was never any question about the evidence against Little,' said Steven.

'Absolutely not,' said Macmillan. 'A perfect DNA match: his semen was recovered from the girl. You can't ask for better than that.'

'So Combe couldn't have done it.'

'No, he couldn't,' said Macmillan. 'Which begs the question, why confess to a crime you didn't commit?'

Steven shrugged. 'Maybe he was confused. You said he was dying?'

'Of cancer. The report suggests that he was quite lucid when he made the confession. He died shortly afterwards but he was adamant that it was Julie Summers he'd killed. The local police think that he was just trying to cause trouble for them by digging up the past. They took a lot of flak over the case on account of the suicide of the original suspect and his mother. The blame for that was laid at their door by the press at the time. They've no desire to see it all over the papers again.'

'Understandable. So where do I come in?' asked Steven.

'Take a look at the case file. If you agree with the police assessment we'll forget it, if not pick away at it, see what you come up with.'

'*He that pryeth into every cloud may be hit by a thunderbolt*,' quoted Steven with a smile.

'But that's what we pay you for,' replied Macmillan, handing over the file and adding, 'Miss Roberts has prepared some extra material for you. Collect it on the way out.'

Steven left the Home Office and took a cab back to his fifth floor apartment in a converted warehouse near the river. It wasn't quite on the river – Sci-Med pay didn't quite run to that – but it was only one street back so he could actually see the Thames through a gap in the buildings along to the right. He made himself some coffee and sat down by the window to read through the background material he'd been given.

He started with the original police report on the crime and found it made harrowing reading. Julie Summers had been a bright attractive schoolgirl who had been babysitting for a local couple on the evening of January 5th 1993 while they attended the husband's works dinner. The couple had been home by twelve but Julie had declined the husband's offer to walk her home as she lived less than half a mile away. She never made it and was found dead some three days later.

Post-mortem examination revealed that she had been raped both vaginally and anally and had been subsequently strangled with her own brassiere. Her panties had been stuffed into her mouth – presumably to prevent her screaming – and three fingers of her right hand had been broken – presumably during the initial struggle.

Steven looked at the photograph of the child supplied to the police by her parents when she first went missing – a pretty girl smiling and eating ice cream – and compared it with the ones taken by the forensics people after her body was found. It was impossible not to feel an overwhelming sense of sadness. Despite his own medical training he actually felt slightly nauseous, maybe because he had a daughter of his own and it was impossible not to wonder, what if?

Just how many of these animals were there? Steven wondered as he paused to look out of the window. How many were out there tonight, just watching and waiting their chance?

He moved on to the photograph the police had taken of David Little. There was certainly no clue from his appearance that he might be one of them but then that was the trouble; lunatics often tended not to look or act like lunatics. How many rapists and killers had subsequently been described by their neighbours as, 'A quiet man who kept himself very much to himself'? The ugliness of evil was nearly always hidden, just waiting its chance or its trigger.

Little appeared every inch the academic, something under five feet seven according to the police height scale he stood against. He had a mop of frizzy hair, narrow sloping shoulders, a thin waspish-looking face, perhaps suggesting petulance or even arrogance, thought Steven, and wore small, metal-framed glasses to complete an image that could have been taken from the Hollywood drawer marked, 'assorted boffins'.

Steven skimmed through the information that Rose Roberts had included in the file about Little's work and had to admit to being impressed. Unlike so many proposed research projects these days, which were little more than cleverly worded attempts at extracting grant money from the research councils in order to keep their proposers in a job, it sounded as if Little's work had a real chance of success. It made the man's conviction and imprisonment all the more tragic.

Little had been thirty-five at the time of the trial; he would now be forty-three, maybe forty-four. He had been married with two children, both girls, who would now be thirteen and ten. They had lived in the same village as Julie Summers, after moving out there from rented accommodation in Edinburgh where they'd been living since their return from the States. This had been in the summer of 1992 when a large, comfortable family house had come on to the market.

It was difficult not to think that Little had had everything going for him at the time of the murder. He had a job he loved, the recognition of his peers, four million pounds in research grants and as much autonomy to apply them as he could ever have hoped for. He had a wife, two kids and a nice home and he had thrown the lot away because...he needed the body of a schoolgirl.

It seemed incredible but Steven knew well enough that, where sex was the driving force, logic and common sense often went out of the window. It was something that had been documented time and again throughout history. You could be President of the USA and still think that a quick blowjob was worth risking your place in history.

Steven noted that a police psychiatric report had found Little to be uncooperative and aggressive but had found no evidence of personality disorder save for his continuing insistence of his innocence and a reluctance to even contemplate his own guilt.

Little's wife, Charlotte, had divorced him within a year of his conviction and had subsequently severed all links with him. She had moved with the girls away from the district and was last known to be staying with her parents in Cromer in Norfolk. She had recently declined an invitation to take part in a Channel 4 documentary about the suffering experienced by the wives and families of convicted killers.

Steven referred again to the supplementary file on Little and saw that his academic record was outstanding. From humble beginnings as the only child of an insurance agent and a nursery nurse, he had gained a first-class degree from Edinburgh University in medical sciences, and a subsequent D.Phil. from Oxford with a thesis entitled, 'Mammalian Cell Differentiation, Cause and Control'. He had gone on to carry out post-doctoral research on transgenic mice at UCLA in California and then come back to do a second post-doc at the University of Leicester in England before returning to the States to join the so-called brain drain with a move to Harvard where he took up a tenure-track position in the spring of 1990.

After two years however, his wife had become homesick and he had succumbed to pressure to at least consider a move back to the UK. Rumours on the scientific grapevine had led to him being offered the job at the Western General Hospital in Edinburgh and this had tipped the scales in favour of a return. Apart from generous funding for his work it had been made clear that he would be granted a personal chair at the university within a year of his return. The idea of being *Professor* Little in sole charge of his own unit had heralded a new life for the Little family. Unfortunately, thought Steven, it had also signalled an end to the short one of Julie Summers.

A list of Little's scientific publications was appended to the file along with a note of his awards and achievements. There was a copy of his medical records, background reports made at the time of the trial and a psychiatric assessment made after his committal to prison. The bottom line was simple. Little was a highly intelligent, if abrasive man and no one quite knew why he'd done what he'd done. He was currently a Rule 43 prisoner in Barlinnie Prison in Glasgow. He did not have visitors.

Chapter Three

The only clue in the files to what went on inside David Little's head was the incident at the University lab at the Western General Hospital in Edinburgh. A computing officer, who had been working on a network connection fault, reported by Little himself, had discovered a large amount of hard-core pornographic material being stored on the computer in Little's office. The man had immediately passed on his findings to the authorities.

Steven suspected that the university would much rather he hadn't in the circumstances. The last thing it would have wanted at that time would have been any kind of a scandal leading to the dismissal of the man they'd gone to so much trouble to recruit and the subsequent loss of grant money and prestige that would mean. The nature of the material on the disk however, and the fact that a written report had been lodged, had taken matters out of their hands and obliged them to call in the police.

Little had denied all knowledge of the offending material and pointed out that his computer – like all the computers in the unit – was open to use by research students and any other members of staff who might care to use it when none other was available. Computers were generally not regarded as personal property within university departments and confidentiality where required was usually effected through password protection and the saving of sensitive material to removable disks.

In the circumstances, both the police and the university authorities were happy to embrace this get-out clause and were able to head off any potential embarrassment by dismissing the whole affair as a student prank. No further action was taken and the business did not reach the newspapers.

'I wonder,' murmured Steven. From what he'd read about Little, the man did not strike him as the type of person that research students would play pranks on. His reputation was such that he would be held more in awe than in any disregard.

Practical jokes were usually reserved for those members of staff that the students held in low esteem and, while it may have been common practice to share computers in the labs, he couldn't really see Little – as head of the unit – having shared his. He thought it strongly possible that Little had downloaded the material himself and that this was in fact an indication of the true nature of the man.

There was also the matter of the incriminating material itself. It comprised a large number of photographs downloaded from a site specialising in sexual sadism practised on young girls. One such print was included in the file and was captioned, 'Tracy learns her lesson'. It showed the back view of a naked girl being whipped by a man wielding a metal-studded strap. The scars on her back were raw and bleeding and the welts on her buttocks made Steven wince.

'Power trips, Dave? Is that what you were all about?' he murmured.

Steven made himself some more coffee and then turned to the newspaper cuttings of the case. Press coverage had been extensive and, in general, the mood of the articles followed a well-established pattern. Horror had been followed by outrage, which in turn had been followed by criticism of the police and then a general outpouring of anger featuring much use of the words 'beast' and 'monster' when the simpleton, Mulvey, had been arrested.

Steven noted that the tabloids, after using up all their vitriol on Mulvey, had been distinctly reticent when it came to their treatment of Little when he had finally been arrested and charged – as if they had been embarrassed by Little appearing on the scene when they had already convicted Mulvey. He saw the clear change of tack when they started to blame the police for the Mulveys' deaths. Little, the real killer, was variously dismissed as quiet, nondescript, inadequate, enigmatic and obsessive. 'The beast with brains', as one of the papers labelled him.

Little's glittering research career was given no mention, in keeping with the Press's tradition of saying nothing good about those who'd been convicted. One of the broadsheets had done a piece on what they saw as an increase in the incidence of professional men being convicted for serious crimes, citing several members of the medical profession who'd been convicted in recent years of the murder of their patients.

After half an hour, Steven concluded that there was nothing of any great significance to be learned from the cuttings. He decided that he needed a break before moving on to the Hector Combe material and checked his watch before deciding that he should phone his daughter before going out to get something to eat.

Jenny lived in the village of Glenvane in Dumfriesshire in Scotland with his sister-in-law, Sue, and her solicitor husband Richard, who had two children of their own, Mary and Robin. She had lived with them since the death of her mother – Steven's wife and Sue's sister, Lisa, who'd died of cancer some three years ago – and she'd now settled in as one of the family. Steven saw her as often as he could and he tried to spend every second weekend in Glenvane, work permitting. In addition he phoned Jenny twice a week to get her news about school and her friends.

'How are things?' asked Steven when Sue answered the phone.

'Absolutely fine,' replied Sue, her great good nature shining through as always. Sue was the most relaxed person Steven knew. She saw the good in everyone and could find positive things to take from situations where others might find only gloom and despair. In this she was almost matched by her easy-going husband, Richard, who was a partner in a law firm in Dumfries where he took care of the commercial property side of the business. The couple had taken Jenny into their family seemingly without a second thought when Lisa had died, something Steven would be ever grateful for. The weeks and months following Lisa's death had been the darkest time of his life.

'How's my little monster?'

'She's fine. I spoke to her teacher at the gate this morning;

Jenny's a born organiser, she said – quite happy as long as everyone does things her way!'

'Sounds like her,' said Steven.

'I'll put her on.'

Steven heard Sue call out Jenny's name and heard the faint reply, 'I'm busy.'

'It's your daddy,' Sue called out.

Steven heard the running feet and then the breathless, 'Hello Daddy, I'm painting an elephant.'

'What colour are you painting him, Nutkin?'

Steven heard Jenny's fit of the giggles. 'Not a real elephant, silly, a painting book elephant!'

When he'd finished talking to Jenny, Steven went out to find something to eat. His culinary skills did not go much beyond heating up packet meals so take-away food tended to play a significant role in his life. Tonight he returned with a selection of Chinese food from the Jade Garden where he was a once-a-week regular. He reheated it in the microwave before taking a Stella Artois from the fridge and moving everything on a tray through to the living room where he watched the early evening news on Channel 4 while he ate.

Trouble in the Middle East, trouble in Ireland and trouble in Zimbabwe, was followed by party political squabbles at home over farm subsidies. There was a warning about dearer food prices and an 'and finally' story about a kitten marooned on a log floating down a river in Kent and the efforts of the emergency services to rescue it. Steven finished eating and switched off.

The file on Hector Combe related a very different story to that of David Little. Little's file – up until the time of the computer pornography incident – was a glowing record of personal achievement and academic success; Combe's recorded a lifetime of mental illness and criminal activity. Born the illegitimate son of a Glasgow prostitute, he had shown a propensity for violence from an early age, being taken into care at the age of seven and failing to fit in with three separate sets of foster parents by the time he was nine. At this point he had already established himself in police records as a juvenile tearaway.

A teenage life of crime punctuated with periods in various corrective institutes and hospitals had established Combe among the criminal fraternity as a true Glasgow hard man – a man without fear and without conscience. He was assessed by the psychiatric fraternity as a borderline psychopath when he was fourteen and had killed his first victim by the time he was eighteen – a twenty-three-year-old man who didn't like the idea of Combe chatting up his girlfriend. Combe had knifed him in the stomach and, according to witnesses, stood over him smiling as his intestines spilled out on to the pavement outside a nightclub in Glasgow.

Amazingly, Combe had successfully managed to plead self-defence after an exercise in witness intimidation carried out by his underworld friends who valued Combe for his powers of enforcement. Anyone threatened with a visit from Hector Combe generally paid up or shut up, whether it was a case of protection money or sorting out ladies of the night who had become a little too keen on privatising their assets.

Combe had gone to prison for the killing but was out again within five years, the psychiatric board having failed to agree his mental status but deciding to give him the benefit of the doubt in their recommendation to the parole board. It was obvious that the Glasgow police could have helped them out with their assessment of Combe as 'one evil bastard' however, this classification had not been recognised in the psychiatric lexicon and Combe had been freed to continue his 'career'.

For the next few years Combe had managed to avoid crossing paths with the police, not that he had mended his ways but assault and rape perpetrated by one of their own on their own went largely unreported by criminal society so Combe managed to stay clear of the courts. The prostitutes he was employed to keep in line loathed him but were too afraid to refuse an 'invitation' when it came, knowing that if they declined he would have them anyway and it would be twice as bad. In the end they might literally lose their face as one girl had after Combe had taken a knife to her.

Although not officially on any wanted list, the police kept track of Combe through exchanges of inter-force intelligence. As an enforcer, he occasionally moved around the country, accompanying gang bosses on 'business trips' to other cities in the UK. The Glasgow police would inform colleagues as a courtesy when Combe was known to be heading their way.

This situation had continued until June of 1995 when Combe had developed an obsession with a girl outside the criminal fraternity who worked in a flower shop in the centre of Glasgow. At first she had been flattered by Combe's lavish attention: money was no object in his line of work and fast cars and good restaurants were very seductive to a girl earning four pounds an hour. She went out with him several times over a period of six weeks but, as she told friends later, she'd never felt truly at ease in his company. She said that she found his mood changes 'odd' and that he frightened her at times. She suspected that he could be dangerous.

After an incident in a pub in which Combe had threatened a barman with a broken glass, she had told him that she wanted nothing more to do with him but Combe had kept pestering her to continue the association, ultimately threatening her with disfigurement should she even consider seeing someone else. In the end, she had felt obliged to go to the police and they had warned Combe off.

Combe appeared to comply but being a good – or indeed, any kind of loser – was not in Combe's make-up. A month later he turned up at the girl's home late at night. After savagely beating her he raped her in front of her parents whom he'd tied up and when he was through, he murdered all three of them, the parents by strangulation, and the girl by cutting her throat.

He had shown no remorse when the police arrested him, maintaining that the girl had simply got what she deserved. He actually appeared to have forgotten that he'd also killed her parents when the police read out the charges. Combe was sent to prison for life, the psychiatrists finally awarding him full-blown psychopath status. Steven paused to pour himself a gin and tonic. He felt he needed it.

Combe had been incarcerated in the State Hospital at Carstairs where he had gone on to cause mayhem whenever possible with sudden eruptions of violence, only calming down in the Spring of '98 when cancer of the jaw had made an appearance on the left side of his face. The disease succeeded in breaking him where the authorities had failed. A desperate attempt to cling to life involving radical surgery to his face followed by intensive chemotherapy when the disease started to spread, took its toll and left him a broken – though still malevolent – shadow of his former self. He had finally died some ten days ago, bitter to the end and lamented by no one, his only legacy being a confession to a crime he could not possibly have committed.

Steven refilled his glass and swivelled his favourite window chair round so he could look up at the sky. He switched out the room lights. It was a clear night and the stars were out despite competition from urban glare. He, like the local police, was puzzled by Combe's confession. According to what the Church of Scotland minister had written in his report, it had not been made out of any sense of remorse but because he believed that he was entitled to some kind of automatic absolution if he confessed to something before dying. But if the whole thing had been a scam to embarrass the police why had he become so angry when the minister, Lawson, had declined to grant him what he wanted? On the other hand, if Combe had really been intent on gaining absolution, why own up to something he hadn't done when there must have been plenty he had?

Contrition of course, was not something that a psychopath could understand, Steven reminded himself. True psychopaths had no concept of conscience or regret although many were clever enough to simulate such feelings in order to get by in normal society. They would learn to say 'sorry' without any understanding of what the term implied, having deduced by observation that if you did something wrong and then said the word, that was an end to the matter – a simple mathematical equation.

Such pretence of course, was occasionally destined to go badly wrong when the same offence was repeated and saying 'sorry' did not have quite the same effect the second time around. Psychopaths couldn't understand why the 'system' had stopped working on such occasions and were often bemused at the exaggerated response of the aggrieved. It therefore made sense that Combe had seen confessing to a previously undisclosed crime as his side of some automatic *quid pro quo,* which would bring him salvation in the afterlife. It also explained his outrage when Lawson hadn't quite seen it that way. For Combe, Lawson had been a fool who didn't know the rules.

Steven found it slightly disturbing to recognise that Combe was exactly the kind of individual who *could* and *would* have committed an offence like the Julie Summers murder while, on paper, it appeared totally out of character for Little. Combe had confessed: Little had always maintained his innocence. The evidence however, said that Little was the guilty man.

Steven closed the curtains and switched the lights back on. He started going through the forensic evidence offered at the trial, not that this was in any way complicated. The DNA pattern obtained from Little's buccal swab, taken at the start of the investigation, was a perfect match for DNA obtained from the semen found at the scene of the crime. Steven held the photographs of the sequencing gels up in front of him and noted that they were clear and identical. 'Game, set and match,' he murmured.

He paused for a moment to wonder why Little had not tried to avoid giving a sample with the other men from the village. He was a medical scientist so he must have known the significance of what he was doing and that his DNA fingerprint would be certain to convict him and yet there was no report of him being unavailable at any time or appearing reluctant to comply with the police directive. In his job, he could easily have arranged to have been out of town at the time, visiting another university perhaps or even going abroad in connection with his work and yet he had apparently been one of the first to have a smear taken.

On further reading, Steven thought that he had found the reason. Traces of detergent had been found on Julie Summers' vulva, in her vagina and anus. The pathologist had ascribed this to an attempt being made to clean her up after the attack. Little must have underestimated the sensitivity of the test, which only required a minuscule amount of semen, or thought that he'd been more thorough than he had in cleaning up after himself.

As he read on, Steven noted that there seemed to be a dearth of any corroborating evidence offered at Little's trial. He found this puzzling. It was most unlike the Prosecution in any trial not to use every scrap of evidence available to them even if it amounted to overkill. They had alleged correctly that Little knew the dead girl but this had never been in question; she'd been a babysitter at his house. They had pointed out to the jury that he lived in the same village and that he was alone that weekend as his wife happened to be away visiting her parents because her father was ill. They had gone on to suggest that, through local chatter, he would probably have known where Julie Summers was babysitting on the night in question and had lain in wait for her. He had then, they alleged, taken her into nearby woods and raped and strangled her before returning home to where his own children lay sleeping.

Little had vehemently denied all this but in the face of such damning evidence all he could manage to say after sentence was pronounced was, 'There has been some awful mistake.'

Despite the conclusive nature of the DNA match, Steven still found himself wondering why no other forensic evidence had been presented. It was possible that the Procurator Fiscal's office had decided that it wasn't necessary but a mention of matching clothes fibres or mud from the scene of the crime on the accused's shoes or even scratch marks on his face might have given a more rounded feel to the prosecution case.

No mention had been made at the trial of the girl's fingers having been broken in a struggle as the pathologist had suggested in his PM report. Why not? Why had there been no mention of scrapings taken from beneath her fingernails in order to establish a forensic connection with Little? As it stood, Steven was holding the entire case against Little in his hands, two high quality sequencing gel photographs, one taken from the cells on the inside of his mouth and the other taken from semen found in the dead girl.

The jury had obviously not shared Steven's concerns about the lack of back-up evidence. The DNA evidence on its own had done the trick as far as the Crown case was concerned and they had taken less than twenty minutes to unanimously pronounce Little guilty. A calculated gamble by the Fiscal? wondered Steven, or was there something else behind it?

He leafed back through the file papers he had read earlier and found what he was looking for. It was a list of the people whose heads had rolled in the aftermath of the Summers case. Among them was Dr Ronald Lee, the forensic pathologist. Interesting, he thought. Why did Lee have to go?

The Rev Lawson's account of Combe's confession seemed to be confused in parts. It was clear that the man had been deeply shocked by listening to Combe's graphic account of what he had supposedly done to Julie Summers and Steven got the impression that what he was actually reading was an edited version of it. Lawson had probably done this because he couldn't bear to repeat some of the details he'd heard.

Steven noted that Lawson had been particularly disturbed by Combe's account of how he'd broken the girl's fingers after she had scratched him. He'd done it methodically, one by one and had made light of it by introducing a children's nursery rhyme. This little piggy went to market... Snap! This little piggy stayed at home... Snap!

Steven felt a chill run up his spine as he recalled that there had been no mention of broken fingers at the trial and none in any of the news reports he'd read. He started to check frantically through the cuttings, willing there to be some mention but still nothing. If that was the case...how the hell had Combe known that Julie Summers' fingers had been broken?

Steven felt his pulse rate rise and he tapped his right thumbnail rapidly against his teeth as he tried to see some way that Combe could have found out about Julie's fingers. Prison talk maybe? Convicts tended to know a lot of things about their fellow prisoners' crimes and the prison grapevine was notoriously efficient. He supposed that it was even possible that Little had come into contact with Hector Combe at some point – maybe during some psychiatric assessment procedure – but he would have to find out for sure before he could rest easy. If it turned out that this was the case he would put Combe's knowledge down to that. If however, it should turn out that there had been no contact between the two, he would be on his way to Scotland to investigate something very disturbing indeed.

Chapter Four

It had just gone midnight when Steven finally admitted defeat. He had failed to find any reference to Julie Summers' broken fingers anywhere in the press cuttings or any mention of them in the extracts of prosecution submissions made at David Little's trial. He sent a brief email to Sci-Med asking them to investigate whether or not David Little and Hector Combe could ever have crossed paths in the prison system and informing them that he would be travelling to Scotland next day on the first available shuttle flight; he'd be in touch.

This was one of the advantages of working for Sci-Med. Red tape was kept to a minimum and investigators were given a free hand to carry out their assignments as they saw fit. Sci-Med administrators were there to support front-line people, not the other way around as had become the case in so many government departments.

As he considered the prospect, Steven found he had mixed feelings about returning to Scotland. True, it was the place where he had met his wife, Lisa – who had been Scots – and where he had spent many of the happiest times of his life, discovering that particular poignancy that beautiful scenery can have when you are in love – but it held bad memories too.

In the early days of their courtship, spending time together had been difficult and largely limited to when Lisa could manage to escape the yoke of caring for an ageing and increasingly demented mother. Lisa had been a nurse at a hospital in Glasgow when he had been sent there during the course of an investigation, which for him had turned into something of a nightmare and from which he had been lucky to escape with his life.

Yet only eighty or so miles away were the rolling hills of Dumfriesshire and the romantic, lonely shores of the Solway Firth where it was so easy to lose your heart to Scotland. It was a region that so many tourists overlooked as they made their way north to the tartan theme parks of the Highlands. This was where the village of Glenvane lay with its little cluster of whitewashed houses and cobbled yards born of an age when horses tilled the land and the pace of life had been slower. This was where his daughter, Jenny, lived and was happy among people who cared about each other. Steven had seen the good side of Scotland and the bad, the generosity of its people and their meanness of spirit. When they were good they were very good but by God, when they were bad, they didn't bear thinking about.

As the aircraft banked over the Firth of Forth to begin its final descent into Edinburgh Airport it afforded the passengers sitting on the left a grandstand view of the two bridges spanning the estuary below. They were bathed in morning sunshine, the huge red cantilevers of the older rail bridge appearing particularly dramatic, standing tall as a continuing testament to Victorian engineering.

As he looked to the west, Steven wondered with some trepidation what the day would bring. He had arranged for a car to be waiting for him at the airport and his plan was to drive out to the village of Upgate in Lanarkshire to speak with the Rev Lawson about his interview with Hector Combe. He was assuming that Lawson would actually be there. There had not been time to contact him or make any more formal arrangement.

As luck would have it, they were testing the prison sirens when he reached Carstairs. At least, he assumed that it was a test sounding in the absence of any sign of any other activity. It seemed reasonable to believe that there would have been plenty had there been a real escape in progress. He still found it an eerie sound however as he looked up at the tall perimeter fence and wondered what the residents in the nearby houses must think when they heard it go off. He imagined doors and windows being double-checked on dark wet nights, fearful glances being exchanged and TV volumes being turned up.

Steven moved through the village slowly until he found the sign directing him to the B road that led over to Upgate, the one that the Rev Lawson would have used on the night of Combe's death. Like most of the roads around here it ran over bleak moorland, making travellers wonder what it must be like to live here in winter and hoping – as they noticed their mobile phone signal disappear – that the car wouldn't break down.

Steven's rented Rover coped without problem and he entered Upgate, looking for a church spire as an indication of where he might find Lawson. There were no other high buildings in the village so he found it without difficulty and turned off into what he read was Mosspark Road to stop outside the less than imposing building of St John's. He guessed that the grimy Victorian villa standing next to it would be the manse. A metal plaque confirmed this when he reached the gate.

He walked up the cracked and weedy front path to knock on a front door that hadn't seen paint in many years. His second knock was answered by a woman in her fifties who seemed more than a little put-out to have callers. The lines on her face suggested that she hadn't smiled much in the last thirty years. 'Aye, what is it?'

'Is the Rev Lawson at home this morning?' asked Steven.

'He's no' here,' snapped the woman.

'Will he be back soon?'

'Depends.'

'On what?' asked Steven, struggling to maintain a civil smile.

'Them at The Firs.'

Steven tried a blank stare instead of asking another question and the woman eventually said, 'The meenester's ill. He's in The Firs. A nervous breakdoon, they say. Ah dinnae ken; a'body's hivin them these days. A load o' shite if ye ask me. Ah kin remember a time when folk got oan with their lives without all this brekdoon and stress nonsense.'

Steven figured that a nod might be the best way to pave the way ahead. After a moment he asked, 'How do I go about finding The Firs, Mrs...?' asked Steven.

'McLellan; ah'm the meenester's cleaner, no' that he pays me ower much. Tak a left at the end o' the street and it's aboot twa miles oot on the Ayr road. Gie him ma best wishes and tell him he's oot o' toilet roll.'

'Will do,' said Steven.

Steven found The Firs without difficulty although he saw the sign a bit late, thanks to overhanging tree branches, and had to back up on the road before negotiating the narrow entrance that led to an imposingly long drive lined with the trees that had, he presumed, lent their name to the house. He parked on the gravel outside the front door of a large red sandstone villa with an ugly concrete box extension tacked on to its left-hand side. A notice board by the side of the steps leading up to the door proclaimed the house's credentials as a Church of Scotland Rest and Recuperation Home. Steven took encouragement from this. If the place wasn't actually a hospital – psychiatric or otherwise – there must be a good chance that Lawson's condition might not be as serious as he'd feared.

'Rev Lawson is here for complete rest,' said the small, bespectacled figure in the charcoal suit and dog collar who introduced himself as the Rev Angus Minch, the man in charge of The Firs. He'd been summoned by the lone woman in the front office who had been having a telephone conversation about the colour of bridesmaids' dresses when Steven had entered. He'd gathered that green was a non-starter.

'I promise I won't keep him long,' said Steven.

'That's not the point,' said Minch pompously. 'Rev Lawson needs complete rest. Every visitor he gets just interrupts the healing process.'

Steven had no wish to enter any kind of argument about 'the healing process', which he regarded as an expression seldom used by health professionals but a particular favourite of quacks and those who liked to imagine they knew more about medicine than they actually did.

'I'm afraid it's important that I speak with him,' he said in a tone that suggested he had the authority to back up his request.

Minch gave a heavy sigh before saying grudgingly, 'So be it. But if Rev Lawson should suffer a relapse over this, I'll know exactly where to apportion blame.'

Steven guessed that Minch was a man well used to apportioning blame: he had that air about him. Moral rectitude
oozed from every pore. Steven nodded acceptance and was
taken by Minch to a small back room on the first floor where
they found Lawson sitting reading in an armchair by the window. He was wearing a dark plaid dressing gown and seemed
calm when Minch introduced him – perhaps too calm, he
thought. He guessed that he was on some kind of medication.
The book he was reading was Arthur Grimble's *A Pattern of
Islands*.

'I'm sorry, Joseph; this chap's from something called the
Sci-Med Inspectorate, whoever *they* are,' snapped Minch with
a sidelong glance at Steven. 'I'm afraid he needs to ask you
some questions. I told him you weren't well but he insists.'

Lawson looked up at Steven over his glasses and asked,
'About the Combe business?'

'I'm afraid so,' said Steven.

'I have already told the police and the prison authorities
everything I know about that...man,' said Lawson. 'There is
absolutely nothing more I can tell you or anyone else.'

Steven wondered about the editing process that had left
Lawson finally with "man". He said, 'I understand your frustration Rev Lawson but there are some more things I must ask
you.'

'Would you like me to stay?' asked Minch but Lawson said
not with a resigned wave of his hand. 'I'm fine, Angus,' he
assured him.

Steven waited until the door had closed behind Minch. 'I
understand that Combe put you through quite an ordeal?' he
said sympathetically.

A vulnerable look appeared on Lawson's face and he paused
as if choosing his words carefully. 'I thought I understood
people, Dr Dunbar: I believed I knew about the darker side of
life, as people like to call it. Upgate isn't exactly *Songs of Praise*
territory. It's an ugly rash on the landscape with a population
more concerned with Orange Order marches than church
socials – more social services than social diary, if you take my

meaning. Continual poverty breeds its own kind of society over the years and believe me, it isn't pretty. It's life at the lowest common denominator. I'm telling you this because I don't want you thinking that I'm some kind of middle-class cleric who's had an attack of the vapours because he suddenly came face to face with the real world. I was stupid enough to believe that I'd seen it all in my years at Upgate but I was wrong.' His voice dropped to a whisper as he added, 'Oh so wrong. Nothing prepared me for Hector Combe.'

'I think you can be excused for not having come across someone like Combe before,' said Steven quietly. 'That's a "privilege" afforded to only a very unlucky few.'

Lawson smiled wryly. 'Do you know,' he said, 'I went there feeling...' Lawson searched unsuccessfully for the right expression, 'in charge, if you like. It was my role to hear the confession of a dying man. I was the one with the power to offer comfort and reassurance. He was supposed to be the one on his best behaviour, the one displaying remorse and contrition, only Combe didn't seem to see it that way. He had some understanding of the situation but it was a perverted one, if you know what I mean? Maybe you don't; I'm not sure I do myself. He didn't really seem to comprehend what sinning and forgiveness was all about.'

'The games people play,' said Steven softly. 'They're a complete mystery to psychopaths but they're clever; they observe; they emulate as best they can, but they can never feel the underlying emotions so sometimes it doesn't quite come off. It's hard to appear contrite when you don't know what the word means.'

'Yes, that's it exactly,' said Lawson, pleased that someone appeared to understand what he was saying, but then a darkness came over him.

'He insisted on telling me every little detail about what he'd done to that poor girl. Every evil, loathsome thing that he'd made her do and what he'd done to her...And you know, he seemed to enjoy telling me. I could see it was giving him a thrill all over again. He was...' Lawson's voice fell to a whisper, 'touching himself under the blankets as we spoke...enjoying it as if he were reliving the experience.'

'He didn't really do these things,' said Steven. 'He was making the whole lot up. He was deliberately trying to shock you.'

Lawson turned in his chair and looked at him without blinking. 'Was he?' he asked. 'Was he really?'

Steven found the doubt in Lawson's eyes so compelling that he did not reply immediately. Instead, he brought a chair over to join him at the window and sat down. 'Psychopaths feed off other people's fear and revulsion,' he said. 'It's like a drug to them. They see it as weakness, an affirmation of their own strength and superiority.'

'So why ask for absolution for something he hadn't done? Why make up something like that?' asked Lawson.

'I don't know,' admitted Steven.

'It doesn't make any sense,' said Lawson, gazing out of the window and shaking his head.

'The police think he was trying to get at them by attracting press attention to the case all over again. I understand they had a lot of bad publicity over their handling of it the first time around.'

Lawson considered this in silence.

'I'm sorry to have to put you through this,' said Steven, 'but I need to ask you about the girl's fingers.'

'Julie!' Lawson suddenly insisted, as if he'd just come out of his valium haze. 'We must stop referring to her as "the girl". Her name was Julie, not "the girl".'

'I'm sorry; Julie; can you remember exactly what Combe said about Julie's fingers?'

'He told me he broke them,' said Lawson, his gaze drifting off into the middle distance.

There was nothing more forthcoming so Steven prompted him. 'Did he say why?'

'She scratched him. She scratched his face so he broke three of her fingers, one for each scratch, he said, one at a time, simple as that. This little piggy went to market... Snap! This little...' Lawson buried his face in his hands, unable to go on, the shake of his shoulders betraying a silent sob.

'Would you like some water?' Steven asked, seeing there was a carafe sitting on the table by the bed.

Lawson shook his head. When he'd recovered his composure he looked at Steven and said, 'If he made the whole lot up, how come he still had the scars on his face? He pointed them out to me; three parallel lines on his cheek.'

Steven was taken aback. Eventually, he said, 'I'm sure a man like Combe was no stranger to scars: he's probably been collecting them since he was old enough to start beating up the other kids. He probably thought that showing you them would make his story sound more real, keep you on the hook.'

Lawson ignored what Steven had said and continued. 'He invited me to touch them... He seemed to know instinctively that it would have been like touching the dead girl for me... It was as if he could read my mind...see my weakness – sense my fears. He was an animal, a clever, cunning, evil animal.'

'Combe is dead, Mr Lawson,' said Steven. 'He's filling an unmarked council grave in a muddy field. The only visitor he'll ever have now will be the rain.'

'His *body* is in a grave,' said Lawson flatly.

Steven's impulse was to say, 'That's good enough for me,' but, out of compassion, he didn't. Instead he said, 'I'll let you chaps worry about other matters.'

'I don't think I know how to any more,' said Lawson. 'I told him that I hoped he would burn in hell.'

'A sentiment shared by the rest of the population of this country, I should think,' said Steven. 'There's only so much emotional baggage that one person can carry around in one life, Rev Lawson, even a man of the cloth like yourself. The world is better off without Hector Combe. Period. End of story. Forget him. Concentrate on the living and the people who need you.'

'Need me?' exclaimed Lawson quietly. 'Sometimes I feel like Canute trying to turn the tide.'

'We all feel like that from time to time,' said Steven. 'The number of people who actually make a difference in our world is painfully small. The rest of us just have to do our bit and hope that our contribution will fit in somewhere.'

Lawson smiled wanly for the first time and said, 'You sound as if you've given the subject some thought?'

'I lost my wife Lisa to cancer,' said Steven. 'When it happened, I saw pointlessness everywhere. Believe me, I'm an expert on it.'

'I suppose it would be too much to hope that it was religion that got you through it?'

'It would,' agreed Steven flatly.

'So...'

'Thoughts of my daughter, Jenny, got me through the worst. I thought she might need me – or at least I convinced myself that it would be better for her if I stayed alive rather than taking "the easy way out", as people mistakenly call it.'

'You're still bitter,' said Lawson.

'I didn't realise it showed,' said Steven.

'It does when you speak of your wife,' said Lawson.

'Maybe in time I'll get over it,' said Steven, 'just as you'll get over your experience with Combe.'

Lawson pursed his lips then said, 'Why did you ask about Julie's fingers?'

Steven considered fielding the question but then admitted, 'I'm trying to find out how Combe knew about Julie's broken fingers. They weren't mentioned at the trial or in any of the newspaper reports of the time.'

'I can tell you that,' said Lawson. 'It's because he did it.'

Steven walked slowly back to the car. Combe could not have committed the crime and yet he'd obviously made a very good job of convincing Lawson that he had. But why? If he had been setting out to make trouble for the police as a final act of malice, why bring in a minister of the church as an intermediary? Why go through the motions of seeking absolution and losing his temper when it wasn't forthcoming? What was that all about?

As he got into the car, Steven conceded that his visit to The Firs had resolved nothing. If anything, it had actually heightened his feelings of unease. The fact that Combe had elaborated on just how he'd broken Julie's fingers to Lawson was something he found particularly disturbing. It was almost as if he had wanted to draw attention to this aspect of the attack and his suggestion that Lawson touch the scars on his cheek as proof of a continuing link to the dead girl was quite bizarre. He wondered if David Little's face had been marked during the attack but most of all he wondered again why there had been no mention of the broken fingers in the prosecution evidence given at the trial. Maybe the answer to these questions would be in the police files. He checked his watch and saw that there would still be time to drive into Edinburgh and visit police headquarters before catching the last London flight home.

Fettes Police Headquarters in Edinburgh had no great claim to architectural merit but the functional buildings were situated in a pleasant area of the city near the botanical gardens and facing the impressive facade of Fettes College, one of Scotland's leading public schools. Steven noted as he drove past that they were also close to the Western General Hospital, where David Little had carried out his research. He had given no warning of his visit so he had to show his ID and state his business to several uniformed men before finally being shown into the office of Inspector Peter McClintock.

'This is a bit of a surprise,' said McClintock. 'Official is it?'

'Not exactly,' smiled Steven.

'You were in the vicinity so you thought you'd just drop by and say hello?' said McClintock.

'You could say,' replied Steven, instinctively feeling that, given time, he could like the man.

'Well if it's not official, do you fancy a pint?'

'Sounds good,' replied Steven, well aware that informal exchanges of information were usually of much more use than those confined to official channels – a bit like the black economy being more efficient than the real one.

'So how come I was shown to your door?' asked Steven as they drove away in McClintock's car. He hadn't come across

McClintock's name in any of the files on the case.

'I was the one who got landed with Hector Combe's confession when it came in. I sent it on to you guys when I found your sticker on the Summers file. Evil bastard, Combe.'

'So I understand. So you weren't actually involved in the Julie Summers case at the time?' said Steven.

'Not directly,' said McClintock a bit too hesitantly for Steven's liking. He let his silence prompt McClintock to elaborate. 'I was a DS at the time so I knew what was going on. I was friendly with a woman DC on Currie's team so you could say she kept me in the picture. I remember she got very upset over the Mulvey affair, I think that's what decided her to leave the force.'

'That upset?' said Steven.

'She reckoned Currie's team were going over the score, to use her words.'

'And were they?'

McClintock paused, pretending he was concentrating on the traffic at an intersection before saying, 'Depends how you look at it. They weren't to know that old mother Mulvey and her simple-Simon son were going to top themselves, were they?'

'Whether they knew or not, they appear to have been the reason for it,' said Steven.

'Whatever,' conceded McClintock. 'Well, the great British public had their way in the end. Four of our lot hit the street on the early retirement train and Jane decided to leave the force of her own accord.'

'Jane's your girlfriend?'

'Ex-girlfriend.'

'Not the best kind of publicity for the force.'

'You could say.'

'But it recovered?'

'Blood under the bridge.'

'So what's Sci-Med's interest in this?' asked McClintock as he returned from the bar carrying two pints of beer. They were sitting in an old-fashioned pub in Inverleith Row where McClintock appeared to be well known judging by the nods and asides made at the bar.

'David Little was a top-flight medical scientist,' said Steven.

'Ah,' said McClintock, putting down the glasses carefully but still slopping some on the tabletop. 'I get it. You're looking for some reason to spring one of your own?'

'Nothing could be further from the truth,' said Steven, bristling at the suggestion. 'The evidence against him was overwhelming.'

'Damn right it was,' growled McClintock.

'On the other hand, if a man like Hector Combe says on his deathbed that *he* did it and that the police fitted someone else up for it – someone who just happened to be a brilliant medical scientist – then we do take an interest.'

'Come on man, that was just Combe taking one last swing at his natural enemy, the police. He was opening up old wounds and rubbing salt into them. It was just his way of saying goodbye. That was Combe all over, evil bastard.'

'Combe knew about Julie Summers' fingers being broken,' said Steven, taking a sip of his beer and watching McClintock's reaction over the rim of the glass.

'I'm not with you,' said McClintock, opening a new packet of cigarettes and lighting one with an old-style Zippo lighter: it made the air smell of petrol.

Steven waited until McClintock had taken a first lungful and exhaled it before saying, 'It was never common knowledge that her fingers had been broken in the attack. It didn't come out in court and the newspapers never got hold of it but Combe knew,' said Steven. 'He made a point of telling the Rev Lawson all about it in great detail.'

McClintock looked doubtful. 'All sorts of details get circulated in the prison system,' he said. 'And nobody knows how they get there in the first place. I bet half the buggers in pokey know where Lord Lucan is. Combe knowing that is no big deal.'

'Probably not,' agreed Steven, 'but all the same I'd like to check the forensic reports on the case before I call a halt.'

'The forensic stuff was all in the file,' said McClintock.

'Only the stuff that was used in court,' said Steven. 'Come to think of it, I'd like to see the full scene of crime report, sample lists, photographs, the lot.'

'Are you sure this is really necessary?' asked McClintock.

'No, but it's what I want to do,' said Steven.

'But why?' exclaimed McClintock. 'If it gets out that someone is taking another look at the Julie Summers case, the press are going to want to know why. They'll start crucifying us all over again.'

'It doesn't have to get out,' said Steven. 'It can be done discreetly.'

'But Christ, man! Little was as guilty as sin,' said McClintock, becoming animated. 'The evidence was rock-solid, a perfect DNA match. What more do you need? A ribbon round his dick proclaiming, I fucked Julie Summers then throttled the life out of her?'

'I want to know about her broken fingers,' said Steven, remaining calm. 'I want to know if the lab found anything under her nails and I want to know why no mention of her fingers was made at the trial.'

McClintock took a long drag on his cigarette and looked at Steven without speaking as if weighing up his chances of winning the argument. Finally, he looked away, exhaled out the side of his mouth and said quietly, 'The prosecution didn't need anything else. They had more than enough as it was.'

'I know they did,' said Steven. 'But I'd still like to know what was available in the shape of back-up evidence.'

A cloud came over McClintock's face and he shifted uncomfortably in his seat. 'There might be a problem with that,' he said. 'Ronnie Lee didn't exactly run a tight ship.'

'Lee was the forensic pathologist?'

McClintock nodded. 'He was also a premier league piss artist.'

'Meaning?'

'Meaning his work suffered. Two or three cases went arse over tit when they got to court because of Ronnie's fuck-ups. Important cases. Big name villains walked free. The Fiscal's office wasn't too amused but nothing was done about it except that they preferred not to rely too much on forensics after that.'

'Let me get this straight,' said Steven. 'You're telling me that the Fiscal's office would present a minimum of forensic evidence because they couldn't trust the lab?'

'More or less.'

'Jesus,' said Steven. 'How long did that situation go on?'

'A couple of years. That's the reason they took the opportunity to get rid of Lee along with the others in the big clear-out after what happened to the Mulveys.'

'Nice to know something good came out of their deaths,' said Steven sourly.

'It's never easy getting rid of someone in Lee's position,' said McClintock defensively. 'People tend to look the other way, make allowances; colleagues cover up as best they can. You wouldn't believe the number of pathologists I've known who've had a problem with the bottle.'

'Yes I would,' said Steven without elaboration.

McClintock smiled and said, 'Sorry, I guess you would. Mind you, can't be easy seeing the sights they see every day of their lives.'

'It's more the smells,' said Steven.

'I'll take your word for it,' said McClintock, screwing up his face.

'Another pint?'

'Why not.'

Steven fetched two more beers from the bar and asked, 'How many of the original murder investigation team are still around?'

'None of the principals,' said McClintock. 'Chisholm,

Currie, Hutton and Lee all fell on their swords. Jane went off to push trolleys.'

Steven gave him a quizzical look.

'Cabin crew, British Airways.'

Steven nodded with a smile. He'd been thinking of Tesco's car park.

'I can't think where the wooden-tops ended up, probably all over the place,' said McClintock.

'What about Lee's forensic team?' asked Steven.

'Couldn't really say. We don't have much to do with the lab on a personal level. We just send in the samples and read the reports.'

'I think maybe I'd like to visit the lab,' said Steven.

McClintock looked at his watch. 'It's a bit late now,' he said. 'They'll be closed by the time we get there. Civil service hours.'

Steven nodded and said, 'Then I'll stay over.'

'Are you sure this is really necessary?' asked McClintock again. There was no aggression in his voice this time. It was more of an appeal.

'I hate loose ends,' said Steven.

McClintock nodded and paused before saying, 'It's as well to know that a lot of people up here are...a bit sensitive about the Julie Summers case.'

'That sounded like a warning,' said Steven.

'I'm just telling you how it is,' said McClintock, 'and asking you to consider just for a moment that you might be playing Hector Combe's game for him.'

'I'll bear that in mind,' said Steven. 'In the meantime, how do I find the forensics lab?'

'Come to Fettes around nine in the morning, I'll run you over.'

As they stepped outside and started walking back to the car, McClintock asked, 'Do you know your way around Edinburgh?'

'Well enough,' replied Steven.

'There are plenty of small hotels in Ferry Road if you're

looking for a place to stay.'

'I'll be fine,' replied Steven.

They drove back over to police headquarters and Steven picked up his own car, saying that he'd see McClintock in the morning. He declined his suggestion that they go out on the town together and have a few more beers, saying that he had some paperwork to catch up on and fancied an early night. Neither was strictly true; he just wanted to be on his own to think over the happenings of the day.

Almost on autopilot, he drove over to the south of the city with the intention of booking in at the Grange Hotel. He'd stayed there twice before when in Edinburgh, the first time with Lisa on an overnight stay after attending a concert during the Edinburgh Festival, the second after Lisa's death when he'd been on an assignment in West Lothian. On that occasion he had chosen to stay there as part of a personal rehabilitation programme – a sort of test to see if he had got over Lisa's death and could revisit places they had known together without the overwhelming sense of grief that usually accompanied such attempts. The Grange was the first of these places to assure him that he had. He could now think about Lisa with fondness and without the awful knife in the guts feeling of raw grief.

It was during the course of the West Lothian assignment that he had met a girl named Eve Ferguson who had convinced him that life had to go on and he had to move on with it. She had done her bit to exorcise the feelings of guilt he'd been prone to when faced with the possibility of an association with any woman other than Lisa.

Eve had been a beautiful, intelligent and down to earth girl who had been quite frank about her career ambitions and whom he might easily have fallen in love with had they had more time together. As it was, she had not seen herself settling down with Steven, acting as Jenny's stepmother and wandering aimlessly around supermarkets – as she'd suspected such a future might hold. It wasn't just children that women pushed round shopping centres in buggies, she had maintained; it was broken dreams and abandoned careers. Eve had been an MSc student at university at the time and wanted to give life her best shot. They had parted on friendly terms.

There had been one other woman in Steven's life since that time and their time together had also been brief. Caroline had been a doctor, a public health consultant in Manchester at a time when a viral epidemic was sweeping the city. She had fallen victim to the virus while working as a volunteer nurse and had died in his arms.

For a while after Caroline's death Steven had found it difficult to believe that he wasn't jinxed when it came to women. The experience of having lost both Lisa and Caroline to disease had profoundly affected him. The old adage that life was what happened to you while you were planning for the future had never seemed more apt. He embraced a new philosophy that demanded he live more in the present and think less of what tomorrow might bring. Making ambitious plans for the future was best left to the young and to those as yet unharmed by the slings and arrows of outrageous fortune.

He was not above using this as an excuse for not considering his personal circumstances in too much detail. On the odd occasion when he found himself alone in his flat, late at night, beset by thoughts of being nearly forty with little or nothing in the way of personal possessions, it was the perfect excuse for wiping such thoughts from his head. He would have another drink and go to bed. Tomorrow could take care of itself.

The only uncomfortable factor in all of this was that he had a daughter, Jenny, and therefore had a responsibility towards her. When Lisa died Sue and Peter had taken Jenny to live with them down in Glenvane. It had been his intention to have her back living with him as soon as possible if only for the selfish reason that he could see that in many ways Lisa lived on in Jenny and he needed to see that. She had Lisa's eyes and, although she was still very young, certain mannerisms that were Lisa's.

The practical problems however, of having Jenny live with

him were quickly to defeat him. His job would simply not permit it. He had considered trying to find a more stable humdrum job that would have meant more regular hours so that he would be home every night but in reality, that was as far as it had ever gone. When push came to shove he had not been prepared to give up his job with Sci-Med. He knew that it was almost certainly selfish but he needed it: he needed the excitement, the unpredictability and even the danger of it on occasion.

As it was, Sue and Peter were more than happy to have Jenny stay as part of their family and Jenny was more than happy to be there. The downside that Steven recognised and accepted was that Jenny would probably end up regarding Sue and Peter as her *real* parents. He would be the man who appeared every couple of weeks, work permitting, bearing smiles and presents. He tried to be more than that, taking an interest in everything that Jenny did at home and at school, but he knew that this was still a good bit short of taking on full parental responsibility. It was a compromise but then compromise was the glue on which society depended.

In the meantime, tonight was proving problematical. Steven arrived at the Grange Hotel in Whitehouse Terrace to find it no longer there. The building was there all right but it was no longer a hotel. It had been bought for private use. He looked at the darkened driveway, now stripped of its welcoming signs, and silently bade farewell to a little bit of his past. He looked up at the night sky as if imagining Lisa might be watching and murmured quietly, 'Sorry love.'

Steven checked into The Braid Hills Hotel a couple of miles away to the west. It occupied a lofty position in the well-heeled south side of the city, which gave it an air of solid respectability, and he was lucky enough to get a room with a panoramic view to the north and west. After looking out over the lights of the city for a few moments he went downstairs and had a drink in the bar where golf club sweaters were much in evidence. He picked up that the four men standing next to him were lawyers, not his favourite profession, believing as he did that in any sphere of human misery you would find a lawyer making a fat living. The ones beside him however, were discussing property prices – their own by the sound of it. 'It's absolutely outrageous!' beamed one with a self-satisfied smile.

Steven exchanged small talk with the barman about the weather and agreed when asked that he was in the city on business without actually saying what that business might be. Steven wondered about that himself as he made his way back upstairs to his room.

McClintock and the local police were clearly unhappy about the prospect of his opening up old wounds where they saw no need and he had a certain sympathy for this view. As they saw it, what had happened was long in the past and the reputation of the force had suffered enough because of it – as had several of the individuals involved although Steven had less sympathy for them. By all accounts, they had fully deserved their early exit from the payroll.

On the other hand, Hector Combe had made such a good job of confessing to the murder that he had utterly convinced the Rev Lawson that he'd done it. His reason for doing this however, was still far from clear and this annoyed him. He hated loose ends. Now, to add to his unease, he had learned that a known drunk with a reputation for incompetence had been in charge of the forensic evidence against Little. If Little had been convicted by anything other than rock-solid DNA evidence he would have been seriously concerned. As it was, he just wanted to see the notes on Julie's broken fingers and establish how Combe had come to know about them.

If they had been broken during a struggle with her assailant, as Lee had suggested, then it might well have been possible for the lab to identify her attacker from material recovered from under her fingernails. He wanted to see this information. Getting hold of it would be an acceptable alternative to trying to find out how Combe knew about the fingers in the first place. Fragments of skin and dried blood identifying David Little as Julie's attacker would make Combe's claims irrelevant.

It took Steven nearly forty-five minutes to cross town in the morning rush hour. He arrived at Fettes Police Headquarters at nearly a quarter past nine to find McClintock in conversation with another officer. Both men stopped talking as he came into view and McClintock adopted a wan smile. 'Thought you'd changed your mind,' he said, looking at his watch.

'Traffic,' said Steven. 'All ready to go?'

McClintock moved uneasily on his feet and cleared his throat unnecessarily before saying, 'Actually, Chief Superintendent Santini would like a word with you before we go over to the lab.'

'Oh yes?' said Steven, making it sound like an accusation.

'I had to tell him you were here and what was going on,' said McClintock.

'No problem,' said Steven. 'Where do I find him?'

McClintock led the way to Santini's office and affected a friendly grin as he waited for a response to his knock on the door.

'Come.'

'Dr Dunbar, sir,' said McClintock, ushering Steven inside and then leaving.

Santini, a rotund figure in his fifties with a tanned complexion and sleek silvery hair, sat back in his chair and made a steeple with his fingers. He didn't smile or make any move to shake hands. 'I understand you have an interest in the Julie Summers case, Doctor,' he said.

'I have an interest in Hector Combe's confession to her murder,' answered Steven. 'But then I'm sure you know that already.' He made a gesture towards the door behind him.

'Always nice to know what's going on in one's own backyard, Doctor, don't you think?'

'Wherever possible,' agreed Steven.

'I called Sci-Med. I've just spoken to John Macmillan. He tells me that there are no official plans to review the Summers case.'

'That's my understanding too,' agreed Steven.

This was not what Santini expected to hear. 'So you are here in an…unofficial capacity?' he asked.

'You could say.'

'I do say,' snapped Santini. 'David Little was convicted on cast-iron evidence, which no one has ever disputed. Hector Combe could not have carried out the crime. He just wanted to create trouble for the police and you – in your *unofficial* capacity – seem to be doing your level best to assist him in that objective.'

'Far from it,' retorted Steven. 'I agree with everything you say. I just want to take a look at the forensic evidence that wasn't used in the trial so that I can be sure in my own mind about something.'

'What?' Santini demanded. He then did a fair impression of a cat watching a bird without blinking, Steven thought.

'Three of Julie Summers' fingers were broken by her assailant during the struggle. I want to know what the lab found under her nails.'

'Maybe nothing,' said Santini.

'If they were broken when she put up a struggle, as your own pathologist seemed to suggest at the time, there's a good chance that something would have been recovered – skin, hair, blood, fibres?'

'The DNA evidence on its own was irrefutable,' said Santini. 'A one hundred per cent match. There was no call for anything else.'

'I know,' said Steven. 'But I'd feel happier to see a piece of corroborating evidence. It would also prove beyond doubt that Hector Combe's assertion that Julie Summers scratched *his* face was nonsense.'

'Of course it was nonsense,' snapped Santini.

'Then corroborating evidence should make everyone happy,' said Steven calmly.

'But it shouldn't be necessary!' exclaimed Santini. 'What in God's name don't you accept about the evidence against David Little?'

'Nothing,' replied Steven. 'It seems irrefutable.'

'But you still want more?'

'I just want to take a look at the forensic samples taken at the time and then I'll be on my way.'

Santini looked down at his desk top for so long that Steven wondered if he had a crystal ball installed in it. Eventually he said quietly, 'That may not be possible.'

'I'm sorry?' said Steven.

'There aren't any samples,' said Santini quietly. 'Ronald Lee, the forensic pathologist at the time, screwed up. The samples were lost.'

'Lost?' exclaimed Steven.

'Destroyed, incinerated, thrown out with the discards, something like that. I'm not sure of the exact details.'

'How long have you known this?' asked Steven.

'Not long, I assure you. I called the head of the forensics lab when DI McClintock told me yesterday why you were here and he went into the lab last night to look out the samples. I just wanted to smooth the way so that you could see what you wanted to see and then be on your way without anyone getting wind of what you were up to. He called me just after eleven last night and broke the news.'

'But this suggests that the lab must have kept this a secret at the time,' said Steven.

Santini nodded and said, 'Presumably Superintendent Chisholm and Inspector Currie were told and they informed the Procurator Fiscal's Office of the situation.'

'And then they all colluded in one great big cover-up,' said Steven.

'It was a very difficult time for the force,' began Santini. 'The press were on our backs and the public were baying for an arrest. The investigating team had screwed up big time over the Mulvey boy and were being pilloried left, right and centre for perceived incompetence. I'm sure it was a case of the force simply not being able to afford another public scandal over a lab mix-up. It's not as if anyone falsified evidence.'

'They just lost it,' said Steven.

Santini swallowed and continued. 'They did have a DNA

match and it was perfect. The Fiscal obviously decided that a conviction could be obtained using that alone and he went ahead with the trial. He was proved right.'

Steven said quietly, 'I take it that this is the real reason Ronald Lee got his marching orders with the others?'

Santini leaned forward and said, 'Yes.'

Steven shook his head as he thought about it.

Santini said, 'I'm asking you as a colleague to let sleeping dogs lie. Hector Combe could not have committed that crime. We got the right man. You know that.'

Steven nodded.

'Well?'

'Even if the samples were discarded, I presume they were logged at the scene of crime?' said Steven.

'I suppose so.'

'I'd like to see the log.'

Santini took a deep breath as if trying to keep his equilibrium and exhaled slowly. 'I'll ask,' he said. 'Anything else?'

'I'd also like to see the medical officer's report on David Little when he was arrested.'

'We should have that here. I'll have to call the lab about the log. If they have it shall I ask for it to be sent over or will you want to go over yourself?'

'I'll go over,' said Steven.

'And then?' asked Santini.

'If I don't find anything untoward I'll call it a day.'

'Good,' said Santini. 'The Julie Summers file can then go back to gathering dust and Hector Combe can continue to rot in hell.'

McClintock looked sheepish when Steven arrived back in his office. 'I just found out myself a few minutes before you got here,' he said. 'What happens now?'

'Your governor is asking the lab if they still have the scene of crime log of the samples that Lee's team took. If they have, I want to see it. I said I'd go over.'

'I'll take you,' said McClintock.

'I've also asked to see the medical officer's report on Little when he was arrested.'

'He's just put my sergeant on to that. Coffee while we wait?'

'Black, no sugar,' said Steven.

McClintock left the office and returned a few moments later, holding two plastic cups by the rims with the tips of his fingers. 'I couldn't believe it when Santini told me about the samples this morning,' he said to Steven as he handed him his coffee. 'You must be thinking we're a right bunch of hicks up here.'

'If there's one thing I've learned over the years it's that there's no such thing as a completely efficient organisation and the bigger an outfit is, the less likely that becomes,' said Steven. 'Scratch the surface and you'll find the flaws. Doesn't matter if it's a hospital or a bank, the police force or the army, they've all got things to hide and usually plenty of staff only too willing to do the hiding.'

'A cynic after my own heart,' said McClintock ruefully.

'Realist,' said Steven.

'It's still bloody embarrassing,' said McClintock.

'It's a damned good thing you got the DNA match.'

'Bloody right.'

McClintock's sergeant knocked and came in carrying a cardboard file holder. 'The chief super said to give you this,' he said. 'It's the MO's report on the prisoner, Little.'

Steven nodded his thanks as the phone started to ring. He heard McClintock say, 'Right, we're on our way.'

McClintock dropped the phone in its cradle and said to Steven, 'Forensics have come up with the log.'

As they drove over to the lab, Steven asked, 'Any idea what happened to your Doctor Lee when he left?'

'Last I heard was that he and his wife had sold up and bought a cottage somewhere up on Speyside. Makes perfect sense I suppose,' said McClintock.

'How so?'

'It's distillery country,' replied McClintock.

'And the others?'

'George Chisholm moved to the south of Spain; spends his time playing golf with former clients I shouldn't wonder. Bill Currie became a security consultant with a big insurance company in Glasgow. Twice the pay for half the effort they tell me. I've no idea what happened to Hutton. Why?'

'Just wondered,' said Steven.

They arrived at the lab and McClintock showed his warrant card when asked to do so. Steven did the same.

'Dr McDougal is expecting you,' said the white-coated woman who had been detailed to escort them. Steven recognised the smell of medical labs the world over, a mixture of chemical solvents and air that had been heated by Bunsen burners, the ever-present hint of something vaguely unpleasant in the air but not enough to permit precise identification. He looked through the glass windows on one side of the corridor as they moved along and counted half a dozen white-coated workers sitting on stools at lab benches. It made him wonder about perception and reality. Forensic science was perceived by the public as being a glamorous occupation. The reality was analysing vomit and poking about in other people's dirty underwear. What did the workers see, he wondered, the glamour or the reality? He noted three high quality Leitz microscopes, a couple of Perkin Elmer spectrophotometers and a wide range of Hybaid DNA sequencing apparatus: the lab was well equipped.

McDougal turned out to be a serious-looking man in his early forties. He was balding at the front and wore spectacles with unfashionably large frames, which when worn on a pear-shaped face that almost narrowed to a point at his chin, gave him the appearance of a large insect. He smiled however and got up to hold out his hand when Steven was introduced. 'I'm hugely embarrassed at not being able to comply with your request,' he said. 'But my predecessor…well, let's just say that things could only get better.'

'I appreciate the problems were before your time,' Steven assured him.

'This is the scene of crime forensics log that you wanted to see,' said McDougal, handing over a large manila envelope.

'May I hang on to this?' Steven asked him.

'Of course, it's your copy. Is there anything else I can do to help?'

Steven was pleased to see that McDougal's desire to help seemed genuine. 'Are any of the forensic team who worked on the Julie Summers murder under Dr Lee still on the staff?' he asked.

McDougal thought for a moment before saying, 'To be honest, there was a bit of a radical shake-up in the lab after Dr Lee's departure. Quite a few people left for pastures new. I think maybe Carol Bain is the only one left from that time.'

'Do you think I could have a word with her?'

'Of course,' replied McDougal. 'Just give me a moment.' He left the room and McClintock got up and said, 'I'll wait outside in the car.'

Steven nodded his appreciation. He was considering opening the manila envelope in the interim when McDougal arrived back with Carol Bain.

Steven's first impression was that there was a woman like Carol Bain in every lab he'd ever known. His guess was that she had been there for over twenty years, did everything by the book and gave unswerving loyalty to whoever was in charge. He'd put money on her not being married and possibly still living with her mother – with whom she went on holiday to the same resort and same hotel every year.

Carol Bain gave Steven a cautious smile and sat down opposite, taking practised care to keep her knees together and turned slightly to the side. She kept her back straight and clasped her hands together in her lap. Her greying hair was swept back and held in a bun; a cameo brooch secured the collar of her high blouse collar.

'Carol has been with the service for, what is it now Carol? Twenty-three, twenty-four years?' said McDougal.

'Twenty-three,' smiled Carol.

'And no time off for good behaviour,' said McDougal.

Carol looked down and smiled wanly as if she'd heard the joke many times before.

'Well, I'll leave you two to talk,' said McDougal. 'Let me know when Dr Dunbar is ready to leave, will you Carol?'

'I understand that you're the only member of staff left from the team who worked on the Julie Summers murder, Miss...Mrs Bain?' said Steven.

'Miss,' said Carol. 'I suppose that's right,' she agreed. 'Dr Lee retired after the case, John moved on to pastures new and Samantha decided that lab work wasn't really for her – she was the most junior member of the team: she'd only been with us a few months.'

'Did you actually attend the scene of the crime yourself?' asked Steven.

Carol Bain shook her head. 'No, it was just John and Dr Lee as far as I remember.'

'John?'

'John Merton, the senior scientific officer on the team at the time.'

'Did you personally deal with Julie Summers' body?'

'No, there was no reason to, I worked on the lab samples that John and Dr Lee brought in.'

'Can you remember which particular aspect you worked on?'

'Of course, the semen recovered from the body. Recovery of the DNA was our top priority. It always is in rape cases.'

'Couldn't have been easy,' said Steven. 'I read that an attempt had been made to clean her up.'

'I don't remember that being a problem,' said Carol. 'There was certainly enough material for our purpose. You don't need much.'

'You actually did the DNA sequencing?' Steven asked.

'John and I both did it. We didn't have an automatic sequencer at the time. We did it manually and independently of each other, pouring our own acrylamide gels and doing everything the hard way. Nowadays we have a machine.'

'Why did you both do it?'

'It was a sensible precaution. DNA sequencing could be a bit iffy in those days. Gels could leak; bands could run together, smudging often occurred. As it turned out, we both got reasonably clean gels with identical banding so there was no doubt.'

'And that was what convicted David Little,' said Steven.

'A one hundred per cent match with the DNA sample obtained from one of the men in the village who happened to be David Little was what did it,' said Carol.

'Dr Lee must have been relieved?'

'It's always good to get a clear result but I suppose you're referring to the loss of the other samples?'

'Any idea how they came to be lost?' asked Steven.

'Not really. Dr Lee had been working on some of them – fibres from the girl's clothes I think. He liked to get involved in the practical aspects of lab work but in reality...'

'He was a bit of a liability?'

'Latterly,' agreed Carol Bain, looking down at the floor again as if uncomfortable about speaking ill of a superior. 'I suppose he must have become confused when returning the Summers samples to the storage rack. Instead of putting them back in the fridge he must have put the whole lot out in the discard tray instead. Everything had gone to the incinerator before anyone realised what had happened. John usually kept a watchful eye on him when he was in the lab but he couldn't do that all the time.'

'So you were left with no scene of crime samples at all apart from the semen recovered? No evidence apart from the DNA profile?'

'Luckily the semen samples were in another fridge – the one next door in the sequencing suite. But it isn't actually true to say that we had no other evidence; we did; it was the samples that we didn't have any more.'

Steven looked at her for a moment, feeling slightly puzzled. 'Are you saying that the samples were analysed *before* they were lost?' he asked.

'Well, yes,' said Carol, as if she'd never imagined anything else.

'I had the impression they had been discarded *before* they could be analysed,' said Steven. 'And that's why no corroborating forensic evidence was offered in court.'

Carol shook her head and said, 'No, I think the Fiscal's office didn't want to risk offering evidence that the defence might conceivably challenge. If defence counsel had asked for an independent analysis of anything we couldn't produce, the prosecution case might have collapsed.'

'Ah,' said Steven. 'So there are reports available for the other samples?'

'The samples had been in the lab for a couple of days before Dr Lee discarded them so some if not all of them must have already been dealt with. It was a very high profile case.'

'I think there's been a misunderstanding somewhere along the line,' said Steven. 'I was led to believe that there was no forensic evidence available apart from the DNA matches.'

'No, it should all be in the files,' said Carol.

'You don't happen to remember anything about it, do you?' asked Steven.

Carol shook her head. 'I'm sorry; it was such a long time ago but I do remember it all pointed to the accused, David Little.'

'Miss Bain, you've been a big help,' said Steven.

'I'll tell Dr McDougal we're through,' said Carol.

When McDougal returned, Steven explained about the misunderstanding, saying that it wasn't the actual forensic samples he needed access to, the reports on them would be fine.

McDougal looked blank. 'I'm sorry?'

'I understand from Ms Bain that forensic analysis was carried out on the samples before they were destroyed. If I could just take a look at the reports?'

McDougal seemed bemused. He held up his palms and hunched his shoulders. 'I'm sorry; I didn't find any record of anything being done. I too was under the impression that the samples had been lost before they could be analysed. There's nothing in the files. Was Carol quite sure?'

'Seemed to be,' replied Steven flatly.

Carol Bain was called back to repeat what she had told Steven.

'Did you actually see the lab reports yourself, Carol?' McDougal asked her.

'I may have done,' said Carol. 'But I have no recollection. It was all such a long time ago. As I told Dr Dunbar, the only thing I remember clearly was Dr Lee saying that the evidence backed up the case against David Little.'

'So the samples *were* analysed,' said McDougal quietly. He turned to Steven and said, 'I don't know what to say. There's definitely no trace of these reports in our records.'

'Maybe they were discarded after the samples were lost,' said Carol. 'I mean, if the Fiscal felt that the evidence couldn't be used then Dr Lee might have decided that there would have been no point in keeping them.'

'That might have been the thinking at the time,' said McDougal, his tone suggesting that this would be quite wrong in his book.

Steven turned to Carol and said, 'If you didn't do any work on the missing samples yourself then the analysis must have been carried out by one or more of the others you mentioned. That would be Dr Lee or Mr Merton or...I've forgotten the other person you mentioned?'

'Samantha Styles. She was the junior SO on the team; she left lab work and subsequently trained to be a nurse. She's a nursing sister now; I bumped into her at the Western General last year when I was visiting my mother. Time flies.'

'Indeed it does,' said Steven thoughtfully.

'Well, Doctor Dunbar, I'm not sure there is much else we can do to help in the circumstances,' said McDougal. 'Was it one particular piece of evidence you were concerned with?'

'It was a detail,' said Steven, recovering from the disappointment of having his hopes raised and then having them dashed by the absence of the paperwork. 'I suppose the main thing to know is that there was corroborative evidence that pointed to David Little.'

Steven left the building and got into McClintock's car.

'Get what you wanted?'

'One of the scientists remembers that the lost forensic samples were analysed before they were lost.'

'Thank God for that.'

'She also remembers Lee saying that the reports backed up the case against David Little.'

'There you are then,' said McClintock.

'But the reports have gone missing.'

'Jesus,' muttered McClintock. He drove in silence for a few minutes before asking, 'Is it really such a big deal?'

'Maybe not,' conceded Steven although, in truth, he wasn't sure himself. He had reservations about the whole affair.

'Let sleeping dogs lie?' said McClintock.

Steven smiled at McClintock's obvious desire to see the back of him.

'I haven't decided yet,' he said truthfully. He saw McClintock's hands tighten on the wheel.

'But the DNA evidence against Little was watertight,' said McClintock. 'And you now know that the lab did have other evidence against him, even if they couldn't use it. What's left?'

'I'd be happier if I knew what that evidence was,' said Steven. He was also thinking that he would have been more comfortable if the pathologist hadn't been a drunk.

In spite of what Carol Bain had said about the reports not being required, why would Lee destroy them? Surely he would just have filed them along with the DNA evidence. Maybe he still had them in his personal files? Steven saw this as a distinct possibility. It could be that they just hadn't been transferred when the case was over and big changes were being made in the lab. 'You don't happen to know where about on Speyside Lee moved to?' he asked.

'You're not thinking of going to see him?' exclaimed McClintock.

'I might,' said Steven.

McClintock sighed slowly. 'Must be eight, nine years since he retired. If he's kept up his drinking you'll be lucky if he knows what day of the week it is.'

They had arrived back at Fettes. As Steven got out the car he said, 'Like I said, I haven't decided yet what I'm going to do.'

'Get wise,' advised McClintock. 'Go back to the sunny south.'

Steven smiled but added, 'If you could find out where Lee is living, I'd be grateful.' He gave McClintock his mobile number.

The sun had come out and Steven decided he didn't want to go back to his hotel room. He wanted to be out in the fresh air, away from the smell of stale tobacco that accompanied McClintock. He needed to stretch his legs and time to think. He opted for a walk through the botanical gardens, which were close to police headquarters and where spring was definitely in the air as he walked along avenues lined with budding trees.

He found a quiet bench near the Chinese garden where he could enjoy the warmth of the sun on his face while he went through the paperwork that McDougal had given him. He started with the list of forensic samples taken at the scene of the crime. It seemed thorough and comprehensive and recorded Ronald Lee and John Merton as the forensic lab staff attending the scene of the crime.

Halfway down the list he found what he was looking for. Scrapings *had* been taken from under Julie Summers' fingernails. A visual examination had suggested that blood and possibly skin were present under the three fingers of her left hand, all of which had been broken. Three separate samples had been taken and were labelled 21, 22 and 23 in the inventory.

Steven raised his head and closed his eyes for a moment, enjoying the sun on his eyelids and thinking that this more or less cleared up any worry he might have had about what Combe had claimed. Biological material had been found under Julie's fingernails and although he hadn't seen the written report, Carol Bain remembered Lee saying that the analysis had positively identified David Little as her assailant. 'Hallelujah,' he murmured. Combe's confession could be buried with the rest of him.

Feeling more at ease, Steven started reading through the medical officer's report on David Little. He only got to the second paragraph before he felt a hollow feeling in his stomach and it grew bigger by the second. According to the doctor who'd examined him, there were no marks on Little's face. The only recorded scar on his entire body was a single three-inch scratch mark on his left forearm.

Steven looked at the date of the report. The examination had been carried out on January 14th, eleven days after the murder. Would scratch marks have had time to heal? He thought not – at any rate, not completely and the examining doctor would have looked in great detail for evidence of any such marking. How could Julie Summers have had Little's blood and tissue under three of her nails when he only had a single scratch mark on his arm? This was something he thought he would now have to ask Lee personally.

Steven called McClintock.

'So you're off back to London then,' said McClintock hopefully. 'You just called to say goodbye?'

'No,' replied Steven. 'I'm phoning to see if you've got that address for Lee?'

'I was afraid you were going to say that,' said McClintock wearily. There was a rustle of paper and he said, 'He lives a couple of miles outside Grantown on Spey in a house on the Ardlung estate called Ptarmigan Cottage.'

'Thanks,' said Steven.

'What decided you to stay?' asked McClintock.

For a moment Steven considered not telling but then he said, 'There was blood and skin under three of Julie's finger-nails.'

'So?'

'According to the doctor's report, there was only a single scratch mark on Little.'

'That's not impossible if she moved her fingers horizon-tally,' said McClintock. 'I mean, if she swiped her hand across his face then...'

'The scratch was on his arm. His face was unmarked.'

'Well, his bloody arm then,' said McClintock.

'Little said his cat did it.'

'He bloody would, wouldn't he?'

'She was murdered in January.'

'What's your point?'

'Little would hardly be out and about in a short-sleeved shirt, would he?' rapped Steven, sounding equally annoyed.

'I guess not,' McClintock conceded. 'But Christ, his sleeve could have been pushed up in the struggle.'

'Maybe,' said Steven in a tone that suggested he thought it the least likely explanation.

'So just what are you going to ask Ronnie Lee, assuming he's still on the same planet after all these years?'

'I'm hoping he might still have the original lab reports on what was found under Julie Summers' nails,' said Steven. 'If he has, I want to see them.'

'You don't let go easily, do you?' said McClintock with a sigh.

'Nope,' agreed Steven.

Chapter Seven

'I understand the local police are getting touchy about your presence,' said John Macmillan when Steven called Sci-Med to say that he would be staying on in Scotland for a bit.

'I'm not unsympathetic,' said Steven, 'but there are one or two things about the secondary evidence that I want to be perfectly clear about. You wouldn't think that should be too difficult but they're certainly making it look that way. Not only were all the forensic samples discarded in some lab screw-up at the time but even the lab reports on them have gone AWOL. I'm reduced to hoping that the police pathologist of the day still has them somewhere, hidden away in his personal files or even in a box under the bed. It's crazy.'

'Does no one remember what was in them?' asked Macmillan.

'Oh yes, I'm told that they confirmed David Little positively as Julie Summers' killer.'

There was a short pause before Macmillan said, 'So what's the problem or am I missing something here?'

'I've seen the inventory of samples taken at the scene of the crime,' said Steven. 'The only real candidate for providing a second *positive* ID of the killer apart from the semen itself was the material taken from under three of Julie Summers' fingernails. Data obtained from the other samples collected at the crime could have provided circumstantial evidence to put him at the scene of the murder but for a *positive* ID it would have to have been the nail samples.'

'Because they could have got DNA from them?'

'Precisely.'

'So?'

'According to the police doctor's report on David Little when he was arrested, he only had a single scratch mark on him and it was on his forearm not his face.'

'A single scratch from three fingernails,' murmured Macmillan thoughtfully. 'Not entirely impossible I suppose...'

'No, but pushing it. I need to be sure about this.'

'I admire your attention to detail,' said Macmillan, sounding as if he didn't. 'Chances are all this will probably turn out to be some filing mistake. Try not to upset too many people.'

'I'll do my best,' said Steven but the line had gone dead.

Steven got an early start next morning and stopped after a hundred miles or so in Aviemore to find something to eat – he had made do with just coffee and orange juice for breakfast so he was feeling hungry. It had rained all the way up and the roads had been busy with commercial traffic sending up clouds of spray so the break was going to be welcome on both accounts. He found a seat in the bay window of a hotel restaurant advertising all-day food and ordered scrambled eggs and bacon and a pot of coffee.

'We don't do pots,' the waitress informed him.

'Well, whatever you do,' said Steven.

'Cup or a mug,' said the waitress.

'A mug.'

Steven looked out of the window while he waited and watched little groups of people in waterproof gear wander aimlessly up and down the main street of the village that promoted itself as Scotland's premier ski resort. The colour of their jackets added brightness to the otherwise grey and depressing scene.

The food when it came was lukewarm and soggy but when the waitress returned to ask in her automated way if 'everything was alright' for him, he simply nodded and said, 'Fine.' The truth was that he hadn't expected any better – although he did wonder what excuse the UK tourist boards would offer this year for falling numbers. He didn't think that lousy food and bad service would even make it to the starting line.

Grantown-on-Spey struck Steven as one of those places where it was always Sunday. There were very few people about and it seemed almost as if a respectful silence was being observed. It had the kind of ambience that obliged people to speak in whispers. Yet when he looked more closely, shops and businesses did after all seem to be open. He asked at the post office for directions to Ptarmigan Cottage and was given clear instructions from a friendly woman who thought at first that he might be the Lees' son. She seemed disappointed when he said that he was just a friend.

Steven spent much of the two miles on the forest-track road leading to Ptarmigan Cottage hoping that nothing was coming the other way. There were so many twists and blind turns in it as it led up through dense pinewoods that the seeds for disaster seemed to be sown at every corner. He completed the journey without incident however, and found himself admiring the cottage and its environs when he finally got out the car. It was painted white and perched on the edge of a steep cliff with magnificent views down the River Spey in both directions. He could understand the attraction the place must have had for Lee when he'd moved there; the idea of living among so much natural beauty after spending such a large part of his professional life with ugliness and decay must have proved irresistible.

He supposed that the cottage itself had probably started out as a home for estate workers but, like so many, it had been modernised and prettified – although not to an unacceptable degree – and sold off to incomers. Through the large picture window of the lounge, Steven saw a woman get out of her chair and come to the door.

'Can I help you?' she asked in a well-educated voice but in a tone that questioned his being there.

'Mrs Lee? My name is Dunbar. I hate to intrude like this but I wonder if I might have a word with your husband?' Steven showed her his ID.

'The Sci-Med Inspectorate,' she read aloud. The formal smile faded from her face and suspicion took its place. 'May I ask what this is about?'

'I'm looking into some aspects of an old case your husband was involved in, Mrs Lee. There are a few things I must ask him.'

'Ronnie retired more than eight years ago. That part of his life is over. There's nothing he can tell you. All that stuff was in the past.'

'Stuff?' asked Steven.

Mrs Lee waved her hands in the air and said, 'Pathology, dead bodies, police evidence, being called out at all hours, all that...unpleasantness.'

'Mrs Lee, I really would like to speak to your husband,' said Steven plainly. 'It is important.'

'My husband is not a well man, Dr Dunbar, and I will not have him being upset. If there's one thing guaranteed to upset him, it's any allusion to his former career. He's still very bitter about the way he was treated by these...bureaucratic pygmies.'

Steven saw the steely resolve in her eyes but he said, 'I need to ask him some things about the forensic evidence in the Julie Summers murder nine years ago.'

Mary Lee closed her eyes and remained silent for a long moment. When she opened them Steven saw the anger there. 'The Julie Summers murder is the last thing on earth he needs to be reminded of,' she hissed. 'These bastards destroyed my husband's distinguished career over that ridiculous Mulvey woman and her idiot son. They completely ignored the fact that Ronnie positively identified the murderer and secured a conviction for them.'

Well, well, thought Steven. It wasn't the first time he'd seen middle-class charm disappear like snow off a dyke to be replaced by fascist rant but he still found it fascinating. He didn't see any point in reminding the woman that it had been drink that had destroyed her husband's 'distinguished career' and that it apparently had been on the skids for some time before the Summers case so he simply said, 'My questions have nothing to do with the Mulveys, Mrs Lee.'

'Then what?' Mary Lee demanded.

'I'm trying to find some missing lab reports connected with the case. I thought your husband might still have them in among his personal papers. If by any chance you yourself could lay your hands on them for me there would be no need for me to disturb your husband at all.'

'Ronnie didn't keep anything of his old life,' said Mary Lee. 'He put it all behind him when we left Edinburgh... Actually,

I remember now, we had a bonfire. Any old papers probably went on top of that.' The sweet smile returned.

'I see,' said Steven. 'In that case I really will have to speak to him.'

Mary Lee's smile vanished again. 'And I've already told you; he's ill.'

'Mrs Lee, I do have the authority to insist,' said Steven. 'I'm sure neither of us wants the involvement of the local police in this but that's exactly what will happen if you continue to obstruct me.'

'You people make me sick,' said Mary Lee, turning on her heel and going back inside the house. As she'd left the door open, Steven assumed that he should follow and did.

'Wait here,' said Mary Lee without turning when they'd reached the living room. Steven stood there while she disappeared for a few moments. When she returned she said, 'Through here. You've got five minutes. Any longer and I'm going to call the press about harassment of a desperately sick man.'

Steven found Lee in bed. A slight figure with white hair and round shoulders, he was wearing pyjamas, buttoned up to the neck and was propped up on pillows, watching a small television, which sat on a table at the foot of the bed. It was currently showing a cooking programme involving teams of competing celebrities playing to the camera. Their animated laughter and show business smiles contrasted sharply with Lee's pinched, angry expression. The yellowness of his complexion spoke volumes to Steven about liver damage but a vague smell of whisky in the air said that it was still a factor in Lee's life.

'What the hell do you want?' snapped Lee, although the effort involved in being aggressive made him cough. 'You've upset my wife.'

'I need to ask you some things about the Julie Summers case.

'Julie Summers, Julie Summers,' intoned Lee. 'Always Julie bloody Summers. We nailed the bastard who did it. What more do you want? More crap about the blessed Mulveys? That was just so much shit from a gutter press who'd nothing better to do with their time than to destroy a few good careers. Rodents!'

'I'm not concerned with the Mulveys,' said Steven. 'It's the forensic evidence in the Summers case I need to talk to you about. I already know that the samples taken at the scene of the crime were lost.'

'These things happen,' said Lee. 'It was an accident, just one of those things. Someone in the lab put them in the wrong rack. We're all human.'

Steven was taken aback at Lee's shifting of blame away from himself and apparent dismissal of such a serious mistake but resisted the urge to point this out. Instead he said, 'I understand that the samples were analysed before they were lost?'

'Exactly, so it was no big deal.'

'But to all intents and purposes the evidence was rendered useless because the Procurator Fiscal couldn't use it in case of a Defence challenge?' countered Steven.

'His decision not mine,' snapped Lee.

Steven was amazed at the arrogance still residing within this alcohol-ravaged shell of a man. He clearly believed that he had done nothing wrong and that he was just a victim of circumstance. 'Did the evidence back up the case against David Little?' he asked.

'Of course it did!' exclaimed Lee, but he broke off eye contact.

'I'm particularly concerned with the scrapings taken from under the girl's fingernails,' said Steven.

'What about them?'

'Did they point to David Little?

'Yes, of course they did.'

'You remember that clearly?'

'Yes, dammit.' Lee still kept his head down.

'You got DNA from them?'

'Yes, how many times do I have to . . ?'

'Who did the DNA fingerprinting?'

'I did.'

'You personally carried out the DNA sequencing on the material obtained from under Julie Summers' fingernails?' asked Steven slowly so that there could be no misunderstanding.

'Yes,' said Lee, finally looking up at Steven.

'What about the hard evidence of that? Sequence data? Gel photographs?'

'It'll all be in the lab in Edinburgh somewhere.'

'It isn't.'

'Then I suppose they must have thrown it out. You'll have to talk to them about that.'

'I already did,' said Steven, choosing to stare directly at Lee. 'No one there ever saw it. They don't think you left it behind when you retired. I hoped you might still have it somewhere but your wife tells me you had a bit of a bonfire before you left Edinburgh?'

Lee looked at Steven, his sunken dark eyes sizing him up for a few moments as he considered what had been said. His reaction made Steven think that this might perhaps be the first time that Lee had heard of any bonfire. 'That's true,' said Lee softly. 'My old files may well have been confined to the flames…ashes to ashes and all that. A bonfire of past vanities, the funeral pyre of a career, sacrificed on the altar of some idiot and his loony mother.'

'Let's see if I've got this right,' said Steven. 'You were responsible for losing the forensic samples and then you followed up by destroying all the lab reports on them?'

Lee's self-satisfied muse was well and truly fractured. 'Just what the hell are you getting at?' he stormed, setting off a round of coughing. It was interspersed with more angry comments when he could catch his breath. 'What the fuck does it matter if a few old lab reports have gone missing. They were never used…because they were never bloody needed! The evidence against Little was overwhelming!'

Lee now entered a prolonged bout of coughing during which his wife came into the room with a glass of water for him. As he sipped it Mary Lee turned to Steven and said, 'Get out! Leave us alone! Can't you see the damage you're doing?'

'I'm sorry,' said Steven. 'But I may have to come back.'

Steven stood for a moment outside the cottage, looking at the view and wondering where to go from here. He was aware of the muted sound of Lee's coughing coming from the bedroom at the back of the house.

'Shit,' he murmured. Lee had told him that he personally had analysed the material taken from under Julie's nails but Carol Bain had suggested that he was incapable of doing that. One of them was lying and he didn't think it was Carol Bain.

The rain gave way to watery spring sunshine as he drove back to Edinburgh. He stopped in Perthshire at a woodland park near Dunkeld to stretch his legs. This was a place he remembered visiting with Lisa in the early days of their courtship. It had been summer and the leafy canopy of the tall trees had shaded the winding paths as they walked by the river on a gloriously warm day. Today sunlight filtered through budding branches and sparkled off the fast flowing water of the River Bran as it carried away the rains of the morning.

Steven sat on a felled tree trunk near the water's edge and flicked pebbles into the flow as he wrestled with the growing feeling of frustration inside him. It should have been such a simple thing for the forensic team to demonstrate that the material under Julie Summer's fingernails had come from David Little but no, the samples had been destroyed and the lab reports were missing – possibly destroyed too. All he had to show for his efforts was the word of a discredited drunk who claimed to have carried out tests himself when one of his staff had already suggested that he wasn't capable of it. What the hell was going on? Why lie about such a thing?

What if the samples had been discarded *before* any analysis had been carried out, he wondered. That would have made Lee's error much more serious and may even have embarrassed him into claiming that they *had* been examined and that the evidence had backed up the DNA findings from the semen. There might even have been collusion among some of the lab staff at the time in a damage limitation exercise.

So had the scrapings been analysed or hadn't they? If he didn't find out the answer to that he knew that the worries he had over the case wouldn't go away. This was the one thing that was stopping him dropping the whole thing and returning to London.

Steven feared that it might be necessary to go back and confront Lee with such an accusation but first, he supposed, it might be useful to have a word with the members of Lee's team that he hadn't yet spoken to, John Merton and Samantha Styles. If they could confirm or even admit to harbouring suspicions that no analysis had taken place then he would go back north again and tackle Ronnie Lee about it.

Steven remembered that Carol Bain had mentioned that she thought John Merton had moved to a job in the medical school when he left Lee's lab. It was after six before he got back to Edinburgh so he left it until next morning to call.

'We did have a John Merton on the staff,' the university's personnel department confirmed. 'He left nearly eight years ago.'

Steven asked for any forwarding address but none was known. He turned his attention to Samantha Styles. Carol Bain had said that she was working as a nursing sister in the Western General but she might well have married and changed her surname in the intervening eight years.

Lothian Regional Health Board did not have a Sister Styles on their register, he was told. 'How about nursing sisters with Samantha as a first name?' he asked.

'The staff aren't filed under first names.'

'The list is computerised, isn't it?'

'Ye...s.'

'Then run a search for "Samantha".'

'I'll have to ask...'

Steven drummed his fingers lightly on the table as he waited.

'We do have a Sister Samantha Egan,' said the voice, 'working at the Western General Hospital.'

'Good show. How do I find her?'

'You'll have to call the director of nursing services at the hospital.'

Steven wrote down the number and called it as soon as he'd rung off.

'Sister Egan is in charge of ward 31,' he was told. He asked to be transferred to the ward and was rewarded by a series of clicks and buzzes until finally the phone went dead. He called the Western General directly and asked for ward 31.

'Ward 31, Staff Nurse Kelly speaking.'

'I'd like to speak to Sister Egan please.'

'May I ask who's calling?'

'Dr Dunbar.'

Steven smiled as he picked up the distant words, 'Never heard of him,' before Samantha Egan finally came on the phone and he explained who he was and what he wanted to speak to her about.

'Ye gods and little fishes,' she exclaimed and laughed before saying, 'I only worked in the lab for a few months. Are you sure it's me you want to speak to?'

Steven said that it was and in person rather than over the phone.

'Well, on the grounds that it can't possibly take very long, why don't you pop up to the ward this morning. Say, eleven thirty?'

Steven thanked her and said he'd be there.

As luck would have it, Steven couldn't find a parking place at the hospital. He ended up leaving the car quite a way down Carrington Road, which ran east from the hospital, down past Fettes Police Headquarters. As he got out, Peter McClintock happened to be passing. He double parked against Steven's car for a moment and got out to ask how he had got on with Ronnie Lee.

'I've had better days,' said Steven. 'Talking to the pot plant in my room would have been equally productive.'

McClintock looked pleased. 'I won't say I told you so,' he grinned. 'I'm surprised the bugger's still alive. So where do you go from here?'

'I'm going to talk to one of the other people who were in the forensic lab at the time,' said Steven.

'You're persistent, I'll give you that,' smiled McClintock. 'But you're chasing rainbows.'

McClintock drove off and Steven walked back up to the hospital and followed the signs to ward 31. He had to pause at the entrance to allow a porter to manoeuvre his laden trolley out through the swing doors. He took the opportunity to ask the man where he would find 'sister'.

'Second on the left,' mumbled the man with a vague wave of his hand. 'Cow's in a foul mood. It's no ma bloody fault if there's no' enough sheets in this bloody hospital.'

Steven smiled and gave him a sympathetic nod as he watched him move off, fighting his trolley over a directional disagreement and mumbling to himself about the injustice of the world. He personally found no evidence of Samantha Egan's foul mood when he knocked and entered her office.

'Dr Dunbar, come in, I'm intrigued,' she said, getting up and coming towards him.'

Steven found Samantha Egan's smile attractive and genuine. For some reason he had been harbouring a mental image of a slim dark woman wearing glasses, with a serious countenance and a permanently severe expression. Instead he found a tall, attractive brunette who seemed anything but severe.

'Oh my God,' she said with mock alarm. 'You haven't come to tell me that I made even more mistakes in the lab than I thought?'

'Nothing like that,' smiled Steven. 'But am I right in thinking that you did work in the forensic lab when Dr Ronald Lee was the consultant there some years ago?'

'Briefly, but not much more than a few months. It was my first real job. Let's see, I got my degree in '91 and then I did voluntary service overseas for a year in Africa so I would have joined the lab towards the end of '92 and then I left in the spring of '93 to train as a nurse.'

'Any regrets?' asked Steven.

'None at all,' replied Samantha without hesitation. 'I did a science degree and I thought I'd be suited to lab work but my time in Africa changed all that – you know the sort of thing, sheltered middle-class girl experiences reality for the first time. There's nothing like a bit of dirt and squalor for completing your education. Anyway, I decided that I needed involvement with people rather than test tubes and Bunsen burners. I needed the smiles, the tears. Labs are cold, sterile places.'

'But you did apply for a job in forensic science,' said Steven.

'Yes, I did,' agreed Samantha. 'I thought maybe it was just me feeling a bit unsettled after my African trip and that I might feel differently after a few months so, as you say, I did apply for the job in Dr Lee's lab.'

'Not a happy time?' asked Steven.

'A strange time,' replied Samantha with an infectious smile, as if she'd been looking for a suitable euphemism.

'Strange?' Steven persisted.

'Dr Lee...' Samantha hesitated before completing the sentence. 'Well, let's just say he had problems.'

'It's all right,' Steven assured her. 'I'm well aware of Dr Lee's "problems".'

'Oh good,' said Samantha. 'Then it was one weird place, if you really want to know. The staff seemed to spend half their time covering up for the fact that their boss was pissed out of his skull!'

Steven smiled and agreed that it must have been odd. 'You must remember Carol Bain?'

'Oh yes,' said Samantha. 'I actually bumped into her last year when she came to visit one of the patients. A nice woman.'

Steven looked at her for a moment as if challenging her assessment.

'Oh, all right,' laughed Carol. 'She was a right cow who related more easily to dead bodies than she ever did to live ones. She seemed to resent me from the word go, so let's say I never found her particularly helpful.'

'How about John Merton?'

'Clever chap, good at his job, taught me a lot but not enough to make me want to stay in lab work. From what I could see, he did most of the covering up for Dr Lee.'

'I understand you worked on the Julie Summers case?'

'I was on the team,' agreed Samantha, 'but I didn't do much.'

'Would you remember who did what?'

Samantha thought for a moment before saying, 'As I recall, it wasn't a particularly difficult case in forensic terms because of the semen found on the dead girl and the perfect match they got with the man from the village. I think Carol did most of the DNA work on it although John did some as well. Dr Lee pottered around with fibres found on the dead girl's clothes. I remember he got a match with fibres also found on the accused man's clothes but then it turned out that they came from furniture in the accused man's house and there was no dispute about the girl having been there – I think she had babysat for them in the past?'

Steven nodded.

'The pantomime really got under way when most of the samples taken at the scene of the crime got chucked out and everyone started running around like headless chickens. Luckily the semen match was so strong that it didn't matter too much. Dr Lee wouldn't admit it was him who discarded the samples but everyone seemed to know it was.'

'What did you personally work on?'

'I was put to work on the scrapings found under the dead girl's nails,' said Samantha.

Steven felt his throat tighten but he gave no outward sign of the surprise he felt at this unexpected revelation. 'What did you do exactly?' he asked.

'I was asked to type the blood that had been found there.'

Steven sensed a certain reluctance in Samantha to continue. 'And?' he prompted.

'I screwed up,' said Samantha, casting her eyes downward and self-consciously rubbing her forehead as if still embarrassed at the memory.

'In what way?' asked Steven.

'I concluded that the blood was group "O" negative but it turned out I'd used distilled water instead of saline in the agglutination tests and got false negatives. The blood was actually "A" positive.'

'Someone checked your findings?

'I was very junior. Someone always checked my work.'

Steven nodded.

'John Merton was very kind about it and blamed the bottles being on the wrong shelves. Thank God it wasn't Carol: she would have shouted my mistake from the rooftops. Anyway, it was that experience that made me decide that lab work wasn't for me.'

'But the scrapings were definitely analysed before they were discarded?' asked Steven, going for the key question with bated breath.

'Oh yes,' said Samantha, lifting a weight from his shoulders without realising it. 'Everything was done.'

Steven had to accept that his theory about the examinations not being done was wrong. Lee may not have carried out the work personally but the work had been done and that was the important thing.

'Did Dr Lee himself get involved in the analysis of the scrapings?' he asked.

'I think he did,' replied Samantha, destroying what was left of the Dunbar theory. 'I don't think he was very good at DNA work but he liked to go through the motions and John was always on hand to keep him right.'

'What was the final outcome?'

'The scrapings confirmed David Little as being the murderer.'

Steven smiled at Samantha and said, 'You have been a tremendous help. In fact, you've just told me everything I needed to know.'

Steven had a lightness in his step as he left the hospital and walked back to the car. He no longer had the feeling of trying to run in soft sand. Samantha Styles had told him exactly what he needed to know; that the material found under Julie Summers' fingernails had confirmed the case against David Little. He could return to London with an easy mind.

Steven checked out of the hotel and drove to Edinburgh airport where he returned the hire car to Hertz before booking himself on the next British Airways shuttle flight to Heathrow. He was standing in the lounge looking out at the rain sweeping across the main runway when his mobile rang.

'Yes?'

'Peter McClintock.'

'And just in time to say goodbye,' said Steven. 'I'm at the airport.' He expected McClintock to be pleased and come back with some kind of a joke but there was a short pause before the policeman said, 'I thought you should know that Ronnie Lee's gone missing.'

'Missing,' repeated Steven.

'And his wife's blaming you.'

'How in God's name could he go missing? He didn't look as if he could stand up let alone go missing.'

'His wife told Grampian Police that he was greatly upset by your questions yesterday and didn't seem himself last night. When she got up this morning his bed was empty. She thinks he must have wandered off somewhere in his pyjamas in the middle of the night. The temperature dropped below freezing last night in the highlands. She's been screaming harassment to anyone who'll listen.'

'Who's listening?'

'Luckily, no one at the moment but Grampian Police thought we'd like to be kept in the picture,' said McClintock.

Steven considered for a moment before making a reluctant decision and saying, 'I've just changed my mind about leaving. I'll stay until they find him. Let me know as soon as there are any developments.'

Steven cancelled his shuttle ticket and went back to the car hire desk.

'Change of heart?' asked the girl.

'Couldn't bear to leave,' said Steven, filling in the paper-work all over again. He saw no point in travelling back across town to the hotel where he had been staying so he checked into the airport hotel instead and called Sci-Med.

'Any idea where he might have gone?' asked Macmillan.

'None at all.'

'But he was disturbed by your visit?'

'He was more angry than disturbed,' said Steven. 'I really wasn't hard on him.'

'So where the hell has he gone?'

'I don't think he was in any physical condition to go very far,' said Steven. 'I'm surprised he made it to the front door.'

'I don't wish to pre-empt matters but did he strike you as the suicidal type?' asked Macmillan.

'Far from it,' replied Steven. 'He was full of bitterness and resentment. He genuinely believes he got a raw deal when they forced him into retirement. According to him, everything that happened was just down to either circumstances or the fault of other people.'

'I think they call it "being in denial" these days,' said Macmillan.

'If you say so,' said Steven.

'And his wife?

'Standing by her man. She seemed to share his view. Neither seemed to acknowledge that being permanently pissed could be a drawback for a forensic pathologist.'

'This could get very messy,' said Macmillan. 'Let's try to minimise the fall-out if this woman starts stirring things up all over again. I like to maintain good relations with our police colleagues wherever possible.'

Steven grimaced as he put the phone down. 'Easier said than done,' he murmured.

Steven remained on tenterhooks for the next couple of

hours, not knowing what to do but feeling uncomfortable about doing nothing. He snatched up the phone when it rang. It was McClintock.

'They've found him. He's dead.'

'Shit,' said Steven.

'Apparently there's a steep drop at the back of his house to the river.'

'There is,' agreed Steven, thinking of the view of the Spey he'd admired from there.

'Some time last night he walked over it, only he didn't make it into the water. He impaled himself on a sharp tree stump after falling fifty feet or so. The local plods are treating it as suicide. Seems like old Ronnie even fucked that up.'

'When's the PM?'

'Tomorrow in Inverness.'

'I want to be there,' said Steven. He wasn't sure why but he didn't feel comfortable with the idea of Lee committing suicide. A man like Lee would have seen that as letting the bastards win.

'Nothing I can do personally,' said McClintock, 'but I can give you the name of my Grampian contact. He's DI Hamish Teal.' McClintock gave Steven the telephone number.

'Thanks for your help,' said Steven.

'Something tells me that a whole lot of shit is going to start flying,' said McClintock ruefully. 'I'd hate to be wearing a white suit.'

Steven could think of nothing reassuring to say. He took a moment to consider before calling Sci-Med to inform John Macmillan of Lee's death. 'I don't think he committed suicide.'

'Anything to back that up?'

'Just instinct.'

'Well, it's served you well enough in the past,' conceded Macmillan. 'What do you want to do?'

'I want to call a code red on it,' said Steven. His request was that his inquiry in Scotland should no longer be regarded as unofficial but that he should be considered fully operational with all that entailed. In effect this would mean that he would no longer be reliant on the voluntary cooperation of individual police officers in his investigation but that his official status as a Sci-Med Inspector on Home Office business would oblige relevant police authorities to cooperate fully with any request he made. He would also be entitled to full back-up from Sci-Med who would see to it that he had everything he needed from simple information to weapons should they be necessary. He would have access to operational funds through two credit cards and access to a special phone line, which guaranteed access to a duty officer at Sci-Med at any hour of the day or night.

'Up to you,' said Macmillan, as he usually did in this situation. The nuance in his voice however, suggested that Steven had better have a good reason in the long run for doing this. 'Do you have your laptop with you?'

Steven said not. He knew that he'd need one for secure electronic communication.

'We'll get one to you. Where are you staying?'

'The airport hotel at Edinburgh.'

Steven was called down to the lobby half an hour later. He was surprised to find McClintock standing there. 'Room service,' said McClintock holding out a notebook computer by the strap of its leather carry case.

'Should I tip you?' smiled Steven.

'I came to tip you,' replied McClintock. 'Santini just about went through the roof when the Home Office directive came in. I think he's considering putting out a contract on you.'

Steven smiled.

'Don't laugh,' said McClintock. 'I'm the hit man.'

'Then let me buy you a beer so you'll leave your prints on the glass,' smiled Steven. He led McClintock through to the hotel bar where he was true to his word.

'Seriously,' said McClintock. 'The powers that be have already been on to Sci-Med asking just what the fuck you think you're up to.'

'And what were they told?'

'Some guy called Macmillan told them that you must have had good reason for putting your inquiry on a more official basis and that was as much as they needed to know. That's what I call backing up your people,' said McClintock admiringly. 'I wish I could say the same for my lot.'

Steven smiled.

'But do you know the best bit?' said McClintock leaning across the table conspiratorially. 'When Santini asked the DCC what would happen if he refused to cooperate with the Sci-Med directive, he was told to look out his lollipop because he would be on school crossings within the week. Like the Titanic, that went down really well!'

Steven almost choked on his beer.

'Don't ever let on to Santini that I told you that,' said McClintock.

'I won't,' Steven assured him. 'And thanks. I'm grateful.'

'I just hope you know what you're doing,' said McClintock, finishing his beer and getting up to go.

Steven found himself hoping much the same thing as he went back upstairs. He connected the modem of the laptop to the phone socket in the room and logged on to Sci-Med where his first message was decoded as DUNBAR GREEN, indicating that he now had full operational status. There followed details of numbers and codes to be used during the course of the assignment. Two credit cards would be delivered to the hotel first thing in the morning. He was also requested to contact the duty officer at Sci-Med directly with any immediate requests.

Steven called and asked that the Grampian Police authority be informed of his being in their area on the following day and that he would like to be present at the post-mortem examination of Ronald Lee. He gave the man the name of the Grampian police officer, DI Teal, that McClintock had given him as a contact name, thinking that this might be quicker than depending on things coming from the top downwards. The duty man called back just before 11 p.m. to say that the post-mortem on Lee had been rescheduled from 9 a.m. to noon to give him time to get up to Inverness. He was given the address of the city mortuary, elementary directions and the name of the pathologist who would be carrying out the autopsy, Dr Robert Reid.

Steven did not sleep well. He was haunted by dreams of Hector Combe laughing at him from the gates of hell while an angry Mary Lee accused him of being responsible for her husband's death. 'Just leave it alone,' advised Peter McClintock repeatedly in the background while Santini stood in the road stopping his progress by holding up a lollipop stick with 'Stop' written on it. Any argument he tried to mount was countered by Combe grinning at him and making a snapping gesture with his fingers as he whispered, 'This little piggy went to market... Snap! This little piggy stayed at home...'.

Steven woke with a start before the third snap and found that he was bathed in sweat. He looked at his watch and saw that it was just after three, the hour when the human spirit was at its lowest ebb and problems were magnified most. He lay slowly back down on the pillow and watched the moving shadows of the tree branches on the ceiling as the wind rose and fell outside. He knew that the sense of unease he felt stemmed from the fact he was acting on instinct rather than on any firm grounds for suspicion. He just had the feeling that something was dreadfully wrong about the Julie Summers case although at the moment it was hard to see exactly what. What did he hope to prove? If he didn't know the answer to that – and he didn't – it was no wonder that the local police were thoroughly pissed off with him.

Steven was on the road by seven in the morning. He had been warned that it might take some time to get across the Forth Road Bridge in the morning rush hour and so it proved with heavy traffic backed up on the approach roads. As he waited, he watched a small helicopter circle mockingly overhead and guessed that it would be reporting traffic conditions to a local radio station, informing commuters that there was a traffic jam where there was a traffic jam every morning.

Once over the bridge and on to the M90, he made good

progress as far as Perth but then slowed as the motorway came
to an end and he was funnelled back on to a trunk road where
the slowest vehicle determined the speed of the convoy until
overtaking became possible – usually on intermittent small
sections of dual carriageway.

Steven still reached Inverness in plenty of time and found
the morgue where the PM on Lee was to be performed before
parking the car and stretching his legs with a walk by the River
Ness until it was time.

The pathologist, Reid, a tall man in his early forties who was
soft-spoken and had a habit of punctuating his remarks with
an unsure half smile and a look at everyone as if to reassure
himself that he wasn't upsetting anyone, greeted him cordially.
The only other person present, apart from a mortuary attendant, was the Grampian policeman, DI Teal. He was a short,
thickset man who acknowledged his presence with a nod.

Reid was already gowned and aproned. He invited Steven to
do the same, indicating a row of clothes pegs with gowns and
aprons hanging from them. There was a wooden-slatted bench
below under which was a neat row of white Wellington boots.
Steven went for full overalls while Teal made do with an apron
over his double-breasted suit.

The attendant brought out Lee's body from the refrigerated
vault and Steven grimaced when he saw that the tree stump
that had skewered Lee had been left in place. It had been sawn
off at the base to permit retrieval of the body from the river-
bank but the jagged stump was still protruding from his chest.
A look of agonised horror was etched on Lee's face as if he had
seen what was coming as he fell.

'Not a pretty death,' said Reid, again with his half smile.

'Poor bugger,' murmured Teal.

Reid started his external appraisal of the body, recording his
findings into an overhead microphone as he did so. When he
said, 'The body has slight contusions to the left side of the
neck and adjacent shoulder,' Steven interrupted and asked if
he could take a look for himself. Reid stepped back and
extended an invitation with a gloved hand. Steven took a

closer look then asked for a magnifying glass before doing so
again.

In the background Reid said, 'I'm not quite sure what your
interest is in this case, Doctor. No one had the grace to tell
me.'

Steven was aware of the pathologist and the policeman
exchanging glances when he didn't answer but for the moment
he pressed on with his inspection, moving down to Lee's torso
and paying close attention to his waist where he concentrated
on more marks he found there. 'I think I've found something,'
he said, straightening up and inviting Reid to take a look for
himself.

'Ah,' said Reid, 'I see what you're getting at. These marks
together with the marks on the deceased's neck would suggest
that he was held firmly from behind before...'

'...being pushed over the cliff,' completed Steven.

'Very possibly,' said Reid.

Teal rolled his eyes skywards and said, 'You're saying this
was murder not suicide?'

'I rather think we are,' said Reid with his half smile.

The policeman nodded as if this were unwelcome news. 'I
don't suppose any prizes are on offer for figuring out what
actually killed him,' he said, eyeing up the wooden stake protruding from Lee's chest.

'No,' agreed Reid. 'But we'll go through the whole business
anyway.' He was about to start the autopsy proper when
something caught his eye and he put down the knife. It was
Steven's turn to swop glances with the policeman when Reid
appeared to take an interest in Lee's teeth, a task made consid-
erably easier by Lee's lips already being pulled back over them
in his pained death grimace. Reid scrabbled around for a pair
of forceps from the tray beside him and extracted a small fragment of material from between two of them. 'Unless I'm very
much mistaken,' he announced, holding it up to the light, 'this
is latex. My guess is that it came from a glove like the ones I'm
wearing at the moment, a surgical glove.'

'Lee's attacker must have been wearing them and Lee bit

him during the struggle,' said Steven. 'Well spotted, Doctor.'

Reid smiled as he put the fragment carefully into a sterile specimen jar. 'Looks clean; I don't think we'll get any DNA from it but it's worth a try.'

'Probably put his hand over Lee's mouth to stop him yelling out,' offered the policeman. He turned to Steven and said, 'I don't suppose you've any thoughts about motive that you'd care to share with us, Doctor?'

Steven shook his head. 'I wish I had,' he said. 'All I know at the moment is that there is some connection with the death of a young girl who died over eight years ago.'

'Julie Summers,' murmured Teal. 'Lothian and Borders are going to love this.'

'That's their problem,' said Steven, noting that Teal must have been briefed about the situation. 'Right now, Inspector, you have a murder on your hands.'

Steven felt a mixture of guilt and relief; guilt at being pleased that Lee had been murdered and relief at having been proved right in calling a code red. It was possible that Lee's death might not be connected to the Julie Summers case but the fact that it had taken place the day after he'd questioned him about it suggested strongly that it had. This upped the stakes enormously. Lee must have confided in someone that Sci-Med was taking an interest in the case and that he had been questioned about the evidence. That someone had seen this as sufficient reason for killing him, but why?

The obvious reason would be to keep him quiet, thought Steven, but quiet about what? What kind of screw-up in the handling of secondary evidence could be so damning that someone would want to kill to keep it secret?

Steven told Teal that he wanted to inform Lee's wife personally about her husband's murder. He hoped that the fact it wasn't suicide would remove the feelings of guilt that always affected the nearest and dearest of the deceased. He also hoped that she might mellow in her attitude towards him personally and help him find out whom her husband had been in contact with over the last couple of days.

'Please yourself but I'll have to send in a forensic team to the house,' said Teal.

'Of course,' agreed Steven. 'Maybe you could check where Mrs Lee is at the moment? She might be staying with friends or relatives.'

Teal left the PM suite to start things moving and Steven left a short time later, leaving Reid to complete the post-mortem. He decided to walk for a bit, mainly to let the fresh air take away the smell of formaldehyde that he feared might still be clinging to his clothes. It was a smell he had loathed from his student days at medical school where they'd used formalin solution to preserve the bodies the classes worked on. The stiffening westerly breeze was today very welcome, carrying on it as it did, the scent of wet grass and pine needles.

Despite being convinced that Lee's murder was connected with his questioning of the man and try as he might, Steven failed to see a motive behind the murder. What could Lee have told him that he didn't know already? That he didn't really examine the scrapings from under Julie Summers' fingernails himself? So what? It didn't matter…unless of course, what was being covered up was the unthinkable, the possibility that the traces of blood and skin *had not matched the convicted man at all.*

'Jesus Christ,' murmured Steven.

Chapter Nine

Steven's mobile phone rang. It was Detective Inspector Teal.

'You wanted to know about Mary Lee's whereabouts,' said Teal. 'She's in Glasgow's Western Infirmary. She took a heart attack while travelling down to her sister's place in Greenock.'

'Shit,' said Steven. 'How bad?'

'Touch and go.'

'I'm on my way,' said Steven. He set out for Glasgow immediately, pausing only to fill the car up with petrol at a station at the edge of town. He still saw Mary Lee as his best chance of finding out who Ronnie had contacted since his visit to Ptarmigan Cottage.

As he drove south he tried to think through all the logical implications if the fingernail scrapings had not come from David Little. Had a second person been involved in the crime and Lee had covered it up? This would certainly provide someone with a motive for murdering Lee – to head off another deathbed confession – but why would Lee want to cover up something like that in the first place? Blackmail? The involvement of a relative?

Although Steven had trained himself to think the unthinkable and explore every avenue, dismissing nothing without cold, logical consideration, he decided that he was on the wrong track. The situation in Lee's lab at the time of the murder was such that Lee simply could not have covered up anything on his own. In any case, it was almost certain that someone else had carried out the tests on the fingernail samples so at least one other person must have known about the findings.

According to Carol Bain and Samantha Styles, John Merton had been riding shotgun on Lee for some time – covering up for his shortcomings, keeping an eye on him in the lab and discreetly checking his findings before reports were allowed to go out. Even if Merton had not carried out the analysis himself he would almost certainly have seen the results of the tests and perhaps even been called upon to verify them. If there had been some kind of a problem with the origin of the scrapings,

John Merton would have known about it.

Steven thought he could see a possible scenario emerge. Lee, either through incompetence or inebriation, had messed up his analysis of the nail scrapings. Merton, in his role of guardian angel, had tried to cover for him but Lee's results were such a mess that they defied interpretation. The small amounts of material available had all been used up, making a repeat analysis impossible and leaving the lab with an embarrassing problem. The temptation might well have been to pretend that the analysis of the scrapings had supported Carol Bain's findings on the semen and to say no more about it. Whatever the truth of the matter, he was looking forward to hearing what John Merton had to say about all this when he finally managed to track him down.

It was just after four in the afternoon when he entered the outskirts of Glasgow and caught what he thought must be the beginnings of rush-hour traffic as he made his way to the Western Infirmary. Progress however, became even slower and it became clear that, despite having a three-lane motorway that cut a great swathe through its centre, Glasgow's traffic was grinding to a virtual standstill because of road-works.

Steven turned on the car radio to provide distraction from his growing sense of frustration but if anything, inane chatter and mindless pop music only made matters worse. After covering less than a mile in fifteen minutes his phone rang and gave him the news he didn't want to hear. Mary Lee was dead.

Although the east-bound traffic did not seem to be moving any more freely than the west-bound, Steven took the next exit when it became possible and circled round to join it, thinking that he might as well make a start back to Edinburgh. A lorry driver flashed his lights and he inched out into the nearside lane to become a piece in a slow-moving jigsaw.

Watching a fat man in overalls, sitting in the passenger seat of the white van in the lane beside him, chew gum and gaze at the nude picture in the tabloid newspaper he was reading made him consider Darwinian evolution for a few minutes. He felt it was anything but cut and dried.

When the traffic in that lane finally started to move, it afforded him a temporary view of the high walls of Barlinnie Prison where David Little had been incarcerated for the past eight years. The file said that he was a rule 43 prisoner – in solitary confinement at his own request. Solitary confinement for life?

Steven grimaced at the thought. How anyone could retain their sanity under such conditions was quite beyond him. He could understand why Little might have opted for rule 43 at the outset of his sentence when, after all the publicity, other prisoners would have been queuing up to establish their credentials as 'regular guys' by beating the shit out of him. In prison as in life, all things were relative. Everyone needed someone to look up to and someone to look down on. Child abusers and murderers were welcome in prison because they made robbery with violence seem almost respectable. Beating up a child abuser made you the Lone Ranger. 'Who was that masked burglar, Mommy?'

On the other hand, it was possible that Little might regard solitary confinement as some kind of penance for his crime. The conditions would be almost monastic – an enclosed order, basic food and endless hours available for contemplation. Perhaps he had even found religion in his now otherwise meaningless existence. He wouldn't be the first and conditions would be absolutely right for it. Disorientation followed by suggestion – the first rule of brainwashing or religious conversion for that matter. But even if he had, how could he hope to come to terms with having carried out such an awful crime? Could atonement ever be achieved or would guilt stretch out before Little like the expanding universe?

Almost to his own surprise, Steven found himself indicating a left turn and edging across to the nearside lane in order to take the next exit. He had decided that he needed to confront Little personally. If there was the slightest chance that the man now acknowledged his guilt he might well be prepared to answer some questions about what had really happened on that awful night and in particular, how he got the scratch mark on his arm.

Although there had been nothing in the files to indicate that Little had stopped maintaining his innocence, there was a chance that the files hadn't been updated for some time. As far as society was concerned, Little had been convicted and sentenced to life imprisonment for the rape and murder of Julie Summers. End of story. Whether or not he admitted it was neither here nor there.

Almost as soon as he had parked the car and started to walk towards the prison his subconscious started searching for excuses not to proceed. Prisons had that effect on him. They were more than just grey, forbidding buildings; they were monuments to human failure, housing a hellish mix of wasted lives and broken dreams, often spiced with evil and violence. They were Pandora's boxes with the lids wide open.

He glanced at his watch. So far, it had taken him fourteen minutes to reach the office of an assistant governor. His path had been impeded by bureaucracy at every step of the way. The natural response of officialdom to any out of the ordinary request was to set up a wall of obstruction. His ID card had been passed around like a parcel at a party. He had been told by one man that he would have to go through official channels and apply in writing and by another that his request was simply not possible... 'Because it wasn't, that's why.' It was only his insistence that a phone call to the Home Office be made that eventually paid off and he found himself in the office of Assistant Governor John Cummings, an angry-looking man with short red hair and a clipped moustache. He had the florid complexion of a heavy drinker but the build of a gym teacher although perhaps a little on the short side.

'Little doesn't see visitors,' said Cummings.

'Has anyone ever asked to see him?' asked Steven.

'That's beside the point,' insisted Cummings. 'He has his books and that's all he needs. He doesn't speak to anyone he doesn't have to. 'He reads and makes notes. That's it. He's shut himself off in his own little world.'

'What kind of stuff does he read?'

'Journals mainly, scientific journals.'

'I'd still like to see him,' said Steven.

Cummings shrugged and said sourly, 'And you have friends in high places, right?'

'Not friends,' said Steven acidly. 'Employers; I believe they just might be yours too if I'm not mistaken.'

Cummings thought for a moment before conceding. 'Well, don't blame me if it's a waste of time and he refuses to say anything. You can take a horse to water etc.' He picked up the phone and gave instructions that David Little be brought to an interview room. He and Steven sat in silence until the phone rang to confirm that this had been done. A prison officer with a badly repaired harelip and impaired speech because of it was detailed to escort Steven to the meeting with Little. He didn't say anything en route but Steven was aware of several prisoners along the way affecting a speech impediment as they passed. Most of them did it almost out of earshot but one did it too close for the officer to pretend that he'd not heard.

'You'll be sorry, Edwards,' the officer spat out the corner of his mouth.

He said it with such venom that Steven had little doubt that the man would, but then he didn't doubt that life in Scotland's toughest jail would be anything other than a constant battle of wills with an undercurrent of threatened violence.

The room allocated for his meeting with Little seemed little different from a cell. It had four bare walls and a high, barred window affording glimpses of passing clouds. Perhaps the rough table and two plastic chairs altered its status, he surmised. 'I want to speak to him alone,' he said to the accompanying officer. The man opened his mouth as if to protest but changed his mind and said, 'I'll be right outside.'

Steven was shocked at David Little's appearance when he was finally brought in. He had only seen a photograph of him, taken at the time of his arrest, but all trace of youth had now disappeared from the man standing in front of him. His head was shaven, his cheeks were sunken and his eyes had retreated into large dark hollows. He was painfully thin. The officer escorting him undid his handcuffs and Steven asked the man to wait outside. He indicated to Little that he should sit opposite him at the table.

'My name's Dunbar,' said Steven, showing his ID card. 'I work for the Sci-Med Inspectorate. I'm looking into certain aspects of the Julie Summers case.'

Little looked Steven in the eye but didn't say anything. Steven thought it was a classic 'You-didn't-ask-a-question-so-I'm-not-replying' response.

'I'd appreciate if you would answer some questions,' said Steven.

Little got out of his chair as if to indicate that the interview was at an end.

'Sit down,' snapped Steven.

Little sat down and resumed his stare.

Steven found it unnerving. It wasn't dumb insolence; it was something more detached. It was the look of a man who had given up on life, someone who was no longer a participant but merely a disinterested spectator.

'I won't bullshit you,' said Steven. 'I don't feel any sympathy for you. What you did to that young girl was beyond the pale. But why you did it is another matter and I'm willing to concede that there are all sorts of mental aberrations that medicine knows very little about. Maybe you're sick. Maybe you couldn't help yourself. But whatever the reason, you can help lessen the aftermath of what happened by answering my questions.'

Little made no response. He simply maintained his stare.

'I'll be straight with you,' said Steven. 'I'm here because a man in the State Hospital at Carstairs, a convicted killer named Hector Combe, confessed on his deathbed to the rape and murder of Julie Summers.'

Although Little didn't say anything Steven saw a change of expression in his eyes. It was only there for a moment but he was almost certain that he saw the veil lift to be replaced by...what? He found that harder to interpret. Sadness was the best that he could come up with but he suspected it was far deeper than that. It was as if, in an instant, Little had caught a glimpse of what his life might have been like had things been different. 'Did you ever meet Hector Combe?' Steven asked.

Little shook his head slowly.

'You're absolutely sure?'

A nod of the head.

'Julie scratched you on the arm,' said Steven. 'Tell me about it.'

Little behaved as if he hadn't heard. His gaze moved off to the middle distance.

'Did you hear what I said?' prompted Steven.

Little remained silent.

'Come on man,' urged Steven. 'You've got nothing to lose by telling me now.'

'I can't help you,' said Little, speaking for the first time and taking Steven by surprise. The voice was calm and cultured.

'Why?' demanded Steven. 'What's the big silence all about? Does shutting yourself off make the guilt easier to bear? If you maintain you're innocent you don't ever have to face up to the guilt? Is that it? If you don't say the words it can't be true? Christ man, you've got a lot of years ahead of you to keep that up.'

Little seemed unimpressed. He looked down at Steven's ID card lying on the table. 'You're a doctor,' he said.

Steven nodded.

Little leaned forward and planted the index finger of his right hand on his right cheek and held it there. 'What do you think this is?' he asked.

Steven took a closer look and saw there was a small purple lesion there.

'And here,' said Little, moving his finger to the side of his neck.

Steven saw another purple mark. His blood ran cold as he recognised what the lesions were. 'Good God,' he murmured. 'Kaposi's sarcoma.'

'Well done,' said Little, without emotion.

'Are you telling me you've got AIDS?' asked Steven.

'I think we can both agree on that,' said Little.

'But...how?' asked Steven.

Little let a long silence elapse before he said, 'When I first came here some of my fellow prisoners – fine upstanding chaps that they are – felt I should be taught a lesson. They decided that I should know what it felt like to be raped – just like my "victim". At least, I think that was the rationale behind it.'

'My God,' whispered Steven. 'And you finished up with AIDS.'

Little's silence was more eloquent than any reply. Eventually he said, 'So you see, I won't have all the years you imagine.'

'But you must be getting treatment,' said Steven, although it was more of a question. The look on Little's face made his blood go even colder. 'The authorities don't know?' he asked almost incredulously. 'You haven't told anyone?'

'No point,' said Little. 'And they haven't noticed although they probably will when the next little pathological 'treat' for me arrives. What d'you reckon? Pneumocystis pneumonia? Tuberculosis? Some creeping fungal infection? Maybe a brain tumour?'

Like Little, Steven knew there was no way of predicting what a person with AIDS would fall prey to next once their immune system had packed in and left them open to the myriad invading forces of the microbial world. 'But surely the prison doctor noticed these marks on you?' he said.

'He might spot a broken leg on a good day,' said Little.

'But my God man, there's a lot they can do to help these days. You should be on combination therapy,' said Steven.

The look on Little's face made Steven suddenly realise that he was overlooking the now obvious fact that Little didn't have much interest in slowing down the condition that was going to kill him.

Little read Steven's mind and said quietly, 'I've really nothing left to lose. My job, my wife, my children, my freedom, my self-respect – all long gone. Ironic really but AIDS is going to be my saviour, my get-out-of-jail card. No more hell on earth, just sweet, beautiful, endless sleep.'

'I don't know what to say,' said Steven.

'Just as long as you don't start suggesting it's God's way of punishing me,' said Little.

'No,' replied Steven. 'I won't do that but I'd still like you to answer my questions if it's all the same to you.'

'I can't.'

'Why not?'

'Because I had nothing to do with Julie Summers's murder.'

Steven shook his head in exasperation but he still felt disconcerted when he saw that the man clearly believed what he was saying. 'For God's sake man,' he protested, 'the prosecution came up with a perfect DNA match for you.'

'So they did,' said Little sarcastically.

'So what are you suggesting? That they made the whole lot up?'

Little's slight shrug seemed to suggest an affirmative.

'How? Why?'

Little shrugged again.

'I'm sorry, I don't believe you,' said Steven.

Little did not show any reaction. He said simply, 'Neither did my wife, the police, the prosecuting counsel, the judge and the jury,' replied Little. 'It really doesn't matter any more. It'll soon be over.'

Steven felt uneasy. Although he felt that continuing denial must be Little's way of dealing with the burden of guilt, the fact that the evidence against him – however good – had come from Lee's lab was still a worry. He got up from the table and Little did the same.

The prison officers came back into the room on hearing the sound of the chairs moving back and Steven watched as Little was led away.

As he left the room, Little turned and said, 'I really didn't kill her.'

'Like fuck you didn't,' growled the officer escorting him.

'Some of them are like that,' said the man with the harelip.

'They go to their grave insisting they were innocent.'

'If I want Mickey Mouse psychiatry, I'll let you know,' snapped Steven, almost immediately regretting it. He was on edge.

'Get what you wanted?' asked Cummings.

'Not exactly. Did you know David Little has full-blown AIDS?' replied Steven.

'Christ, you're kidding!' exclaimed Cummings.

Steven's accusing look removed any doubt.

'Jesus Christ, that's all I need,' complained Cummings as he picked up the phone and punched in four numbers. 'Is the Doctor still there? Gone? Shit.' Cummings slammed down the receiver and looked at Steven. 'You're sure about this?' he asked.

'He's got Kaposi's sarcoma on his face and neck. It's usually a sure sign.'

'How on earth would he get...?'

'Male rape,' interrupted Steven.

'Christ,' murmured Cummings. After a moment he thought he saw an objection and said, 'But he's been on rule 43 for years.'

'AIDS can take several years to develop,' said Steven.

'Of course,' conceded Cummings. 'I wasn't thinking straight. Look, I'll get on to the doctor at home and tell him to get his bloody finger out and organise some treatment for Little. Best I can do.'

'He may refuse. He wants to die.'

'I'll have to see what the rule book says.'

'I want to take a buccal swab from Little,' said Steven.

Cummings seemed shocked. 'What for?'

'I want to check his DNA profile.'

Cummings stared at him as if he couldn't believe his ears then he said, 'That's all we need, a rumour starting that Little is innocent. You do know what you're doing?' he asked.

Steven remained impassive.

Cummings made a steeple with his hands and covered his mouth and nose for a few moments before seeming to conclude that any argument would be pointless. He simply asked, 'What do you need?'

'Just a cotton swab and a sterile tube.'

Harelip was detailed to take Steven first to the sickbay to pick up supplies and then to David Little's cell.

'I thought we'd said our goodbyes,' said Little, who was sitting reading a copy of the science magazine, *Nature*.

'I'd like to take a buccal smear from you,' said Steven.

'What for?'

'DNA fingerprinting.'

'Is this some kind of sick joke?'

'I want to compare it with samples taken at the scene of Julie Summers' murder. A second opinion if you like. Something your lawyer should have done.'

'He believed I was guilty from the outset. That was obvious.'

'So what was your defence?' asked Steven.

'My lawyer said he was willing to enter a plea of insanity but that there was no point in arguing about technicalities: the evidence against me was so overwhelming.'

'Who was your lawyer?'

'Paul Verdi of Seymour, Nicholson and Verdi.'

'What did you say to that?'

'I said it was all some awful mistake. There must have been some mix-up in the lab but no one would listen, not even Charlotte. I'll never forget the look on her face when...'

'About that swab?' said Steven, wanting the conversation to end.

'There's no point,' said Little.

Steven looked at him. 'Scared of what I'll come up with?' he asked. 'Think you might have to face up to your guilt after all?'

Little didn't reply. Instead he opened his mouth and allowed Steven to rub the cotton-tipped swab around the inside of his right cheek.

'Tell me one thing,' said Steven as he carefully placed the swab inside a sterile tube, making sure that the tip did not touch anything else. 'How did you get the scratch you had on your arm when you were arrested?'

'Our cat, Romeo, did it.'

Ronald Lee's murder made it into all the papers next morning. The story was generally presented as a highland tragedy, a mindless killing followed by the death of the victim's wife, suggesting a devoted couple who clearly couldn't live without each other. Two of the nationals however did note that Lee had been the forensic pathologist involved in the murder investigation of Julie Summers. One of them also recalled that he had taken early retirement in the aftermath of the case.

'Lothian and Borders Police have been on to the Home Office again,' said John Macmillan when Steven called Sci-Med. 'Suffice to say they're hopping mad about your latest exploit.'

'And what would that be?' asked Steven.

'They say you've visited David Little in prison and taken a sample from him for DNA analysis. They're complaining that you're giving everyone the impression that there was something wrong with the original one.'

'Well, that certainly got around fast,' said Steven. 'That's actually why I'm calling. I do want the DNA fingerprinting done again if only for my own peace of mind. I'd also like it to be done locally rather than send the samples to London so I need a name, someone independent of the police and forensic services up here.'

'You don't really think that Little could be innocent, do you?' said Macmillan.

'I don't know what to think right now,' said Steven.

'But the DNA evidence against him was...'

'Overwhelming, yes, I know,' interrupted Steven. 'But all the same, I just know there's something badly wrong with the Summers case. I keep looking for reassurance but so far I haven't found any. There are just too many question marks.'

'All right,' sighed Macmillan. 'We'll make arrangements for the sequencing and get back to you. Anything else?'

'I'd like to know the current whereabouts of a man named John Merton who was on the staff of the forensic lab at the time of the murder. He left when Ronald Lee was put out to grass and worked in the medical school for a while but then he moved on.'

'We'll do our best,' said Macmillan.

Next Steven called McDougal, the current head of forensics in Edinburgh, to ask if he had any objection to giving him access to the semen samples recovered from Julie Summers.

'I personally don't have any objection,' said McDougal although he sounded puzzled. 'Is there a problem?'

'I hope not,' said Steven.

'I dare say you won't be alone in these sentiments,' said McDougal. 'I read about the deaths of Ronald Lee and his wife in the papers this morning. I even had a journalist phoning me to ask if I had anything to say on the matter.'

'Did you?' asked Steven.

'Only that I never knew the man.'

'One more thing: when I come by to pick up the samples, could I have another word with Carol Bain?' Steven wanted to ask her about John Merton.

'I'll tell her to expect you,' said McDougal.

Steven said that he would be over some time in the afternoon and then called Peter McClintock at Fettes Police Headquarters to ask if he'd meet him at lunchtime in the pub they'd used before in Inverleith Row.

'Being seen with you is not exactly a good career move right now,' said McClintock. 'Your prison visit has been the talk of the steamie all morning.'

'The what?'

'I forgot you were English,' replied McClintock. 'In the days when men were men and women were grateful, the steamie was a communal washhouse for cleaning clothes. It was where Scots housewives used to meet and exchange gossip.'

'Right. About that drink?'

'One o'clock. I'll be the one wearing a blonde wig and swearing I don't know anyone called Dunbar.'

Steven saw that he had about an hour to kill so he sat down

and tried to get his thoughts in order. Telling Sci-Med that he had a bad feeling about the case wasn't going to be enough to sustain continued investigation for much longer. He would need something more concrete to offer Macmillan next time they spoke. There had been a distinct edginess in Macmillan's voice when they'd spoken earlier and Steven suspected that he was being subjected to Home Office pressure.

The duty officer at Sci-Med phoned as he was driving across town to meet McClintock. He told him that Sci-Med had arranged for a molecular biologist at the University of Edinburgh – a woman who had already signed the official secrets act for other aspects of her work – to carry out the semen and buccal swab analysis he'd asked for. Steven asked the man to send the relevant information to him as a text message. He was in heavy traffic and couldn't stop to note down details.

'I think Mr Macmillan would like a word with you before you hang up,' said the man.

Steven had to tuck the phone between head and hunched shoulder as he used both hands to turn the car into a side street to start looking for a parking place. His action attracted a disgusted look and shake of the head from a woman pedestrian who was waiting to cross the road. He gave her a half smile by way of apology.

'When do you plan taking the samples over?' asked Macmillan.

'This afternoon,' replied Steven, wondering why Macmillan had asked.

'If these new lab tests should suggest that David Little was not the killer of Julie Summers...' began Macmillan hesitantly, 'then of course the case must be reopened and to hell with any fall-out...'

'But?' prompted Steven.

'If the tests should confirm that the semen was in fact David Little's...'

'You'd like me to stop upsetting people and come back to London?' said Steven.

'Do you have a problem with that?' asked Macmillan.

'I suppose not,' conceded Steven. He understood the difficulty of Macmillan's position and recognised that there were limits to how long he could go on rocking the boat.

'Good,' said Macmillan. 'As long as we understand each other. Keep in touch.'

McClintock was already in the pub in Inverleith Row when Steven arrived. Steven saw that he had got himself a beer and was eating a sandwich so he did the same and joined him in the corner.

'So, do I get an invite to the opening?' asked McClintock between bites of a cheese sandwich.

'Of what?' Steven asked.

'The Steven Dunbar Forensic Lab Service,' replied McClintock.

'Highly amusing,' said Steven.

'But you are going to do the DNA fingerprinting again?' Steven confirmed it.

'Look,' said McClintock, leaning across the table, 'I know Ronnie Lee was a tosser but Christ, you're surely not suggesting that the whole lab was crooked and made the whole lot up?'

'If I didn't have doubts I wouldn't be asking for the tests,' said Steven.

McClintock stopped eating and looked at Steven in astonishment. 'Christ, you are,' he whispered. 'You really believe that Little was stitched up.'

'I didn't say that,' countered Steven. 'But there's something wrong.'

'You *think* there's something wrong,' corrected McClintock. 'And on the basis of that you're prepared to throw shit 360 degrees.'

'It's not a question of throwing shit but I am telling you, there's definitely something wrong,' insisted Steven. 'I've tried bloody hard to find evidence to show that I'm imagining it but frankly, it's been like looking for snow in July. The samples are missing; the lab reports are missing and when I ask the pathologist about it he takes an assisted walk off a cliff. The only thing left to me to check is the DNA evidence myself.'

'Have you asked McDougal to do it?' asked McClintock.

'No.'

'You don't trust anyone round here, do you?'

'Trust is like faith. I try hard not to rely on either,' said Steven.

'What did you want to see me about?' asked McClintock.

'I wanted to tell you personally why I was doing this. I suppose I hoped you'd understand.'

'And you'd get the inside gen on how the local plods were taking it,' said McClintock.

'No,' said Steven. 'I know how they're taking it. They've been on to the Home Office.'

'Good,' said McClintock. 'Then you'll know not to park on any double yellow lines in this city. You'll go down for life.'

Steven smiled wanly and said, 'You told me that the Fiscal's office was wary of relying on evidence that came from Ronnie Lee's lab. They presented as little as possible?'

McClintock nodded. 'Like I said, they lost a number of cases when everything seemed to be cut and dried. Just when they felt sure their man was going down, defence counsel would pop up and question some aspect of the forensic evidence. Suddenly, it didn't stand up any more. Case dismissed and egg on face all round.'

'Can you get me details of these cases?' asked Steven.

'Are you thinking of having them reopened too?' asked McClintock.

'You never know,' said Steven calmly.

'Bugger me, you've got balls Dunbar: I have to give you that. If I was making enemies at the rate you are I'd be spending most of my time in the bog, I'm telling you.'

'But you will get the details for me?' asked Steven.

'I'll see what I can do.'

'Another beer?'

'Maybe coffee.'

When he got back to the car, Steven checked his phone for

the Sci-Med text message he'd asked for. He called the number he'd been given at Edinburgh University and asked to
speak to Dr Susan Givens.

'Speaking.'

'My name's Dunbar. I understand the Sci-Med Inspectorate
has been in touch?' said Steven.

'Indeed they have, Doctor. I take it you have the samples?'

'I'm just about to pick them up from the police lab. Will it
be all right if I bring them over this afternoon?'

'I have a meeting at two, so any time after three? Say three
thirty?'

'Three thirty it is then,' said Steven. 'And you are in the
Institute of Cell and Molecular Biology, room 923?'

'That's right. It's the tower building on your left as you
enter through gate 4 in Mayfield Road.'

Steven drove across town to the forensics lab and was
shown immediately into McDougal's office where he sensed
that McDougal seemed a deal less friendly than last time.

'All ready for you,' said McDougal with a weak attempt at a
smile as he pushed a polystyrene container sealed up with yellow tape across his desk. 'There are two samples of semen and
the wash obtained from the buccal swab of David Little taken
at the time. They're all in crushed ice. I take it you've already
made arrangements for the analysis?'

Steven confirmed that he had without saying more.

'I can't say I wish you luck because I've no official idea of
what you're setting out to do. I'd be lying of course, if I pretended that I couldn't work it out for myself. Let's say, I wish
you a result which shows that you're wasting your time.'

'Fair enough,' smiled Steven.

'There's one thing I think you should know,' said
McDougal.

'What?' asked Steven.

'I was asked yesterday to carry out a discreet analysis on
these self-same samples.'

'By whom?'

'People with an impressive amount of scrambled egg on

their hats,' replied McDougal.

'And?'

'I declined.'

'Can you do that?'

'I'll find out over the next few days,' said McDougal with a nervous smile.

'Why did you refuse?'

'I don't want anything to do with what went on in this lab in Ronald Lee's time. I'm not going to be tainted by association. I'm gambling that they won't want me fuelling the fires of publicity by resigning on a matter of principle.'

'Seems a safe enough call,' said Steven. 'Let's hope for everyone's sake that the scrambled egg stays on their hats and doesn't slip down on to their faces when the results come back.'

'Amen to that,' said McDougal. 'You wanted a word with Carol?'

Steven nodded and McDougal excused himself in order to go find Carol Bain.

Carol Bain, when she came in, sat down in the same prissy fashion as she had on the occasion of their last meeting, crossing her legs and smoothing her skirt. 'How can I help you, Doctor?' she asked.

'You can tell me about John Merton,' said Steven simply.

'I haven't seen John for years. As I said before, when Dr Lee retired John left too. He worked in the medical school for a while and then there was some talk of him setting up his own business but that's about as much as I know.'

'Any idea what kind of a business?' asked Steven.

Carol shrugged. 'I don't remember him having any other hobbies or interests outside science so I presume it would have to have something to do with that. That's about as much as I can tell you.'

'The last time we spoke, you told me that John took it upon himself to look after Dr Lee in the lab, make sure he didn't mess up too many things, minimise the damage and generally keep an eye on him.'

'That's right,' agreed Carol.

'Why?' asked Steven. 'Why did he do that?'

'Just John's nature, I suppose. I'm not sure I know what you mean,' replied Carol.

'What do you think would have happened if John Merton hadn't covered for Dr Lee?'

Carol thought for a moment and said, 'I suppose matters would have come to a head much sooner.'

'Perhaps that might not have been a bad thing?'

Carol moved uncomfortably in her seat. 'In retrospect, I suppose not,' she conceded. She raised the palms of both hands, trying to fend off an unpleasant notion. 'Who can say?' she said. 'What's done is done. It's always easy to be wise after the event.'

'John wasn't always successful in protecting Dr Lee, was he?' asked Steven.

Carol looked defensive.

'I mean there were occasions when things slipped through, things that defence counsel exposed and exploited. It must have been a bit embarrassing?'

'I suppose.'

'Guilty men walked free on occasions?' asked Steven.

'Unfortunately yes,' said Carol in a low voice.

'Did John apply for the position of head of the lab when Ronald Lee was forced into retirement?'

'No,' said Carol with a decisive shake of the head. 'There was no question of that.'

'Why not?

'He wasn't medically qualified. That's a requirement.'

'I see,' said Steven. 'Well, thank you for your help, Miss Bain.'

Steven checked his watch as he left the building and saw that he had forty minutes to kill before his meeting with Susan Givens. It would only take him ten minutes to drive to Edinburgh University's science campus in Mayfield Road so he stopped at the first hotel he came to and ordered some coffee. It came on a silver tray accompanied by a small plate of shortbread fingers.

Steven sat in the lounge, which at 3 o'clock on a Wednesday afternoon was deserted. This encouraged him to take up cup and saucer in hand and wander around the room viewing the eclectic mix of artefacts that for some reason hotel lounges always managed to accumulate. He supposed that there might be a large warehouse somewhere that prospective hoteliers called up in order to buy assorted junk by weight. 'Forty kilos of Victoriana please.'

He moved to one of the large windows and looked out on the car park and what had once been an impressive orchard beyond. It now lay neglected and overgrown, a tangled mess of intertwined boughs and ill-defined paths, one of them leading to the tumbledown remains of a greenhouse without glass. It looked a mess but only because the human eye searched for order and functionality. Here, nature was simply reclaiming her own. The tangled branches had buds on them. They were very much alive. In a few years there would be no trace left at all of man's efforts to order the garden because the green stuff had one big advantage over cinder paths and brick walls, it had DNA, the self-replicating life force. It was no contest.

Susan Givens was discussing experimental results with one of her research students, a Chinese boy, when Steven arrived.

'I'll be with you in a moment,' she smiled.

Steven took in the stunning view of the city from the window of her office, which looked out due north to Edinburgh Castle. The conversation continued in the background.

'The graph shows big rise,' said the Chinese boy enthusiastically.

'But so does the control culture,' countered Susan, holding up two sheets of graph paper in front of her and comparing them critically.

'Not so much,' insisted the boy. 'I think result is significant.'

'The control doesn't show as big a rise because you've plotted it on a different scale from the experimental culture,' said Susan. 'I think you should go away and plot them on the same scale and then you will see there's no significant difference.'

The boy left her office, peering closely at the graph he held up to his face, the paper almost touching his glasses. Susan shut the door behind him and turned, wearing a smile. 'You know,' she said, 'it's amazing just how much people see because they want to see it...'

Steven found her smile disarming. 'Not a breakthrough then,' he said.

'Not even a tap on the door.'

Susan Givens was a good-looking woman in her mid-thirties, slim and dark-haired with a smooth olive skin. She exuded a confidence that suggested she might be capable of spotting a phoney at two hundred yards on a foggy night.

'I understand you'd like me to carry out some DNA work for you, Doctor?' she said.

Steven handed over the polystyrene box and said, 'This contains a number of semen samples, which were collected at the scene of a rape and murder of a young girl eight years ago. This is a buccal swab extract taken at the time from the man who was subsequently convicted for the crime. It was the matching of these two that sent him down for life.' Steven took out another small packet from his briefcase and said, 'This is a buccal swab that I took myself from that same man yesterday. I need to be sure they convicted the right man.'

Susan took the samples and asked, 'Is there any reason to believe that they didn't?'

'Every reason and no reason at all,' replied Steven.

'And I thought bullshitting was the province of my students.'

Steven smiled. 'I'm sorry, I have no concrete reason to believe that there's a problem but there are factors surrounding the case that have made me feel uneasy. I need to be sure there has been no mistake.'

'You said eight years ago?'

'The girl, Julie Summers, was murdered in January of 1993.'

'I'm just trying to think how good DNA fingerprinting was at that time,' said Susan.

Steven opened his briefcase and took out the forensic lab's photographs of the DNA gels. 'These are what the forensic lab submitted in evidence,' he said.

'They're good,' said Susan admiringly. 'In fact, they're very good indeed. I didn't think they had the software at that time...'

'Software?'

'I'm sure it's nothing significant but I don't think these are photographs of the actual DNA gels they ran in the lab. Call me suspicious, but they're too clean. They've almost certainly been tidied up – or digitally enhanced, if you prefer. It's my guess that someone used Adobe Photoshop or some other imaging software on them.'

'You're telling me they've been altered?' asked Steven, feeling a surge of excitement at the prospect.

'That might be going too far,' said Susan, taking a closer look, this time using a magnifying lens. 'They've probably just been cleaned up for aesthetic reasons.'

'Is that normal practice?'

Susan shrugged and said, 'It's more common than people let on. There's really nothing wrong with it as long as it is confined to tidying. If of course, people were to use it to actually add or remove elements to or from the gel then you'd be entering the realms of scientific fraud.'

'Would it be easy to add or remove elements, as you put it?' asked Steven.

'Very,' replied Susan. 'Once the hard data is converted to a computer image, the world's your digital oyster.'

'I can understand the temptation, particularly in a research lab,' said Steven. 'If the presence or absence of a single band on a gel can make the difference between an exciting result and nothing.'

'But the repercussions can be equally great,' said Susan. 'If a researcher were caught doing that, his or her career would be over.'

'Have you ever known someone to try?' asked Steven.

'Scientific fraud has always been with us,' said Susan. 'And we're not just talking about ambitious students taking shortcuts. Scientists of world renown have fallen from grace over it. Common or garden arrogance is usually the cause. Some scientists believe so strongly in their theories that they dismiss their continued failure to come up with supporting evidence as some kind of technical difficulty. Frustration leads to manipulation of the data to show that what they believe must be true – or worse still, they've occasionally been known to browbeat their research students into coming up with data to support their pet theories. This is why we have rigorous peer review of work before it gets published in the journals.'

'Foolproof?' asked Steven.

'No,' replied Susan. 'But it stops the more overt rubbish getting through the net. Apart from that, science has its own inherent safeguard.'

'How so?'

'Science is conservative with a capital "C". If you try to publish work that sounds entirely new and radical, the scientific establishment won't like it. Every aspect of your paper will be examined in minute detail by career scientists who will go through it with a fine-tooth comb, looking for reasons not to publish it. The work really has to be well done and that's as it should be. Unfortunately, the other side of the coin is that if you submit work that supports the scientific establishment's view of things, you will have a much easier time of it. Your paper will sail through the refereeing process. People see what they want to see.'

Steven nodded.

'So now you can guess what ninety per cent of the research journals contain,' said Susan with a wry smile.

'Nothing of any great import at all?' ventured Steven.

'Right,' laughed Susan. 'They are full of work that amounts to little more than the crossing of t's and the dotting of i's, people telling each other what they want to hear, work confirming what has already been shown to be so. Some scientists have turned saying the same thing over and over again into a minor art form. But in a world where scientific achievement is equated with the number of papers you've had published, what else can you expect?'

'You make it all sound rather depressing,' said Steven. 'But I suppose it's the best system we've got.'

'It is,' smiled Susan. 'But that doesn't make it good.'

'How easy would it be to fake a DNA fingerprint match?' asked Steven.

'If we're talking about altering the actual gel data to make it appear that one person's DNA fingerprint matched another's, impossible I'd say. They are just so highly individual.'

'So you couldn't see anyone attempting it?'

'Frankly, no.'

'How about simply photographing the same gel twice and pretending that they came from two different sources?'

'It would be quite obvious that the photographs had come from the same gel. There are always lots of little distinguishing marks in the polyacrylamide – that's the jelly that the gel is made from. A first-year student would spot it right away.'

'Could these marks not be removed by using the software you spoke about earlier?'

'There are just so many of them when you look through a magnifier that you would be left with something that had so obviously been doctored that no one would believe it anyway.'

'Good,' said Steven. 'So if you come up with a DNA match from the sample I've just given you it means that this man is guilty beyond doubt.'

'If the DNA from the buccal swab you took matches the DNA from the semen then it's perfectly safe to say that they came from one and the same man – unless of course, he has an identical twin somewhere,' said Susan.

'He hasn't,' said Steven.

'In that case, leave me your number and I'll be in touch.'

Chapter Eleven

Steven felt positive about his meeting with Susan Givens. She seemed impressively competent and her assertion of how difficult it would be to fake a DNA fingerprint had reassured him. He was on the way back to his hotel when Sci-Med called with details of John Merton's whereabouts.

'He set up a business called Genecheck some seven years ago,' said the duty officer. 'It seems to have been very successful.'

'What do they do?' asked Steven.

'Commercial DNA sequencing, paternity checks, inheritance lines, that sort of thing.'

'Sign of the times,' said Steven. 'Where about are they?'

'Nearest to you would be Glasgow – 471 Shamrock Street.'

'They have more than one place?'

'They're listed in seven UK cities, only one in Scotland though.'

Steven checked his watch and did a mental calculation before concluding that he could comfortably cover the forty-odd miles to Glasgow and find Shamrock Street before the end of the business day. He had however, failed to take account of the road works in Glasgow and it was nearly ten minutes to five when he drew up outside the building which housed Genecheck on its second floor.

'I wonder if I could have a word with Mr Merton,' Steven asked the attractive girl who was in the process of tidying her desk before leaving.

'Who?'

'John Merton... I think he owns the company?'

'Oh, I see,' said the girl, 'that Mr Merton.'

'Uh huh,' said Steven.

'Sorry, I've only been here a few months. I've not actually met Mr Merton yet. Mr Kelly is the manager here. Can I ask what it's about?'

'It's a private matter,' said Steven.

'Usually is with our customers,' smiled the girl.

Steven showed her his ID. 'Perhaps I could talk to Mr Kelly?'

'Of course, Doctor. Just give me a moment.' She relayed Steven's request over the intercom on her desk and Steven heard the affirmative response. He was shown into another office, light, bright and furnished in modern style. A small, thin man, well-dressed in a pinstripe suit, stood up and asked in a gentle Irish accent what he could do for him.

'It was actually John Merton I wanted to see,' said Steven, 'but I understand he's not around here very much?'

'The business has really taken off,' said Kelly.

'Have you been with him long?'

'Almost from the outset. This was the first branch. I think he's up to seven now and thinking about a move abroad.'

'I didn't realise there was that much call for DNA sequencing among the public,' said Steven.

'Neither did we,' laughed Kelly. 'How wrong we were. You wouldn't believe just how much doubt there is out there over whose child is whose. It's quite frightening. Skeletons are falling over each other to get out of cupboards! Apart from that we get quite a lot of veterinary work; race horses mainly.'

'Well, it's an ill wind...' said Steven.

'Quite so,' agreed Kelly. 'No complaints.'

'I need to talk to John about his previous life in the forensics lab in Edinburgh. Perhaps you can tell me how to get in touch with him?'

'Easier said than done most of the time,' said Kelly. 'He moves around so much that we've had to start communicating by email when we have something to say to each other – not that there's that much call to. The place runs itself. Would you like me to have him get in touch with you? That might be easier.'

'I'd be obliged,' said Steven, giving Kelly his phone number and email address.

'Would you like to see around?' asked Kelly.

Steven declined. 'I think I've seen enough labs recently.'

When he got back to his hotel he found a large manila

envelope waiting for him at reception. It was addressed to Dr S. Dunbar and marked, PERSONAL. It had, according to the woman behind the desk, been delivered by hand.

Steven took the envelope upstairs to his room and, despite a dislike of melodrama, held it up to the light and felt all around its edges before deciding that it contained just paper. Inside he found six photocopied sheets of A4 and a small, otherwise blank card bearing the inscription, 'From someone who should know better and must remain anonymous.' The word 'anonymous' was underlined twice. Steven smiled when he saw that the papers contained details of three prosecution cases that had been abandoned due to problems arising with the forensic evidence when Ronald Lee was in charge. McClintock had come up with the goods.

He decided that he would spend the evening going through it but first he would phone his daughter. He was due to visit her next Saturday on his fortnightly visit to Glenvane but he wanted to know in advance if there was anything special that she might like to do. It turned out to be swimming.

Steven had worked his way through three large gin and tonics by the time he stopped reading through the reports that McClintock had given him and leaned back in his chair to rub his eyes. Just as McClintock had said, these cases had collapsed because of challenges from the defence over forensic evidence offered by the prosecution. The three cases in question were spread over a period of eleven months and in each instance the accused had been a well-known criminal with previous convictions for the sort of offence they had been charged with. He now understood the reluctance of the Fiscal's office to rely on evidence coming from Ronald Lee's lab. Losing these cases must have been hugely embarrassing for them.

It must have been humiliating for Lee and the lab too, thought Steven. In fact, the only people who could possibly have been happy about the outcome were the three criminals and their respective lawyers. Steven's jaw dropped when he read that the defence lawyer involved in all three cases was

Paul Verdi of Seymour, Nicholson and Verdi, the man who had handled David Little's defence.

The immediate feeling that he had stumbled across something sinister was replaced after a few moments' thought by the possibility he might be seeing conspiracy everywhere. It wasn't as if Verdi had managed to get Little off too. Quite the reverse, he hadn't mounted much of a defence at all. Suggesting to his client that an insanity plea might be his only course of action wasn't exactly Perry Mason stuff.

The three men cited in the other cases had clearly been guilty but they had been acquitted through lab mistakes, which had been cleverly exposed by Verdi until the judicial system had had no alternative but to acquit them. The thing that troubled Steven was the fact that these three acquittals had been achieved by the same man who hadn't even bothered to ask about the lack of corroborating evidence at David Little's trial or indeed request an independent examination of what evidence there was.

Steven called McClintock's mobile number.

'Didn't I tell you never to call me at home?' joked McClintock conspiratorially.

'I need you to tell me about Paul Verdi.'

'Shit, you really have a nose for sniffing out trouble,' said McClintock. 'Basically he's a crooked little shit with the morals of an alley-cat, a lawyer's lawyer, shall we say.'

'Not your favourite sort of people then?' said Steven.

'Money-grubbing bastards the lot of them,' growled McClintock. 'Sometimes I think I prefer the villains. At least they're not bloody hypocrites.'

'So what about Verdi?'

'The only good thing about Verdi is that he stopped practising a while back. Nothing but rumour and innuendo, you understand, but the word on the street was that he was asked to resign his partnership. He now pursues "business interests" in the city.'

'Which are?'

'I think they call it "the leisure industry". He's behind a

chain of knocking shops called "Cuddles Executive Saunas".'

'Jesus,' said Steven.

'You might well need him on your side if you're thinking of tangling with Verdi and his pals. They're none too cuddly,' said McClintock.

'Thanks for the warning,' said Steven. 'Do you know why he was asked to resign his partnership?'

'No, it was all kept very hush hush at the time, probably because these legal bastards didn't want to shit on their own doorstep. Seymour and Nicholson is a long established firm in the city. They took on Verdi when he was young and ambitious with the idea that he should build up the criminal work for the firm. The principals are a couple of silver-haired patricians of the old school, part of the Mafia that didn't originate in Sicily, pillars of the Edinburgh establishment who could teach Bill Gates a thing or two about networking. Verdi was a shit-kicker from the schemes who got through law school because his old lady scrubbed floors and wanted something better for her little boy.

'Verdi succeeded beyond their greediest dreams because he knew where his clients were coming from. He understood them, knew how their minds worked and what motivated them. The nearest Seymour and Nicholson had ever been to violence was clapping along to the Redetsky march at a New Year's Day concert. Verdi became the name the villains of this fair city called out whenever we came to call and he became a bit of a thorn in our side – if not a pain in our arse. He kept getting the bastards off.'

'He was good then?'

'Depends on your point of view,' replied McClintock. 'Verdi knew damned well that his clients were as guilty as sin. Can you call defending these bastards "professionalism"? Doing your job when you know bloody well that they will go straight back on the street and do the same damned things all over again?'

'Know what you mean,' agreed Steven.

Well, one thing's for sure, Seymour and Nicholson managed

to accommodate any qualms they might have had when faced with the tide of money that Verdi was bringing in. They made him a full partner.'

'But something went wrong?' Steven persisted.

'We did have our suspicions about Verdi when prosecution witnesses changed their mind about giving evidence on occasions but nothing was ever proved.'

'You thought he might be intimidating them?'

'Not personally and, like I say, we never managed to pin anything on him.'

'Maybe the mere hint of anything like that would have been enough to have Seymour and Nicholson drop him? Reputations and all that.'

'Maybe,' agreed McClintock. 'But it must have been something pretty bad to have a couple of lawyers say goodbye to a golden goose.'

'You do know that Verdi defended David Little?' asked Steven.

'I do. Are you going to tell me this means something?'

'No, at the moment I'm just wondering how a man like that took the Little case,' said Steven.

'What do you mean?'

'From what you've told me, Verdi was into defending big name criminals, presumably for big fees to match. Little had a mortgage and a car loan. There wasn't even any PR in it for him. Little was public enemy number one at the time. Defending him wasn't exactly going to be a shop window for his talents.'

'Good point,' said McClintock. 'It's something I hadn't thought about. I've no idea.'

'Maybe I'll ask him,' said Steven, noting McClintock's reminder of how sure the case had been against Little.

'Remember what I said about tangling with the fun people of the "leisure industry",' said McClintock.

'I will and thanks for all your help.'

'Don't know what you mean,' said McClintock.

Steven poured himself another gin and sank back down into

his chair. 'Shit,' he murmured as he reflected on another twist in the case. A question mark hung over Ronald Lee; a question mark hung over his lab and now a question mark hung over Little's lawyer. He closed his eyes and wondered what to do next. It would be Friday before he got the DNA result from Susan Givens so maybe he would pay a visit to the offices of Seymour and Nicholson.

He looked up the phone book for their address and found it was in Edinburgh's 'new town'. This was an area of Georgian squares, streets and crescents built to the north of the castle and much favoured by the city's professional classes. 'Where else?' he murmured. He wrote down the number in Abercromby Place and was about to close the book when he had second thoughts.

He looked up Cuddles Executive Saunas and found three listings. One was in Rose Street, a narrow lane running parallel to Princes Street on its north side, another was in Salamander Street, down by Leith Docks, and the remaining one was situated in a side street close to the city's Haymarket railway station. Steven noted down these addresses too. This was just in case he got round to asking Paul Verdi why such a hotshot lawyer had made such a lousy job of defending David Little.

Steven was just about to get ready for bed when the phone rang and an unfamiliar voice asked, 'Dr Dunbar?'

'Yes, who is this?'

'My name is John Merton; I understand from Tom Kelly that you were looking for me earlier today? How can I help you?'

'Good of you to get back to me so quickly, Mr Merton. I wonder if we could meet up. I'd like to ask you some questions about your time in the forensics lab in Edinburgh.'

'Good Lord, that was a long time ago,' said Merton. 'Another life, you might say. That's going to be a bit difficult, I'm afraid. I'm in France at the moment and then I plan on going on to Germany. I'm not due back until the end of next month. Is there anything I can help you with over the phone?'

'No reason why not,' said Steven. 'Perhaps you'd like me to call you back?'

'No problem,' said Merton, sounding amused. 'I think the business can stand it.'

'I hear it's going well,' said Steven.

'Certainly beats working for the university,' said Merton. 'What can I do for you?'

'I'm looking into events surrounding the Julie Summers murder back in 1993 and the part the lab played in the trial of David Little. Do you remember the case?'

'I'm not liable to forget it,' replied Merton. 'It was a very high profile affair at the time; in all the papers. Come to think of it, I might still be in the lab if it hadn't been for that case. I left in the aftermath. What do you want to know?'

'I understand there was a problem with the samples collected at the scene of the crime.'

'There certainly was. Old Ronnie chucked them out, poor old bugger. His career went with them.'

'I've talked to everyone on the team at the time, Dr Lee, Carol Bain, Sister Egan...'

'Who was that last one?'

'Sister Egan at the Western General... Sorry, Samantha Styles that was,' said Steven. 'She got married.'

'Oh, Sam,' exclaimed Merton. 'Nice lass, didn't realise she'd become a nurse, good for her.'

'I understand from Carol and Samantha that you...looked out for Dr Lee in the lab.'

'Someone had to,' chuckled Merton. 'I kept hoping the powers that be would recognise he had a drink problem and arrange help for him but no, they preferred to bury their heads in the sand and pretend nothing was wrong.'

'Until the Summers scene-of-crime samples were lost,' said Steven.

'That was more or less the last straw,' agreed Merton. 'Not that it made much difference in the end. The DNA evidence was watertight.'

'What other evidence was there?' asked Steven.

'Let me think... Julie scratched Little's arm. We got a perfect DNA match for the material taken from under her fingernails.'

'You did?'

'Most certainly.'

'And a report was prepared to that effect.'

'I did it myself,' said Merton.

'It's just that all the reports have gone missing...'

Merton let out a long sigh. 'Ye gods, you know, hearing this is bringing it all back to me, just how awful that place was. Getting out was the best thing I ever did.'

'Sounds like it,' said Steven. 'You've no idea where the reports might be?'

'If they're not in the lab case files, none at all,' said Merton. 'Sorry.'

Steven relaxed and said, 'Mr Merton, I think that's all I needed to know. You've been most helpful.'

Chapter Twelve

It rained heavily on Thursday morning, giving the city a dark, gloomy, depressing air as Steven's taxi made its way slowly through Edinburgh's morning traffic to the new town premises of Seymour and Nicholson. He'd decided not to drive because of likely parking problems and knew he'd made the right decision when congestion forced them to halt yet again at the West End of Princes Street. The clatter of the taxi's idling diesel engine vied with the sound of the rain on its roof as clouds of cold exhaust from neighbouring vehicles drifted upwards in the chilly air.

'What's this prat doing?' growled the driver as the bus ahead seemed to take an eternity at the stop. 'How long does it take to hand out a few tickets for Christ's sake?' grumbled the man.

'There's no hurry,' said Steven.

'Maybe no' for you, pal, but ah've got a livin' tae make,' snapped the driver.

Steven abandoned his calming initiative.

The bus eventually moved off to ironic cheers from the taxi driver and they continued down into the Georgian new town.

'Abercromby Place, you say?' said the driver.

'That's right,' said Steven, adding the number.

'I think that's at the far end. It bloody well would be...'

The cab turned into Abercromby Place where the driver leaned forward over the wheel to look up at the numbers as they moved along. He had slowed to a crawl, which annoyed a Volvo driver behind who couldn't get past because of parked cars. He tooted his displeasure, which set off the cab driver on another rant. 'What's your problem pal?' he yelled out the window, and then turning to Steven, he added, 'See Volvo drivers? They're all the bloody same. Think they own the bloody road.'

Steven adopted a neutral smile and got out. He paid the driver, aware that they were still holding up the car behind.

'No hurry, pal. Let the bugger wait,' advised the driver.

Steven gave the man a ten pound note, told him to keep the change and stood on the pavement for a moment as the cab drove off slowly with the Volvo estate only inches from its bumper and its driver gesticulating furiously.

Steven turned away from social interaction in the city and looked up at the imposing blue door of Seymour and Nicholson. It stood tall and wide at the head of a flight of stone steps flanked by recently-painted black iron railings. A polished brass nameplate on the wall at the side cited the names and credentials of those who worked within.

The door was slightly ajar so Steven pushed it open and passed through an inner, tiled porch and then through a frosted glass door where he was met with the smell of air that had been dried-out by electric heaters.

'Can I help you?' asked the young girl who appeared at a sliding glass panel. Steven saw this as a test of his theory that the person asking this question never could.

'I wonder if I might have a word with either Mr Seymour or Mr Nicholson,' Steven asked, knowing that the reply would be, as indeed it was, 'Do you have an appointment?'

He admitted that he didn't and showed her his warrant card.

'One moment please,' said the girl, peering at the card as she walked away with it.

Steven could hear whispering female voices while he waited. He heard an older woman finally say, 'I'll deal with this, Marlene,' and the girl reply, 'Yes, Mrs Woodgate.' His theory remained intact.

Mrs Woodgate appeared at the sliding panel, all glasses and blue-rinsed hair, and asked, 'You're some kind of policeman?'

'You could say,' agreed Steven.

'Can I ask what this is about?'

'Fire regulations,' lied Steven.

'Fire regulations?' repeated the woman, sounding alarmed.

Steven nodded. 'There's a problem.'

'I see, well, I'll just see which one of the partners might be available first.'

'Thanks.'

Steven only had to wait a couple of minutes before the woman reappeared and pressed a button to release the electronic door lock, which allowed him to enter the offices proper. 'Mr Seymour will see you,' she said, leading the way up carpeted stairs to an elegant room, which had three tall Georgian windows, all looking out on to Abercromby Place. A tall silver-haired man got up from his desk to greet him.

'I'm afraid you have me at a disadvantage, Doctor,' he smiled, showing even white teeth. He reminded Steven of advertisements for holidays in the sun for the over fifties. 'I don't think I've come across the Sci-Med Inspectorate before.'

'No reason why you should,' replied Steven, saying briefly what they did.

'But I understood there was a problem with fire regulations,' said Seymour, sounding puzzled and looking concerned in an exaggerated way.

'My business is not for your outer office,' said Steven. 'It concerns a man named Paul Verdi.'

Steven could have sworn that Seymour paled slightly but after faltering for a moment the urbane smile returned and Seymour said, 'I'm afraid I can't help you there; Mr Verdi is no longer with us. He left some...let me see; it must be seven years ago at least.'

'But he was a full partner in the firm?'

Seymour conceded with a shrug. 'He was, but after a deal of heart searching, Paul felt that he'd had enough of law. I think he felt frustrated by its...constraints. He decided to embark on a change of career and went into business for himself I understand; the sort of move that takes courage.'

Steven paused before saying, 'So Paul Verdi gave up a full partnership in an old established city law firm...to do what exactly?'

'I think there was some talk at the time of involvement with health clubs, gymnasiums, keep-fit, that sort of nonsense,' Seymour added with what he obviously thought was a disarming smile. 'Not my cup of tea at all although I believe they've become very popular. The truth is we've completely lost touch with one another. These things happen; people move on.'

'So you'd be amazed to learn that Paul Verdi runs a number of sauna parlours in the city?' asked Steven.

Seymour looked uncomfortable. 'Why are you really here, Doctor Dunbar?' he asked.

'Paul Verdi was by all accounts a very successful criminal lawyer and yet he gave it all up to run a chain of knocking shops,' said Steven. 'Make sense to you?'

Seymour winced at the vulgarity, his mouth set into a tight, thin line. He said, 'Mr Verdi's business interests are of no concern to me or this firm. You still haven't answered my question; why are you here?'

'I'll be frank with you, Mr Seymour,' said Steven. 'I think Mr Verdi left under a cloud. I'd like you to tell me what that cloud was. I think it may have some relevance to a case I'm working on.'

Seymour considered for a moment before saying, 'It would be true to say that we had a difference of opinion over certain matters.'

'What matters?'

'Paul was very successful but there was a question mark over how he went about things. He wasn't...'

Steven filled in the gap with a silent, 'One of the old school.'

' – conventional in his handling of certain cases,' completed Seymour.

'Could we be talking about witness intimidation, Mr Seymour?'

'There were rumours,' admitted Seymour. 'We simply couldn't have anything like that associated with this firm.'

'Of course not,' said Steven, waiting for Seymour to continue. When he didn't, he said bluntly, 'Rumours however, wouldn't be enough to get a man like Verdi to fall on his sword and opt out of a full partnership in a firm like this, would they?'

'I don't think I understand what you're getting at,' said Seymour.

'You would have needed more than rumours to confront

Verdi with,' said Steven. 'You must have had absolute positive proof of something he'd done and I'd like to know what it was.'

'I really don't know what you're talking about,' said Seymour, putting up mental shutters and looking at his watch.

'I think you do, Mr Seymour. You and your partner must have had something big on Verdi, something clearly criminal but instead of calling in the police – as you should have done – you gave him the chance of resigning in return for your silence. That way he could keep his freedom and you could get rid of a rotten apple and keep your all-important reputation. Justice would be the only thing to suffer but hey, you can't have everything.'

'How dare you!' exclaimed Seymour.

'Oh, I do dare, Mr Seymour,' replied Steven calmly. 'Now are you going to tell me what it was that Verdi was involved in?'

'I have nothing more to say to you,' said Seymour.

'You will not be prosecuted: you have my word...'

Seymour appeared to waver for a moment but then shook his head.

'Verdi conducted the defence of David Little in the Julie Summers case,' said Steven, suddenly changing tack. 'Why?'

Seymour looked surprised. 'It was a favour,' he said. 'Little's wife worked for him: Charlotte was his secretary.'

It was Steven's turn to be taken aback. 'His secretary,' he repeated.

'Yes, a nice woman, she'd been living in America: the whole family had. We all felt so sorry for her and the children when her husband was charged. Paul did the decent thing and offered to defend him.'

'But not with any great vigour,' said Steven.

'He was clearly guilty,' countered Seymour.

Steven nodded thoughtfully before changing tack again in an effort to unsettle Seymour. 'Verdi was also involved in defending three high-profile criminals who got off through elementary errors he exposed in the forensic evidence. Did

these cases have anything to do with his subsequent downfall?' he asked.

'I have nothing to say,' said Seymour.

Steven could sense that Seymour wasn't going to budge.
'Very well,' he said. 'You are obviously determined not to tell
me. My previous offer of immunity from prosecution is with-
drawn. When I find out what Verdi was up to and if it seems
appropriate, I'll throw the book at you and your firm.'

Seymour swallowed but didn't respond.

As Steven left, he passed an elderly lady waiting in the outer
office: she was wearing a fur coat. He couldn't help but think
of a sheep who'd come to be fleeced. Outside on the street, he
was about to hail a taxi when he thought better of it.
Recollections of his earlier cab ride and his recent experience
of dealing with the legal profession decreed that he sample
fresh air and avoid contact with humanity for a bit.

It had stopped raining so he started walking uphill towards
Princes Street. Edinburgh Castle stood high on its rock,
wreathed in low cloud. The citizens scurrying below would
come and go but it would go on oblivious. Discovering that
David Little's wife had worked for Paul Verdi had come as a bit
of a shock to Steven and was still making him feel uneasy
although he couldn't think why. He supposed that there was
no reason why staff in legal offices shouldn't get perks just
like any other people in commerce. They would probably get
cheap conveyancing when they bought houses just as bank
staff got cheap mortgages and airline staff cheap travel. So
what disturbed him so much about Verdi having taken on
David Little's defence for that reason? he wondered.

The fact that Verdi was a crook was the obvious answer.
Seymour had more or less confirmed what McClintock had
suspected, albeit without giving away any of the details. He
felt sure that Verdi had been ousted from the partnership. The
state of play was now that the evidence against Little had come
from a lab run by a drunk whom no one trusted and his
defence had been conducted by a crook who'd been ousted
from the profession. But the evidence was sound and there

was little or nothing the defence could have done against that, he reminded himself. So why did he still feel uneasy?

The cold and damp was getting to his bones; he needed coffee and warmth. He had been walking on the south side of Princes Street, looking down at the well-kept gardens which sat in the shadow of the castle and where once there had been water but which had become so polluted with the detritus and sewage of the residents of the old town that it had had to be drained. A respectable front on a murky past, he thought with a wry smile as he turned away to cross over to where the shops were.

'Any spare change, mister?' asked a boy huddled in the doorway of one of them. He couldn't have been much more than eighteen years old and looked cold and miserable, wrapped up in a blanket as he was and with cold sores all along his bottom lip. Steven gave him a pound and a smile born more of embarrassment than warmth.

'He'll only spend it on drink,' rasped a passer by.

Steven almost retorted, 'Shut up, you sanctimonious bastard,' but he didn't. He ignored the comment, got his coffee and sat down to look out at the rain, which had just started again. It was rare for him to feel so bad about humanity at this time of the morning – it usually took him till well after eight in the evening.

He recognised that if he were to continue trying to find out the reason for Verdi's professional demise, it would mean tackling the man himself and he didn't feel optimistic about the outcome of that. Why should Verdi tell him anything? He'd counted on Seymour's weakness being his fear of losing his reputation but he'd managed to hold out. Verdi by all accounts had none to lose. Still, he reasoned, if you didn't put the ferret down the hole you didn't find out if the rabbit was there. He finished his coffee and called McClintock.

'Where do I find Paul Verdi?'

'Shit, you can't be serious,' said McClintock.

'Needs must,' replied Steven. 'You were right about his legal partners getting rid of him but I couldn't find out what they had on him exactly.'

'And you think Verdi will tell you?' exclaimed McClintock, as if it were the most ridiculous thing he could imagine. 'Why should he, for Christ's sake?'

'Maybe I can play one off against the other,' said Steven. 'Rattle their cages and see what happens.'

'You'll get your arm bitten off,' said McClintock.

'It's worth a try,' said Steven. 'Just while I'm waiting for the lab result.'

'Try playing chicken on the East Coast mainline. It's probably safer,' said McClintock. 'Why are you so interested in Verdi? I thought that bloke Merton had told you what you wanted to know. Why fly off at a tangent?'

'I think I've just worked that out for myself,' said Steven. 'The cases you showed me collapsed because of sloppy forensics. But I don't think they were down to screw-ups in the lab.'

'Of course they were,' insisted McClintock. 'It's all down there in black and white.'

'Oh yes, but I don't think the screw-ups were actually screw-ups if you get my meaning,' said Steven.

'Not really,' said McClintock.

'I think they were deliberate,' said Steven.

'Jesus Christ,' breathed McClintock as realisation dawned. 'You think that someone in the lab deliberately fucked-up so that Verdi could get his clients off?'

'In a word, yes.'

'Sweet Jesus,' murmured McClintock, now sounding almost reverential. 'No one came up with that one before. Are we talking about Ronnie Lee?'

'He's certainly a strong candidate,' said Steven. 'Maybe he wasn't as pissed as people made out. It probably took a great deal of deviousness and cunning to get the faulty evidence past the others in the lab and through to the court stage.'

'Where Verdi would be waiting for him with a cut of a big fat cheque that he'd got from his client,' said McClintock.

'Exactly. It's possible that Verdi and Ronnie Lee had a thing going. Lee would plant flaws in the evidence and Verdi would expose them. The same said clients would then pay out hand-somely to both parties.'

'Jesus, it's a thought,' agreed McClintock. 'It might also put Verdi behind Lee's death. He might have got nervous when he heard you'd started asking questions up north.'

'That's also possible,' agreed Steven.

'But what has this to do with David Little?'

'Nothing,' admitted Steven. 'Apart from the fact that Verdi defended him and Little's wife Charlotte was his secretary at the time.'

'I didn't know that,' admitted McClintock. 'But at least you've found out why Verdi defended him.'

'Yep,' said Steven, reminding himself that this is how he should have viewed the news himself instead of allowing it to fuel his feelings of uncertainty.

'Maybe this isn't a job for a one man band anymore?' suggested McClintock. 'Why not talk to Santini?'

'Let's keep things the way they are for the moment,' said Steven. 'At least until I've had a chance to talk to Verdi.'

'Okay,' said McClintock. 'Verdi lives in a gin palace in a place called, Silverton Gate. It's a small, exclusive development of four or five houses by the shores of the Forth near Aberlady. His is called Aberlee. You don't get much change from three-quarters of a million for one of these babies. It's on the North Berwick road. Know it?'

'I'll find it,' said Steven.

'Verdi's business doesn't really start running till the sun goes down so there's a good chance he might be home in the afternoon,' said McClintock. 'Who says crime doesn't pay?'

'Not me.'

'Be careful.'

Steven took a cab back to his hotel. He connected his lap-top to the Sci-Med server via his mobile phone and checked for new mail. There wasn't any. He checked his watch and saw that it was nearing twelve thirty. He didn't want to arrive at Verdi's place until after lunchtime so he thought he'd grab a sandwich in the hotel bar before driving the twenty miles or so down to East Lothian. He caught up with the newspapers while he ate.

Ronald Lee's murder had dropped from being front-page news a few days ago to a couple of column inches on page eight. Police were reportedly still searching the ground around Lee's house and conducting door to door inquiries in neighbouring Grantown on Spey. The chief constable of the local force had rejected the idea of asking Strathclyde Police for help with the investigation but the paper – which had made the suggestion in the first place – had somewhat undermined him by listing just how little there had been in the way of murder cases in his region in the past twenty years.

Steven slowed as he saw the sign ahead announcing Silverton Gate and signalled a left turn. There followed a succession of signs stressing the fact that this was private property and no through road to anywhere. The houses, when he finally reached them, were, as McClintock had suggested, very large and very modern. Stone had been used extensively in their construction to create an air of timeless respectability but Steven thought the Greek-columned portico on Aberlee a step too far.

Aberlee enjoyed a prime position, facing the sea and with views across to Fife and the hills beyond. It had a six-foot wall around it with security cameras mounted at each corner. High-railinged gates afforded a view of the front entrance at the head of a semi-circular drive surfaced with white granite chippings. A dark green 7 series BMW sat there, its fat front wheels turned out at a roguish angle.

Steven walked over to the communicator set in the wall to the left of the gates and pressed the brass button. He pulled up his collar against the wind while he waited.

'Yes?' asked a woman's voice.

Steven asked if Verdi was at home.

'Who wants to know?' asked the woman.

'My name's Dunbar. I'm with the Sci-Med Inspectorate.'

'He's busy.'

'So am I. Tell him please.'

Steven turned his back to the wind and pulled his collar up even higher.

'Yes, what is it?' asked a man's voice.

'I need to ask you a few questions, Mr Verdi.'

'What about?'

Steven was becoming tired of holding a conversation with a grating in a wall. 'About your time as a partner with Seymour and Nicholson.'

'Christ, that was years ago.'

'We can talk here or at the local police station if you prefer,' said Steven.

Verdi did not reply. Instead the electronic lock on the gate buzzed and the latch snapped open. Steven took this as his cue to enter and walk up the gravel drive. If he'd thought the Greek pillars a bit pretentious they paled to nothing when he came across the classical statues he could now see standing in the lawns. He half expected to do battle with a Minotaur guarding the entrance to Aberlee when a woman appeared there instead. She was dressed in a waxed cotton jacket, beige slacks and green Wellington boots. She was struggling to hold on to the door while simultaneously restraining two black Labradors who clearly sensed they were about to be taken for a walk.

The woman didn't introduce herself. She simply said, 'You'll find him through there,' gesturing with the angle of her head towards a ground floor room. With that she left and Steven entered, thinking that who was taking who for a walk was a moot point.

'Mr Verdi?' asked Steven, knocking on the door, which was half-open.

'In here.'

Verdi was a small, fashionably dressed man with dark hair and an olive complexion that spoke of his family's Mediterranean origins. He did not get up when Steven came in but he did look up from the papers on his desk, wearing a neutral expression. 'I hope this won't take long,' he said.

'Shouldn't,' said Steven. 'I'd like to know why you resigned your partnership with Seymour and Nicholson. I've heard their version, now I'd like to hear yours.'

Verdi's eyes opened wide. 'What the hell has that got to do with you?' he said angrily.

'I'm just giving you a chance to defend yourself,' said Steven. 'These new-town chaps made some pretty damning accusations about you. I'd like to hear your version of events before I think about instigating proceedings.'

Verdi, who had been thrown off balance by Steven's all-out assault, took a few moments to compose himself. Steven could sense that the initiative was slipping away from him with each passing second. Eventually, Verdi leaned across his desk and rasped in a low voice, 'Just who the fuck are you?'

Steven showed his ID and Verdi slid it back across the desk to him as if it were of no interest. 'I've got nothing to say to you. Get out.'

'Then what Seymour told me is true?' said Steven.

'Seymour told you fuck-all,' snapped Verdi. 'Just like you're going to hear from me. My private life has nothing to do with you or anybody else.'

'It does when it involves criminal activity,' said Steven. 'That's really why you had to come off the new town gravy train, isn't it?'

'No, I got sick of working with a bunch of public school toss-pots who spent most of their days sending notes to each other like kids in primary 6 so I left. All right? That's all there was to it.'

'Apart from your deal with Ronnie Lee's lab,' said Steven.

Although he remained outwardly impassive, Steven felt distinctly unsettled by the dark look that appeared in Verdi's eyes. It was the first indication he'd had of just how dangerous the man might be.

'I've no idea what you're talking about,' said Verdi coldly.

'I'm talking about your defence of three well-known criminals and the flawed forensic evidence you exposed to get them off.'

'The lab was incompetent,' said Verdi. 'If he hadn't been

wearing the right school tie, Lee would have been out on his arse years before.'

'Somehow, I don't think he was *that* incompetent,' said Steven.

'You're pissing in the wind, Dunbar and I'm a busy man.'

'Ah yes, Cuddles,' said Steven.

'What kind of car did *you* drive up in?' sneered Verdi.

'Filthy lucre, Paul,' said Steven getting up to leave. 'Can't buy you love...or class.'

'Get the fuck out of here.'

'Just out of interest,' said Steven, pausing and turning round. 'You weren't such a hot shot with your defence of David Little. What was the deal there?'

'Little got what he deserved,' said Verdi. 'He was guilty. Now get out!'

Feeling bad about his clash with Paul Verdi, Steven set off back to Edinburgh and sought comfort in the fact that the rain had given way to some afternoon brightness. He found sunshine therapeutic. He stopped the car by the beach near Longniddry and got out to admire the sparkle on the waves as seagulls wheeled overhead and a solitary windsurfer, clad in hooded wet-suit, braved the cold of the Firth of Forth. He sank his hands deep in his pockets and set off for a walk along the beach.

His gambit of trying to put Verdi on the back foot by going on the offensive hadn't worked and now he was in no doubt that he had made a potentially dangerous enemy. He hadn't really expected Verdi to cave in and confess all but he regretted allowing his instant dislike of the man to have played a part in his conduct of the interview. He saw this as weakness. The only positive thing that he could take from the encounter was a strengthening of his belief that there really had been some kind of criminal association between Verdi and the forensic lab during Lee's time. The look in Verdi's eyes when he'd broached the subject had told him that he was on the right track. Proving it however, would be quite a different matter.

Steven took a handful of pebbles down to the water's edge, and started skimming the flat ones out over the surface, taking childish pleasure in counting the number of skips they made before disappearing. His mood changed however, when another childhood game came to mind and with it, dark thoughts of Hector Combe and Julie Summers. 'This little piggy went to market. Snap! This little piggy...' With a shudder he returned to the car and resumed his journey.

He had just joined the bypass, intending to skirt round the south of the city to avoid town traffic, when his phone rang. It was McClintock.

'The brown stuff's about to hit the fan big time,' said McClintock.

'Make my day.'

'The word is that some screw at the Bar-L has just funded his summer hols by blabbing to the papers. He's told them about you having the DNA tests on Little repeated. The *Record*'s going to run the story tomorrow.'

'Shit,' said Steven.

'The brass are spitting nails.'

'Thanks for the warning,' said Steven.

'Have you seen Verdi yet?'

'I'm on my way back at the moment. I don't think we'll be exchanging Christmas cards.'

'Jesus, is there anyone left that you haven't managed to alienate?' asked McClintock.

'You're right,' said Steven. 'I should give up the assertiveness classes.'

'When will you get the results?'

'Tomorrow,' replied Steven.

'If Little's still in the frame, I suggest you leak that information as quickly as possible. It might help stem the damage.'

'Will do,' said Steven.

The morning papers did not make for good reading as Steven worked his way through a second pot of coffee at breakfast. The police force's worst fears had been realised and the press took the opportunity to list their failings in the Summers case all over again. The Mulveys' suicides and the subsequent resignations were revisited in detail along with a new suggestion that the police still hadn't got it right. There was an implicit suggestion that new DNA tests heralded the case being reopened by the Home Office. One of the tabloids ran with the headline, 'Will Julie Ever Rest in Peace?' while another jumped the gun with, 'Julie Case Re-opened.'

Steven half expected it to be the police when his phone went off but it was Susan Givens at the university.

'I've got your results,' she said. 'Want to come over?'

Steven resisted the urge to ask her what she'd found over the phone and said that he'd be there in half an hour. His next caller was John Macmillan.

'How in God's name did this happen?' Macmillan

demanded by way of greeting.

'I take it you've seen the Scottish papers then,' said Steven.

'The fax machine has been spewing out little else for the last hour. How did they get on to it?'

'A prison officer at Barlinnie,' said Steven.

'Damn him.'

'I'm just about to go over and get the results of the tests,' said Steven. 'That at least should put an end to conjecture.'

'If they confirm Little as the killer, Lothian and Borders Police are going to add humble pie to your diet for some time to come. Call me when you know.'

As he drove over to the science campus at the university Steven found himself uncertain of what he was hoping for. He was in what the papers liked to call a no-win situation. If Susan Givens confirmed the earlier DNA fingerprint findings, then Hector Combe's claims were nonsense – as common sense decreed they must be – this would signal an end to the affair and he would have achieved nothing but the re-opening of old wounds. If, on the other hand, she found discrepancies which pointed to a miscarriage of justice, it would be too late to rescue David Little: he was already on death row and there was no way back.

'Good morning,' said Susan Givens. She slid a copy of *The Herald* newspaper across her desk towards him. 'I see that your concerns have been made public.'

Steven glanced at the heading, 'Ill-fated Summers Case to be Re-opened?' and nodded. 'I could have done without that,' he said.

'I'll bet,' said Susan, getting up and moving over to another desk where she switched on a light box of the type used by doctors to view X-rays. Instead of being on the wall this one lay flat on the desk. She placed two photographic negatives side by side on the surface.

'The DNA profile on the left is the one I obtained from the David Little buccal smear that you took at the prison the other day; the one on the right is from one of the semen samples stored by the forensics lab.'

'They're the same,' murmured Steven, seeing immediately that the band patterns were identical.

'They are,' agreed Susan. 'Your man is guilty.'

Steven felt a sensation of extreme tiredness sweep over him. He hadn't realised that he'd been so tense and now he felt positively deflated. 'Good,' he said. 'Thanks for that.'

Susan put another photograph on the light box and said, 'This is the DNA fingerprint of the original buccal smear taken from Little at the time of the murder. As you can see, it matches the others. It was taken from him all right. There was no mix-up.'

'Game, set and match,' said Steven. 'I'm grateful to you, Doctor.'

'There is one odd thing,' said Susan, rearranging the photographs and handing Steven a hand lens. 'If you look closely you'll see a phenomenon we call ghosting.'

Steven bent down to examine the photos and asked, 'Do you mean these faint extra bands?'

'That's right. They weren't present on the prints that the prosecution submitted in evidence.'

'So you were right about them cleaning up the pictures?' said Steven.

Susan shrugged. 'Some might argue that the extra bands have something to do with long time storage of the samples.'

'But you don't think so?'

'I'd still bet on a clean-up,' said Susan.

Steven, remembering their earlier conversation about what kind of alteration was acceptable, asked the question.

'A toughie,' smiled Susan. 'Usually ghosting occurs as the result of small amounts of material leaking away from the inoculation wells and causing faint bands at the side of the main track – a simple mechanical fault, if you like – but these are different. The extra bands aren't ghosts of the originals because they occur at different positions and they also occur in the same track as the major bands.'

'What do you think that means?' asked Steven.

'Possibly breakdown products because the samples are old.'

'But if that were the case, they wouldn't have been present on the original gels so there would have been no need to clean them up?' suggested Steven.

'Good point,' conceded Susan. 'The truth is I simply don't know.'

'Would an expert viewing these gel photographs at the time have noticed that they had been cleaned up?' he asked.

Susan said, 'Almost certainly. The technology wasn't good in these days. Gels were usually a bit messy so a very clean one would immediately have aroused suspicion.'

'If it had ever been shown to an expert,' murmured Steven, thinking about Verdi's failure to question the prosecution evidence.

'I take it it never was?' said Susan.

Steven shook his head and said, 'Do you think the presence of these ghost bands would have been grounds for questioning the evidence?'

'No,' said Susan firmly. 'I daresay some lawyers might have tried it but the bottom-line as far as science is concerned remains that the semen came from David Little. There's no doubt about that.'

'As long as that's clear,' said Steven; he took another look at the gel photographs lying on the light box and murmured, 'Truth lies at the bottom of a well.'

'Who said that?' asked Susan, smiling at the pun.

'It's a Greek proverb,' said Steven.

'*Timeo Danaos et dona ferentes*,' said Susan.

'I fear the Greeks...'

'Even when they bring gifts,' completed Susan. 'Virgil. A Roman sentiment.'

Steven smiled and said, 'Thanks for your help. I appreciate it.'

'You're welcome. I'm sure the university will charge the Home Office handsomely for it.'

'Don't you get paid personally?'

'That's not the way the university does things,' smiled Susan.

'Then maybe I could buy you dinner?'

'That would be very nice,' said Susan, sounding at first surprised and then pleased. 'Thank you.'

'I'll be away this weekend – I'm going down to Dumfries to see my daughter – but I'll be back on Monday. How about Monday night?'

'Fine,' said Susan.

Steven left, saying that he would call her at the university on Monday to finalise arrangements. He was already looking forward to spending the evening with her. He suspected she knew a lot about a lot and he enjoyed the company of bright women.

Steven wondered which of the three he should tell first, Macmillan, McClintock or David Little. He decided on Little because it seemed only right although he knew that Little was a man almost beyond caring. Forty-five minutes later he was standing in an assistant governor's office at Barlinnie, hearing him say, 'I think we know who talked to the papers but we can't prove it.'

Steven nodded. He didn't much care because the damage had been done. He was not interested in apportioning blame after the event. 'The tests confirmed Little as being Julie's murderer. I'd like to tell him personally,' said Steven.

'Well, thank Christ for that. Claiming wrongful conviction seems to be a national sport these days. Little's been moved. He's not well. I'll get someone to take you down.'

Steven had to wait for a few minutes before being escorted to see Little by the same prison officer who'd accompanied him on the last occasion, the man with the harelip. Steven would have put money on him being the source of the leak but he didn't give any outward sign of this. He did wonder however, if the same man was under suspicion by the prison and this was why he'd been detailed to accompany him again. This time the authorities might be counting on him leaking the new result to the papers.

As they walked along the corridors it became clear that the prisoners had their own ideas about what had been going on. A muted chorus of, 'McGregor's off to sunny Spain, Viva

Espana,' broke out to mark their progress and brought an angry flush to the cheeks of the officer. Steven pretended that he had heard nothing. His inner feelings of amusement evaporated in an instant however, when he saw the state of Little.

Little had been moved to accommodation of the type used for prisoners who were ill and required medical care but who were not going to be moved to hospital for whatever reason. Little was lying on his bed, staring up at the ceiling and taking rapid, shallow breaths. If anything he seemed even paler than last time and his cheekbones were making him look positively skeletal.

'It's you,' he said hoarsely. 'Come to tell me it's all been a horrible mistake.' He tried to laugh but a cough beat him to it and seemed to rattle his very ribs. He picked up a metal bowl that sat beside his bunk and spat into it. His lack of energy and coordination made it a messy business and bloodstained sputum trickled down his chin as he fell back on the pillow, seemingly exhausted.

Steven took out a couple of surgical gloves from the box by the sink and put them on. He picked up a pack of surgical wipes and cleaned Little's face before dumping both gloves and the used wipes in the pedal bin marked 'Biological Waste'.

'No, I haven't,' he said. 'The tests proved beyond doubt that it was your semen they found in Julie Summers' body.'

Little shook his head despairingly and resumed his survey of the ceiling. 'It just cannot be,' he murmured. 'I didn't do it.'

Steven remained impassive.

'Christ!' exclaimed Little angrily after a moment's thought. 'I actually allowed myself to believe that you were going to come up with something where the others failed or didn't even bother. And what happens? I get kicked in the balls again. Fuck! I just can't win.'

Little's emotional outburst brought on more coughing and Steven gloved up again before helping him through it. He held his bony shoulders while Little hacked in protest at the pneumonia that was attacking his defenceless lungs. A sudden clunk in the bowl made him look down to see with revulsion that one of Little's teeth had come out of his gum and now lay in the bowl attached to a stringy piece of bloody tissue. Little's gums had been retracting with his severe weight loss. 'I'll get you some help,' Steven said.

Little spat out some blood from his mouth and held up his hand. 'No,' he said, looking at Steven with eyes that were dark pools. 'Just fuck off, will you?'

Steven arranged for medical staff to see to Little before walking back to the office with McGregor.

'I take it you had bad news for him then,' said the officer. 'Good. Maybe that'll stop the bastard playing the injured innocent from now on.'

'Si,' said Steven as the strains of 'Viva Espa a' broke out again.

Steven called Macmillan from the car park and gave him the news.

'I won't pretend I'm not relieved,' said Macmillan.

'I've just told Little,' said Steven. 'And now I feel awful.'

'You raised his hopes?'

'I didn't mean to, but yes, I did. For whatever reason – and don't quote the Boys' Own Psychiatry Manual at me – the man still clings to the delusion that he's innocent. He must have seen me as the saviour he's been waiting eight years for. For my part, I just had to make sure the DNA tests were right.'

'You intentions were honourable,' said Macmillan. 'You've nothing to be ashamed of.'

'Thanks,' said Steven.

'As to whether Lothian and Borders Police are going to share that view, that's another matter. Have you told them?'

'Not yet. I'll call DI McClintock before I drive down to see Jenny tonight.'

'When will you be back in London?'

'I thought I might take a couple of days off at the start of the week to clear up here and say thanks to a couple of people. I'll see you Wednesday, Thursday at the latest.'

'You are going to let this go now, aren't you?' asked

Macmillan.

'That's what I agreed,' replied Steven.

'But the bad feeling remains?'

'Yes.'

'See you Wednesday.'

Steven drove back to Edinburgh haunted by images of Little's tooth falling out of his gum and the dead look in his eyes when he'd told him to get out. Even if the man's proclaimed innocence was down to self-delusion, the feelings inside his head must surely be the same as if he really were innocent, he reasoned, and that must come pretty close to being hell on earth. The loss of wife and family, eight years of solitary confinement, the onset of full-blown AIDS and now he had just done his bit to make matters worse. Talk about kicking a man when he was down.

Steven lingered in the shower when he got back, hoping the warm water would wash away some of the stress of the day. He bowed his head and closed his eyes, listening to the sound of the water cascading off his shoulders, using it as white noise to block out all other thoughts. He sought the temporary absolution that would allow him to leave his professional self behind and step into the role of being Jenny's father again. He wanted to join her world, unfettered by thoughts of his job, thoughts that she must know nothing about with its cast of Hector Combes and David Littles. Tomorrow he would take her and Sue's two kids to the swimming pool in Dumfries and be an ordinary father and uncle doing what ordinary folk did at the weekends. This was the plan but first he would have to call McClintock. He did that, sitting on the bed, rubbing his hair with a towel.

'Thank Christ for that,' said McClintock when Steven gave him the news. 'I'm so relieved I won't even say I told you so.'

'Kind of you,' said Steven. 'We'll have a beer before I go back to London, huh?'

'Sure thing. Are you going to tell the papers?'

'That's being taken care of,' said Steven.

'Fair enough. Don't feel too bad about this. You were right

about there being a lot wrong with the Summers case but at least we didn't stitch up the wrong guy.'

'There's still some mileage in taking a look at Paul Verdi's involvement with the police lab at the time though,' said Steven.

'We can talk about that before you go,' said McClintock. 'Want to make it tonight?'

Steven apologised, saying that he was going down to Dumfriesshire. He'd call and fix up something when he got back.

Following one of his practised rituals of the changing of lifestyles, he put on a pair of black Levi jeans and a Nike sweatshirt instead of one of the dark suits he wore during the week. He pulled on a pair of K-Swiss trainers and finally slipped on a tan leather blouson before grabbing his travel bag and heading for the car park. All that was required now was that his mind would play along with the game. It got off to a bad start when he found himself humming *'Viva Espa a'*.

He pressed the remote button on his key to unlock the car door but nothing happened. He tried twice more before realising that it was already unlocked. He must have forgotten to lock it when he'd got back from Glasgow. He didn't usually forget to do that but then his mind had been on other things. He got in and turned on the radio, searching briefly through the stations for some middle-of-the-road music, before starting the car.

Ella Fitzgerald was singing 'Take the A train', when the man who'd been hiding in the back of the car suddenly sat up and clamped something over Steven's face. He held it there with vice-like fingers. Steven's attempts to get to grips with his assailant were hampered by the seat's headrest and by the time he'd changed tactics to trying to prise the man's fingers off his face, the sweet heady scent of chloroform had subverted his senses and lulled him into unconsciousness.

Chapter Fourteen

It was such a lovely dream. He was afloat on a sea of well-being where only gentle waves of happiness disturbed the calm of blissful content. It was warm and light and bright and the colours were so vivid that he couldn't focus on anything long enough to take in shape, but then geometry was a thing of the past. A kaleidoscope of beautiful, fragile images came and went in a seemingly endless carnival of bliss.

Then, out of the rainbow whirls came the girl, the blonde, smiling girl who knelt down beside him and started rubbing warm oil into his chest in a slow circular motion. She did it gently with her fingertips and then harder with the heels of both hands, alternating with perfect regularity so that he could anticipate when the change was coming.

Steven's heart was full of love. He smiled at her as if the sun were inside him instead of above and shining down on both of them from an azure sky. He reached up to run his fingers through her silky blonde hair and trace the line of her slim tanned shoulders as she worked the oil into his skin. They knew each other so well. Love and affection just flowed between them.

Steven caught his breath as her hands started to move down on him and he responded by bringing his hands up to cup her breasts and marvel at their firmness. She paused for a moment to undo her bra top and slip it off, shivering as Steven gently used his fingernails to tease her now hard nipples.

With a knowing smile, the girl sat astride him and moved backwards to work both hands between his thighs. He groaned with pleasure and closed his eyes as for a moment he was transported back to the past. He was fourteen years old and Miriam Barnes was introducing him to the mysteries of the opposite sex in the youth club hut in Patterdale. A few of them had stayed behind after the Friday night dance – ostensibly to clear up – but with teenage hormones raging, an alternative agenda was always on the cards. One of the kids had turned the lights out after putting on some music and at some point, he and Miriam had found themselves in the storeroom where the camping and games equipment was kept. They had made a makeshift nest out of bits and pieces and lay down to explore each other in the dark. She had tugged down his zip to slip her hand inside his jeans while he had rejoiced in the swell of her young breasts and the glorious journey his hand made up under her skirt to slip inside her panties. All this while outside in the hall the others were pairing off to the sounds of Pink Floyd's soulful, 'Wish You Were Here'.

Miriam had brought new meaning to his life that evening, one that was to leave a smile on his face for days. His sense of wonder was perhaps never to rise again to the heights it had scaled on that occasion...until now.

This girl was more skilled than Miriam and knew how to ensure that what might well have been a sprint became an odyssey. Using her mouth and hands she took him to the brink then reined him back. Such pleasure was not unknown to him but the sense of wonder was as great as that first time so many years before.

The girl moved up on him and guided him expertly inside her. Three short squats and she had impaled herself on him to begin gyrating her hips in a slow rhythmic grind, making him wonder if it were possible to die of pleasure. He tried to share this thought with her but found that he couldn't get the words out. It didn't matter: she just smiled and put a finger to her lips then continued on her mission.

There came a point when Steven grew impatient with his passive role. Male hormones were demanding that he take charge. He wanted the girl beneath him. He needed to dominate her, thrust deep and hard into her until this beautiful journey came to its rightful end.

He reached up to take her by the shoulders but she recoiled from him. She was no longer smiling. Something had broken the spell: she was now detached, distant and alarmingly different.

Feeling confused, Steven looked at her questioningly but in an instant the dream evaporated and the world exploded inside

his head. Pleasure gave way to searing pain as he was rolled off
the bed and blows rained down on him. His body shuddered
as boots thudded into his ribs and fists smashed into his face.
The pain soared until the bright lights and colours of a few
moments ago yielded to an agonised spiral downwards into
seemingly infinite blackness.

The dream had become a nightmare. He was in such pain
that he couldn't move without stabs of protest coming from
his injured body. The bed was hard and it was wet; he could
feel it grazing his cheek. In fact, it wasn't a bed at all; it was…a
pavement…it was raining…and it wasn't a dream.

Steven's eyes flickered open to see flashing blue lights
reflected in a puddle in the gutter where he was lying. There
were people nearby but he felt that he couldn't turn his head
just yet. He went on gazing at the puddle, watching a cigarette
butt and a chewing gum wrapper float hither and thither on
the rippled surface as a slight breeze rose and fell away again.
He moved his attention to some moss growing in a join in the
pavement as he tried to determine which part of him was hurting most. The vague sounds nearby however, were starting to
become distinguishable words.

'I don't fucking believe it, Mike,' said a man's voice. 'Do
you know who this guy is?'

'Surprise me,' said another man's voice sourly.

'None other than Dr Steven bloody Dunbar.'

'You're joking!' exclaimed the other man, now sounding
very interested. 'The Home Office guy the boss has been shitting bricks about?'

'The very same. Take a look. Her Majesty's Sci-Med
Inspectorate.'

Steven, who had now regained full consciousness, realised
that his warrant card had been taken from his pocket. He tried
to move without much success but the two men above him
noticed the attempt and knelt down beside him. He could see
now that they were policemen. He could smell boot polish and
the wet serge of their trousers.

'Just you stay put, pal,' said one. 'An ambulance is on its

way. You've had a bit of a doing.'

'And well deserved too,' said the other. 'If what we've been hearing is anything to go by. Santini is going to love this. Man o man. Yes siree. I can almost feel promotion in the air.'

The two policemen started laughing as they stood up.

Steven, wondering just what the hell they found so funny, tried to raise his head to demand an explanation. The arriving ambulance however, drowned out his words and two different uniforms jumped out to take centre stage.

After an examination by two paramedics, during which it was established that none of his limbs had been broken, Steven was helped up and into the back of the vehicle after waving away a stretcher. The last thing he saw before the doors were closed was a lilac neon sign on the wall of the building outside. It said 'Cuddles'.

'You were lucky,' said the young woman doctor in A & E.

Steven closed his eyes and felt sure that if he had fallen into a mincing machine and lost all his limbs, someone would be sure to come up to him and say these self-same words.

'No broken bones,' continued the severe-looking young woman. 'Just bruised ribs and a variety of cuts and bruises that should keep you out of mischief for a bit. We'd like to keep you in overnight though, just as a precaution. You took quite a beating about the head. We'll do some tests. Any idea how long you were unconscious?'

'What time is it now?' Steven asked.

'2 a.m., give or take.'

'Since the back of six last night.'

'What?' exclaimed the doctor. 'Are you serious?'

'The last thing I remember is getting into my car around six last night. Someone grabbed me from behind and then...nothing until I came round in the gutter.'

'Well, memory loss is not that uncommon after head trauma. It'll probably come back to you. In the meantime the police would like to have a word if you feel up to it?'

Steven nodded. As he waited, he ran his hand over the strapping that had been applied to his ribs and then explored his face for lumps and bumps, grimacing as he came across each of them. He was counting the butterfly stitches above his right eye when two plain-clothes officers entered. Neither smiled but they exuded an air of smugness as they introduced themselves that put Steven on his guard.

'There's not much I can tell you,' he said. 'I didn't really get a chance to see who attacked me.'

'We know who "attacked" you,' said the elder of the two, glancing at his colleague and endowing the word with a degree of mockery that put Steven's hackles up.

'Who?'

'The men who…restrained you are bouncers at the Cuddles sauna near Haymarket. According to these gentlemen, you came over all nasty with one of their girls and started knocking her about when you didn't fancy the bill she presented you with after you'd had your wicked way with her. They claim they acted purely in defence of the girl. They tried reasoning with you but you insisted on playing the hard man so they had no other option than to give you a bit of a smack. The lady in question, health club assistant Miss Tracy Manson, will be pressing charges for assault.'

'This is ludicrous!' exclaimed Steven. 'I've never been in the damned place in my life.'

'Aye, right,' said the younger of the two policemen, a ginger-haired DC with a face like a ferret. 'What's your story? You had a quiet night watching the telly before going out and head-butting the pavement outside a sauna at two in the morning?'

Steven fixed him with a look.

'Come on, Doctor,' said the ferret's boss, changing tack. 'Your job here in the city was over and you fancied a bit of rest and recreation before going home. Perfectly understandable, we're all men of the world. Things just got a bit out of hand. These things happen and the supposed extras that some of these tarts try to load the bill with are a nonsense…'

'Stop right there,' said Steven. 'I don't know any Tracy Manson; there was no bill and I have never been in Cuddles sauna in my life. I was attacked last night around six when I got into my car and...I don't remember any more.'

'Well now, isn't that convenient,' sneered the ferret.

'You're beginning to annoy me, sonny,' said Steven in an ice-cold monotone.

'Enough, Roberts,' said his inspector. 'We mustn't forget that Dr Dunbar is a senior colleague of ours and has full Home Office backing.'

'No, boss,' said the ferret with a grin.

Steven bunched the fingers of his right hand and the ferret noticed. 'Is that what Tracy Manson got then?' he asked. 'A bit of a thump for being a greedy girl?'

Steven held his temper in check although it was touch and go for a moment. 'Are you charging me?' he asked.

'Not just yet,' replied the inspector. 'We've not finished our inquiries but you won't be going anywhere will you, Doctor?'

Steven swore softly as they left. He lay back on the pillow, wondering just what the hell was going on. The young doctor, whom he could now read from her badge was Dr Cynthia Reeves, came back into the room and asked how he was feeling.

'Worse,' replied Steven.

'How so?'

'Part of my life has gone missing and I don't like what certain people are intent on filling it with. I can't remember a damn thing after I got in the car last night.'

'Can you remember where you were going?'

Steven thought for a moment before saying, 'Oh God! I was on my way to see my daughter Jenny. God almighty! Sue and Richard will be wondering where I am. I'm supposed to be taking Jenny and the other two swimming this morning. I've got to phone them and tell them what's happened.'

'Easy,' said Cynthia, restraining him. 'All in good time. It's three in the morning. The whole world's asleep.'

Steven was persuaded to relax for the moment. He calmed down and lay back to start thinking again about the previous evening. 'I got in the car and then...nothing. I can't remember anything. No wait! There was a smell, a cloth on my face. Chloroform! It was chloroform! I remember now.'

'That would explain the slight skin burns on your face,' said Cynthia. 'They're not consistent with a beating but direct contact with chloroform would fit the bill perfectly.'

Steven thought out loud. 'But they couldn't have kept me under all that time with chloroform,' he murmured. 'They must have used something else.' He started examining his arms, beginning with the inner aspects.

'What are you doing?' asked Cynthia.

'Looking for puncture marks,' said Steven, grimacing at the discomfort involved in the search. 'Look! There it is,' he said finally, pointing to a tiny mark on the inside of his left elbow. He lay back again while Cynthia examined it and agreed that it could have been left by a hypodermic needle.

'Did you take a blood sample when they brought me in?' asked Steven. His recollection of events at that time was still a bit hazy.

'Yes, for the usual routine.'

'Can you rescue some of it and send it to the biochemistry lab for analysis?'

'Sure, what are they looking for?'

'Any drug they care to come up with,' said Steven.

'I'll see to it. Now you get some rest.'

Rest was the last thing on Steven's mind as the door closed and he was left alone with his thoughts. He was still in considerable pain despite having been given analgesics but it was the mental anguish that was really getting to him. He'd been set up by Paul Verdi but proving that to a police force who were obviously quite happy to see him discredited in any way possible was going to be difficult. He had to think ahead, try to anticipate the opposition's next move.

It only took a few moments to figure out that they were holding all the aces. He'd been unconscious for something like nine hours and couldn't prove anything about his whereabouts during that period. To argue that he had never visited the Cuddles sauna or met the Manson woman wasn't going to convince anyone, particularly as he'd been found lying in the gutter outside the place. He could see that the court's reaction to such a claim would be much the same as that of the ferret-faced policeman. Proving his innocence was going to involve proving that he had been unconscious at the time of the alleged assault and was being held at some unknown location against his will.

With a bit of luck the biochemistry lab would come up with the evidence he needed about the involvement of drugs but as for the rest, he wasn't quite sure where to begin. He supposed his car would be as good a place as any. Forensics might be able to come up with evidence of the attack on him and maybe some clue as to his assailant. It would also be vitally important to establish his intention of travelling down to Dumfries when he'd got into the car. Luckily Peter McClintock knew that to be the case.

Steven phoned Sue at 7 a.m. to tell her what had happened.

'Oh my God Steven, are you all right?'

'A bit bruised and battered but otherwise okay,' Steven assured her. 'The kids must have been awfully disappointed?'

'You could say,' conceded Sue. 'I let them stay up as long as I could last night but then I told them that something very important to do with your job must have come up at the last moment and they shouldn't count on you taking them swimming today. The truth is that Richard and I were both very worried. It was so unlike you not to call.'

'Now you know why,' said Steven.

'Do you know why you were attacked?' asked Sue.

'I think I'm being framed,' said Steven.

'For what?'

'An assault on a young woman in an Edinburgh sauna.'

'Oh dear,' said Sue. 'I've heard about these places. Sounds messy. Is it going to make the papers?'

'I hope not but there is a chance,' said Steven.

'I just hope it doesn't make the nationals then,' said Sue. 'Jenny thinks you're the nearest thing we've got to Batman when it comes to fighting crime. I take it the police realise that you've been set up?'

'That could be another problem,' said Steven.

'Oh double dear.'

'I'm a bit short of friends all round at the moment.'

'Well, you know you can always rely on us,' said Sue.

'I do and I thank you for it.'

'When do you think we'll see you?'

Steven thought for a moment. He thought about the look on the kids' faces when they woke up and learned that they weren't going swimming after all. 'Tonight,' he said.

'But you're in hospital!' said Sue.

'Not for much longer. I'll drive down later today and take the kids swimming tomorrow.'

'If you're sure?'

'I'm sure.'

Peter McClintock arrived just after eight when Steven was breakfasting on tea and toast.

'Well, well, well,' he said, standing in the doorway for a moment with his arms folded and a smug smile on his lips. 'You English blokes certainly know how to party.'

'Don't you start,' complained Steven. 'I've had just about all I can take.'

'Looks like it too,' said McClintock, coming closer to take a look at Steven's cuts and bruises. 'So what happened?... Not that I'm going to believe a word of it.'

'I left the hotel about six last night to drive down to Dumfriesshire. There was someone waiting for me in the back of the car. Shit! I should have realised when I found it unlocked but I didn't. He held a chloroform rag over my face. After that I don't remember anything until I came to in the gutter outside one of Verdi's sauna parlours.'

'Not quite the same story the sauna staff are telling,' said McClintock.

'Come on,' protested Steven. 'You know damn well that Verdi is behind this. He was warning me off.'

'It's your word against theirs.'

'You do believe me, don't you?'

McClintock took his time before saying, 'I'm not the one you have to convince and Verdi's not the only one you have to worry about right now. Santini smells blood. He figures it's payback time. The word is he's going to send the papers up to the Fiscal's office today with a recommendation that you be formally charged.'

'Vindictive little bastard.'

'He speaks kindly of you too,' said McClintock.

Steven told McClintock about the needle mark on his arm. 'I should get the biochemistry report later today. Do you think you can at least stall him until that comes through?'

McClintock looked doubtful. 'Santini would like to see you suffer the same sort of embarrassment he reckons you're putting the local force through. I'm not sure that he'll listen.'

'Even if he knows that I'm not guilty and I'm not.'

McClintock shrugged.

'Well, at least I know where I stand,' said Steven. 'Do you think your forensic people will go over my car or will I have Sci-Med appoint an independent lab?'

'I'll get on to McDougal this morning unless of course, you still have doubts about our lab's competence?'

'No,' replied Steven. 'There's nothing wrong with McDougal.'

'What are they looking for?'

'Evidence of chloroform having been used plus anything else they can come up with on the guy who was in the back.'

'Is that it?'

'Tell me about these saunas,' said Steven.

'Saunas!' snorted McClintock. 'Everybody knows they're knocking shops but it's council policy to leave them alone. The city prides itself on its liberal policy towards sex for sale. As well as the saunas the whores can work the streets unchallenged in certain designated areas. It suits everyone except the poor buggers who live there but then if you are going to have winners, you have to have losers. That's the way it goes.'

'And Tracy Manson?'

'Not known to me but I can ask around if you like.'

'Please,' said Steven.

'One thing's for sure,' said McClintock as he got up to leave. 'You certainly got under Verdi's skin. Makes you wonder why.'

'I hope it makes a lot of people wonder why,' said Steven.

'Where's your car?'

'I'm assuming it's still in the car park at the hotel. If it's not, I've no idea.'

'Better give me details,' said McClintock.

Steven asked McClintock to hand over his jacket and he took out his wallet to find the hire car documents, which he handed over adding, 'I've been told not to leave town.'

'Routine,' said McClintock.

'I'm going down to Dumfries to see my kid.'

'Naughty boy,' said McClintock.

'Can I expect the cavalry to come calling?'

'Leave me a contact number,' said McClintock. 'I'll do my best to head them off at the pass.'

'Thanks. I owe you.'

Steven left hospital just after eleven, having been given the all-clear about head injuries and having arranged that the bio-chemistry report on his blood be emailed to him as soon as it became available, with a copy going to Peter McClintock at Fettes Police Headquarters. He took a taxi back to his hotel and saw that his car was not in the car park. He didn't know if this was because the police had already removed it or whether it hadn't been there when they'd come for it. He decided not to ask; he'd let them sort it out. He pulled up his collar to hide his facial injuries and looked to the side as he walked through the lobby before going directly to his room, where he called down to make arrangements for another car. He called Sci-Med to tell John Macmillan what had been going on.

'Anything broken?' asked Macmillan.

'Just my pride,' replied Steven. 'But there's another problem. Chief Superintendent Santini, the man who's been bending ears in your neck of the woods, sees this as a chance to get back at me for poking around in his dirty linen cupboard. He's all for prosecuting me for assaulting the sauna girl.'

'Damnation,' said Macmillan. 'What the hell does he think he's playing at?'

'Who said policemen aren't human?' said Steven dryly.

'I'll do what I can to apply pressure from this end,' said Macmillan.

Looking at his face in the bathroom mirror, Steven decided that he might need some cosmetic help to hide the worst of his bruising, otherwise Santini might dig up an additional charge of frightening the horses. He had two black eyes, a stitched cut above one of them and severe swelling under his left cheekbone. His bottom lip was swollen where two of his teeth had gone clean through it. For the moment, he decided that a scarf worn around the lower part of his face – if he could lay hands on one – would suffice. He put on a pair of sunglasses before nipping down to the hotel shop where he found he was able to buy a navy blue scarf and a woollen hat – albeit with

Scottish lion rampant motifs on them. Self-consciously wearing his new disguise, he made one other stop at a shop in the
nearby Gyle shopping centre where he bought presents for
Jenny and Sue's kids – books on the sea and what lay beneath.
The assistant on the till eyed him suspiciously; unable to
decide whether he was a film star trying to avoid recognition
or a shoplifter on a mission. She asked a series of auxiliary
questions involving his postcode and mother's maiden name
before finally accepting his credit card.

Steven got into Glenvane just after seven. The pain he'd
been in from his bruised ribs on the drive down had left him
exhausted and it was good to get out of the car and stretch
himself, albeit gingerly. Sue sensed that something was wrong
when she saw him from the window and told the children to
wait inside for a moment while she came out to the car. Steven
took off his dark glasses and gave a smile his best shot.

'My God, Steven, you really shouldn't have come,' said Sue.
'You must be hurting?'

'It looks worse than it is,' said Steven. 'Maybe your make-
up box can help? I meant to get some stuff on the way but
when it came down to it I wasn't quite sure what to ask for...'

'We'll see what we can do in the morning,' laughed Sue.
'What are you going to tell the kids?'

'That I had a bit of an accident,' said Steven.

'Daddy, daddy,' said Jenny as Steven walked up the path to
find her standing in the doorway.

'Hello Nutkin,' said Steven, who'd put his dark glasses back
on. 'How's my girl?'

Jenny looked puzzled. 'It's not sunny,' she said unsurely.

'Daddy had a bit of an accident yesterday,' said Steven,
squatting down in front of her. He took off his glasses and
said, 'I fell down some stairs.'

'Oh,' said Jenny, putting her hands up to her cheeks. 'You're
all sore.'

'I'll be all right again in a few days, Nutkin; the main thing
is I can take you guys swimming tomorrow just like I promised. Sorry it's a day late.'

Later, with the children safely off to bed clutching their new books, Richard poured three large whiskies and put another log on the fire. 'You know, I used to envy you the excitement in your job,' he said. 'Now I'm not so sure. Maybe property conveyancing has its good points after all.'

'An occasional quibble about the bill is about as rough as it gets,' agreed Sue. 'I think I like it that way.'

'At the moment you're making it sound attractive to me too,' agreed Steven with an attempt at a grin, which immediately changed to a grimace of pain.

'You really shouldn't have come,' said Sue. 'The kids would have understood.'

'Promises are important,' said Steven. 'I'll take them to the pool tomorrow and then we'll all feel good.'

'If you're sure,' said Sue.

'I won't be able to get in the water with them: my ribs are strapped. Still, they can do the swimming and I'll keep watch on them from the side.'

Richard got up and fetched the whisky bottle. 'You need some more anaesthetic,' he said, refilling Steven's glass.

In the morning, Sue set out to disguise the worst of Steven's bruises with make-up, something that caused much hilarity among the children, but when she'd finished, Steven had to admit that he was now much less likely to attract public attention although he still opted for the dark glasses. Sue and Richard set off on a shopping trip to Glasgow and he drove the children up to Dumfries, happy at hearing their excited chatter in the back of the car and grinning at their exaggerated claims about who could stay under water the longest. Although his ribs were aching, he was a world away from his other life and that felt therapeutic in itself.

Mary was putting the other two through their paces by insisting that they swim through her legs underwater and Steven was thinking how nice childish laughter sounded when his phone rang.

'It's Peter McClintock; where are you?'

'Dumfries swimming pool.'

'There's been a development,' said McClintock.

Steven could tell from his tone it was nothing good. 'Go on,' he said.

'The bastards have come up with a video.'

'What kind of video?' asked Steven.

'Let's just say that you're the star of the film in question. Well, you and Tracy Manson to be fair to your leading lady.'

'But I've never met the woman in my life,' insisted Steven.

'You're going to have a hard time making that stand up in court,' said McClintock. 'Mind you, everything else is going to, if you get my meaning.'

'Jesus,' murmured Steven. 'You're telling me that I was drugged but I wasn't unconscious?'

'Sounds more like you're telling me that.'

'God, I can't remember a thing.'

'If I had a quid for every time I've heard that in court...' said McClintock. 'I think you should get back here as soon as you can.'

'I'll drive up tonight,' said Steven. He clicked off the phone. The good feelings of the day had evaporated.

Steven was ready to leave when Sue and Richard arrived back from Glasgow.

'You really should be on sick leave,' said Sue when Steven told her he'd have to get back to Edinburgh.

'I really don't think that would help right now,' said Steven. He hugged the kids and promised he would be back as soon as he could manage and that they'd all go swimming again.

'And you'll come in the water next time,' said Jenny.

'You bet,' said Steven.

The weather was foul all the way back to the capital, with a westerly gale driving rain across the motorway and forcing drivers to constantly correct for the buffeting of the side-wind. Steven was glad to reach the city limits where he decided to go straight across town to Police Headquarters rather than call in first at his hotel. He had to find out what the police had on him.

Steven found Santini sitting in McClintock's office. This

put an immediate chill in the air.

'How are you feeling?' asked McClintock, mainly to break the awkward silence.

'Like any other man who's about to be framed by the police I should think,' replied Steven, lowering the temperature still further.

Steven saw McClintock close his eyes when he said it.

Santini looked for a moment as if he were about to explode but he reined in his temper and simply said, 'Show Doctor Dunbar the video, will you, Peter.'

McClintock made to get up from his chair but paused when his computer beeped him with incoming mail. He said, 'It's the biochemistry report on Dr Dunbar's blood.' His finger hit the print button.

McClintock was about to hand the report to Santini when Steven intervened and took it from him, anxiously scanning the contents.

'God,' he said. 'It's a wonder I didn't end up with scrambled eggs for a brain.' He handed the report back to the policemen who read it in turn.

'What's this in English?' asked Santini.

'The main player is LSD,' said Steven. 'With a full supporting cast of three other recreational drugs. They could have killed me.'

'This changes nothing,' said Santini.

'What are you talking about, changes nothing?' said Steven through gritted teeth.

'Finding LSD in your blood hardly exonerates you from anything,' said Santini. 'The fact that you were stoned out of your mind might well explain the whole episode and might well open the door to further charges in my book.'

'Are you for real, Santini?' exploded Steven. 'Or do they wind you up in the morning with the other toy soldiers?'

'That's right, Dunbar, keep digging,' fumed Santini who had gone bright red in the face. 'You decide when the hole is deep enough.' He turned to McClintock and said, 'Play the video.'

Steven had to sit through an explicit video film of himself

making love to a young blonde woman although, to be fair, she was making all the running. He thought the look in his own eyes made him look more like the village idiot – albeit a happy one – than James Bond claiming another conquest.

'The unconscious Doctor Dunbar,' sneered Santini. 'Or should I say, the narcotically challenged Dr Dunbar...for reasons we have yet to establish.'

Steven let the comment pass.

'Should I let it run?' asked McClintock.

Santini shook his head but to McClintock's surprise, Steven said, 'Wait! Don't stop it.'

Steven was recalling snatches of the dream he thought he'd been having before being beaten up by Verdi's thugs. In the dream the girl had been almost indescribably beautiful with silken blonde hair and smooth olive skin. In reality the girl astride him in the film looked the part. Her features were coarse beyond her years, her hair was like dyed straw with dark roots and the colour of her skin had been decided by a UV lamp, which her naturally fair skin had not taken too kindly to. There were a couple of angry red patches on her neck and upper back. But there were several other marks on her back that Steven's attention had been drawn to and these were the reason he'd asked for the film to continue.

'He's about to tell us that it's not really him in the film,' said Santini to McClintock with a self-satisfied little smile.

'Can you wind it back a little?' asked Steven.

McClintock did so.

'There! Stop there!'

The frame was frozen at a point where the camera was locked on Tracy Manson's back.

'Well, well, well,' murmured Steven. 'I was wrong. I said that I'd never come across the woman before in my entire life but I was wrong. I have seen her before.'

McClintock and Santini exchanged glances. 'I can't wait,' said Santini.

'She played a part in the Julie Summers case.'

McClintock closed his eyes as if expecting an explosion.

'What the hell are you talking about, Dunbar?' asked Santini.

'At one point before the Julie Summers murder, you were called in to investigate pornographic material found on a computer used by David Little at the Western General Hospital. I recognise the scars on Tracy Manson's back. She was the girl who was being whipped.'

Santini was speechless for a moment but only for a moment. 'There's just no stopping you, Dunbar, is there?' he exclaimed. 'It's one damned fool assertion after another. You hardly pause for breath, do you?'

'I try to keep busy, Superintendent,' replied Steven, still feeling good from his discovery.

'You can tell from the scars on her back that this girl featured in pornographic material found on David Little's computer nearly nine years ago? Do you know the video off by heart?' asked McClintock.

'Never seen it in my life,' replied Steven, deliberately being unhelpful because he felt like it.

'Then how could you possibly...?'

'Before I came up to Scotland, Sci-Med prepared a file for me on David Little. There were a couple of still photographs taken from the stuff they found on his computer in it. It's the same girl.'

Santini's shoulders sagged. He turned to McClintock and said, 'You'd better check, will you?'

'A bit amazing, don't you think?' said Steven as McClintock left the room.

'And where is this supposed to lead us?' asked Santini who was now wearing defeat like a cloak around his shoulders.

Conversely, Steven was feeling confident again. He said, 'Paul Verdi owns the sauna where this girl works. Paul Verdi was responsible for handling David Little's defence. You tell me, Superintendent.' He left out the 'you are the fucking policeman after all.'

McClintock returned after a few minutes and said to Santini with an almost apologetic shrug of the shoulders, 'He could be right, sir.'

McClintock showed Santini a series of photographs that he had already put into matched pairs. 'The girl looks about eighteen in the Little film: she looks more like thirty-five in the sauna video but she could be around twenty-seven and the scars on her back do match up pretty well.'

'So where the hell do we go from here,' murmured Santini, causing Steven to stifle another comment about it being his job to decide that.

'It would be too much of a coincidence for this girl to have been on Little's computer by chance,' said Steven. 'It's my guess that Verdi is behind the website that put it on the net in the first place. That's probably why they had a video camera conveniently to hand when I was abducted.'

'That hasn't been established yet,' said Santini but it sounded like sour grapes and this showed in McClintock's eyes when he glanced at Steven.

'We could raid the Cuddles saunas, sir?' suggested McClintock.

Santini looked doubtful. 'I don't want any suggestions of police harassment coming from that mob just because they happened to catch one of our lot *in flagrante* so to speak.'

Steven shook his head slightly in protest at what he saw as Santini's stubbornness. 'A raid sounds good to me,' he said.

McClintock's phone rang and he answered it. He was about to say that he was busy but found it important enough to continue listening. He made a series of jotted notes on his desk pad and thanked the caller. 'Forensics, sir,' he said. 'The report on Dr Dunbar's car. They didn't find any sign of a chloroform-soaked rag, I'm afraid.'

Santini looked pleased. Steven felt dejected.

'But they did find an empty plastic box that looked as if it might have contained computer disks at some time.'

'That's mine,' said Steven.

'Well, apparently one corner of the box was deformed; melted was the term they used,' continued McClintock. 'Some plastics are soluble in chloroform according to the lab and this box was made out of one of them. They reckon that someone hiding in the back of the car could have dripped chloroform on to it.'

Steven looked upwards and offered silent thanks.

'I see,' said Santini thoughtfully. 'Taking a broad overall view...' Santini paused as if the words were paining him. 'It would appear that you are off the hook for the time being, Doctor.'

'Innocent is the word you're looking for,' said Steven.

'Yes well, all's well that ends well, eh?'

'About the raid on Verdi's saunas, sir,' said McClintock.

'I think we're on safer ground now,' said Santini with a weak attempt at a smile of reconciliation. Have a word with Vice, will you, Peter? We don't want to be treading on anyone's toes.' With that, Santini got up and left the room.

'Well, that all went splendidly, I thought,' said McClintock, tongue in cheek.

'Are you going to hang around for the hit on the saunas?'

'Wouldn't miss it for the world,' replied Steven.

'It'll give you another chance to get up Santini's nose if nothing else.'

'I still think there's a link to the Julie Summers case,' said Steven.

'So what's your new tack? That Verdi set up Little over the computer download?'

'I suppose,' said Steven.

'But the computer business was before Verdi even knew Little,' said McClintock. 'Come to think of it, it was before Verdi was even in the sauna business. He was still with Seymour and Nicholson at the time.'

Steven nodded and said, 'And his secretary was?'

'Shit! Little's wife,' said McClintock.

'The very lady,' said Steven. 'I think maybe this calls for a trip to Norfolk to have a chat with Mrs Little.'

'You think she could have been in on it?'

'It's possible. But as to why she should have wanted her husband involved in a scandal like that – your guess is as good as mine.'

'When will you go?'

'When will you raid the saunas?'

'It'll take a couple of days to set up. Say Wednesday.'

'I'll go Tuesday if I can clear it with Sci-Med.'

When he finally got back to his hotel, Steven removed the strapping tape from his ribs and ran a deep bath. He lowered himself gingerly into the warm suds and stayed there for more than half an hour, not realising how uptight he'd been about the possibility of prosecution until the threat had been removed. Now, relaxing in the warmth, listening to Miles Davis playing 'Kind of Blue', life suddenly seemed a whole lot better. He was still in some physical pain but when it came down to a choice between that and mental anguish, it was no contest. Even the protests of his ribs when he periodically leaned forward to top up the hot water was nothing compared to the prospect of Jenny hearing bad things about her father had Santini gone ahead with his malicious prosecution. Little bastard.

He thought about what he was going to say to Macmillan and where the Tracy Manson development might take him if – and it was a big 'if' – he were to be given the go-ahead to follow it up. The trouble was that it wasn't strictly Sci-Med territory and he had agreed to pull out of Edinburgh if new DNA tests showed that Little was the guilty man beyond doubt. But Verdi's involvement with the girl on Little's computer was a coincidence too far. He hoped he could convince Macmillan to let him follow his nose for just a bit longer? Santini's behaviour towards him had removed any concern he might have had about the sensitivities of the local police. Any shit that life cared to throw at Santini was fine by him. With a bit of luck Macmillan might feel the same.

When he'd dried himself – using gentle dabbing with the towel over the black and blue bits – he reapplied the strapping to his ribs, feeling and looking a bit like a ballet dancer getting it all wrong. He got dressed and called Macmillan at his home number to give him the news about the report from the hospital lab and the forensic findings of chloroform involvement. Predictably, Macmillan was relieved.

'I don't know what the damned man was thinking about,' he

said. 'You'd expect better from a man of his rank.'

Steven shook his head silently in disagreement. Over the years he had learned not to be surprised at the tactics of those at the top and had concluded that that was often how they'd got there in the first place. Courtesy, civility and concern for others were little more than veneers to be applied after the tooth and claw fight to get exactly what and where they wanted to be.

'When will you be fit to travel back?' asked Macmillan.

'Actually I was thinking that there's still the business of why Verdi thought he should beat me up in the first place,' began Steven tentatively.

'I'm not with you,' said Macmillan, sounding as if he sensed he was about to be subjected to some unwelcome pressure.

'I don't know if you remember but pornographic material was found on David Little's computer in his laboratory at one point.'

'I remember,' said Macmillan. 'He wasn't prosecuted.'

'No, but the girl featured in the porn found on his computer just happens to be the same girl who was involved in framing me at Verdi's sauna,' said Steven, playing what he hoped was his trump card.

'You know that for sure?' asked Macmillan.

Steven told him about the matching scars on her back and Macmillan gave a long sigh. 'Absolutely bizarre,' he said.

'Paul Verdi has to be the common denominator,' continued Steven. 'And because this happened before the murder, the only connection between him and David Little was Little's wife, Charlotte: she was Verdi's secretary at the time. I thought that maybe I should go have a word with her but only if you're agreeable, of course?'

'I'd rather hoped that we'd seen an end to this affair,' said Macmillan.

'There's still something untidy about it,' said Steven.

'So you keep saying.'

The seconds seemed to pass like hours before Macmillan said, 'All right, go talk to her. We'll review the situation after that.'

Steven put the phone down and smiled. To hell with the pain it caused him. He checked that he had an address for Charlotte Little in the file – he had – and then decided on an evening of self-indulgence. He would watch the live Sunday night football match on the Sky Sports channel and have a few beers while he did so. He would then have a good night's sleep with a day off to look forward to before driving down to Norfolk on Tuesday.

'You did say somewhere with subdued lighting?' said Susan Givens, sounding as if she couldn't believe her ears. 'Not somewhere with good food or nice surroundings?'

'I know it sounds odd but you'll understand later,' said Steven who had phoned her next morning to make arrangements for the dinner he'd promised her.

'I'm beginning to wonder about you,' said Susan.

'Trust me, I'm a doctor,' said Steven.

'So am I, so let's cancel that one out, shall we?' replied Susan. 'There's a Spanish place down in Dundas Street called *Los Gemelos*. Its electricity bills can't be too large as I remember. I could hardly read the menu last time.'

'I'll call it,' said Steven. 'Pick you up at seven thirty?'

'Maybe I'll bring a torch,' said Susan and gave him her address.

'Good Lord,' said Susan when she saw Steven's bruising. 'Now I understand your affection for the dark. What on earth happened?'

'I got mugged,' replied Steven, who wanted to leave it at that and Susan seemed content with his reply until they were in the restaurant sipping Rioja by candlelight and waiting for their starters.

'So, were you mugged by chance or for a reason?' she suddenly asked, her eyes watching his.

'It wasn't unconnected with the case I'm working on,' Steven confessed.

'The rape and murder case?'

Steven nodded.

'Why?'

'They wanted to warn me off,' said Steven.

'But from what you told me and from the tests I carried out, there was no problem with the conviction you'd been worried about?' said Susan.

Steven nodded. 'Maybe I was getting too close to something else,' he said.

'Gosh, I'm glad I wasn't asking the questions,' said Susan, unconsciously touching her cheekbones in sympathy. 'Do you often get beat up?'

'Not often.'

They paused while a plate of tapas was laid between them on the table.

'Why did you become a doctor?' asked Susan.

'The usual reason,' replied Steven.

'Care and concern for humanity?' asked Susan with a tongue-in-cheek smile.

'My folks wanted me to be one,' smiled Steven back. 'There's nothing like becoming a doctor for making your mum happy.'

Susan smiled. 'I admire your honesty,' she said. 'So you really didn't want to be one?'

Steven shrugged. 'At that age, if your mother and father want you to do medicine and your school wants you to do medicine and the rewards seem attractive enough, you end up doing it. You do it without really thinking what it's going to be like to spend the rest of your life dishing out pills for depression, lancing boils and telling people they've got six months to live. It takes a special kind of person to do that the way it should be done and they are far fewer on the ground than people imagine. I suppose I'm just not that kind of person. I don't like people enough.'

'So what kind of person are you, Steven Dunbar?' asked Susan.

'It's easier to say what I'm not,' smiled Steven. 'I often look at the recruitment pages and think, God, I'm the exact opposite of that. Maybe I'm just a selfish loner.'

'Well, we can't all be Mother Theresa,' said Susan, 'any more than we can all be dynamic, self-starting team players, giving a hundred and ten per cent to the Acme brush company or whatever. Some of us have too much imagination and that's a dangerous thing. It tends to be socially subversive. We ask questions so we're made to feel guilty.'

'A comfort,' smiled Steven.

'Did you ever practise?'

'I did my registration year and then I joined the army. I trained in field medicine and generally played boys' games with what the papers like to call an elite regiment.'

'Games?' probed Susan.

'If you come back, they're games,' said Steven. 'It's more serious if you don't.'

Susan gave a little shake of the head. 'Different world,' she said. 'So why did you leave?'

'It's a young man's thing. I was looking at middle thirties and getting cold feet about having to convince some drug company that I was a dynamic, self-starting, team-playing company man – in order to earn a living – when I got lucky and landed the medical investigator's job with Sci-Med.'

'Doesn't look too lucky from where I'm sitting,' said Susan, eyeing Steven's bruises.

'It has occasional drawbacks,' conceded Steven. 'But it's the kind of job where I can do things my way. They set me a puzzle and I try to make sense of it.'

'You must have had to change the way you think,' said Susan thoughtfully.

Steven looked at her as if impressed. 'Absolutely right,' he said. 'It was the single biggest change I had to make. I had to switch from thinking along logical lines, using acquired knowledge and experience, and start thinking laterally, tangentially and in any other direction you care to mention. I had to learn to think the unthinkable, consider the impossible, and discard no detail in case it might become valuable at a later date or when some other fact came to light. How did you know that?'

Susan smiled and said, 'It's largely what I had to do when I decided to make research my career. Medicine's not the only profession with lots of misfits in it. The situation's much the same in science. Like being a doctor, being a research scientist carries a certain social status with it, so the job attracts its fair share of exam passers, people who have qualifications coming out their ears but don't have the imagination of a turnip. They can remember facts and think logically but that's as far as it goes. The ability to think like a researcher is something you can't teach. You either have it or you don't. The best you can do as a teacher is to encourage students to try and look at problems from different angles. Like you say, think the unthinkable, consider the impossible. Whether of course, they are capable of doing it is something else again.'

Steven smiled, pleased that they seemed to be on the same wavelength. The waiter arrived with their Canarian-style dish and they paused to make admiring comments about its presentation before Steven asked, 'So what unthinkable thoughts are you working on at the moment?'

To Steven's surprise Susan seemed to freeze and look him straight in the eye. She wasn't smiling so he imagined that he had offended her in some way. 'I'm sorry...' he began. 'I didn't mean to...'

Susan shook her head as if to indicate he was misinterpreting things. She said, 'The ghost bands that appeared on the gel, I've just thought of a reason.'

Steven put down his knife and fork.

'An unthinkable reason,' said Susan. 'The semen sample you gave me to analyse contained semen from two men, not one. They were just present in vastly different proportions...'

Steven felt a shiver on the back of his neck and his mouth became dry.

'The victim must have had sex earlier with someone else,' said Susan.

'But she was thirteen years old. She'd been babysitting on her own all evening,' said Steven.

'It's not unknown for thirteen-year-old girls to have

boyfriends,' said Susan. 'And she wouldn't be the first babysitter to invite her boyfriend round to keep her company.'

'From all accounts she wasn't the type,' said Steven. 'According to her mother and even her friends, she'd never had a boyfriend and wasn't particularly interested in boys. If anything, she was a bit behind her contemporaries in that respect. Horses were her passion. She spent all her free time helping out at the local stables.'

'I see,' said Susan.

'So what does that leave?'

'Like I said, it was probably an unthinkable idea,' said Susan.

'Let's not throw it out just yet,' said Steven. 'Supposing you're right and these ghost bands are actually the DNA profile of a second man...'

'Yes?'

'The original forensics report suggested that some attempt by Julie's attacker had been made to clean her up after the assault...but yet the scientists involved had no difficulty in getting enough semen to carry out their analyses...' murmured Steven, remembering what Carol Bain had told him.

'Which suggests that the cleaning had taken place before the rape, not after?' said Susan.

'Which brings us back to earlier sexual activity,' said Steven. 'Would it be possible to amplify the ghost bands up and display them on their own?'

'The computer can do it. What are you thinking?'

'All the males in Julie Summers' village were DNA fingerprinted at the time of the murder. We could run a second check against the new DNA fingerprint. See if we can find a second match.'

'If the boy was her own age he might not have been tested,' said Susan.

'You're right,' said Steven. 'It was probably over sixteens but it's worth a try.'

'Don't ask me how long it's going to take,' said Susan. 'I'll be as quick as I can.'

* * *

Later, as Steven lay in bed, thinking about what Susan Givens had come up with, he had to admit that a rendezvous with a secret boyfriend would seem to be the most obvious explanation for the ghost bands on the gel if they really did indicate the presence of a second man's semen. Julie would have washed afterwards and that would explain the relative difference in amounts. It would also account for the traces of soap found by the forensic lab in the samples taken at the time. Fine, except that he still felt sure that Julie didn't have a boyfriend. The girl who emerged from the files hadn't even reached the first, stumbling, fumbling, holding-hands stage of life. But there was something else bothering him, something that he couldn't quite put his finger on; then he realised what it was. It was a small detail but one he now remembered. The lab had reported the presence of a small quantity of *detergent*, not soap. He got out of bed and searched through his file on the murder. He felt his pulse rate rise as he found the relevant section. The lab had not only reported the presence of detergent, it had also identified it as one he was familiar with, *Virkon*.

Steven paused, looking at the name and then moved on to the next paragraph where Ronald Lee had opined that the rapist had made some attempt to clean Julie up after the event. Lee had omitted to note that *Virkon* was a detergent used in microbiology labs. You wouldn't find it under the sink in the bathroom or in any domestic situation. This fact, which Lee had overlooked – perhaps because he was so familiar with the product himself – had just become highly significant. The chances of Julie Summers having washed herself with *Virkon* after having sex with some secret boyfriend were, in his estimation, virtually zero.

'So where the hell did the *Virkon* come from?' he murmured as he got back into bed and turned off the light. His eyelids became heavy before any answer was forthcoming other than the possibility that Lee's lab had contaminated the samples themselves. After a last check to see that he'd set the alarm on his watch, he planned on having an early start, he fell asleep, thinking that, on past performance, that was entirely possible.

* * *

The address he had for Charlotte Little was that of her parents who lived in the seaside town of Cromer on the north coast of Norfolk. Steven wondered about that as he turned off the main road south and slowed down for Norfolk country roads. He could understand her having gone back to her parents with the girls after the trauma of the trial and Little's conviction but to still be there some eight years later, he found a bit odd. It was of course possible that her former marriage to a child killer had interfered with the formation of new relationships. He remembered the note in the file recording Charlotte's refusal to appear in a television programme about the experiences of families of convicted offenders. But even at that, he thought she might have moved out into a place of her own. What details there were of the divorce settlement suggested that she had got everything.

Steven had never been to Cromer before but he liked what he saw. He had a soft spot for the English seaside resort and Cromer, on a bright spring day, seemed an excellent example. It even had a pier with a theatre on the end of it. It had beach huts and the traditional big hotel on the front – in this case the Hotel De Paris. He smiled and murmured, 'Let not ambition mock the sons of weary toil.'

He had coffee and a sandwich in a cafe that afforded him a view of the sea and asked the proprietor where he might find Windsor Gardens.

'Along to your left when you leave. Up the hill and it's the second on the right. Nice bungalows, they are.'

Steven found number 37 and rang the bell. An elderly woman with white hair and a fair complexion with rosy cheeks, which gave her a freshly scrubbed appearance, answered it. A bit like Snow White might look in her sixties, thought Steven.

'Mrs Grant? I wonder if I might have a word with your daughter, Charlotte Little?'

'Grant,' replied the woman, her initial smile disappearing. 'Charlotte Grant. Who are you? What do you want?'

Steven showed her his ID and the woman took the card, simultaneously putting on the spectacles that hung on a gold chain round her neck. She held them there, half on, half off.

'Sci-Med Inspectorate,' she read. 'What's that all about? What do you lot want with Charlotte?'

'I have to ask her some questions. There's nothing to be alarmed about, I assure you.'

'Charlotte's not here at the moment. She's walking the dog with my husband.'

'Then she'll be back soon?' said Steven hopefully.

A look of resignation appeared on the woman's face. 'You'd better come in.'

She led the way through the hall, across the lounge and out into a small sunny conservatory with views across the nearby cliffs to the sea. Steven accepted the offer of tea and stood, admiring the view until the woman returned with a tray.

'I do hope you are not going to upset Charlotte. She's had so much to contend with in life. I sometimes wonder how she's kept her sanity.'

'It can't have been easy for her,' agreed Steven.

'My daughter is a very intelligent girl, Dr Dunbar, but when it comes to picking men...'

'She's hopeless,' said the petite woman in her late thirties who had just appeared in the doorway of the conservatory. She was wearing a white roll-neck sweater and jeans tucked in to wellington boots. Her dark hair was cut in a fashion that made Steven think of a pixie.

'Hello dear, I didn't hear you come in,' said her mother.

'Dad's just coming up the hill. I came on ahead to put the kettle on. I didn't know you had company.'

Introductions were made and Steven noticed a nervous tic begin to play on Charlotte's left cheek. 'I'm afraid I have to ask you a few questions, Mrs L...Ms Grant? I shan't take up much of your time. Promise.'

'About David?'

'Indirectly.'

'I'll leave you two on your own,' said Charlotte's mother,

picking up the tea tray and bustling off.

'She's nice,' said Steven.

'I don't know what I would have done without her and Dad,' said Charlotte. 'They've always been there to pick up the pieces.'

'You've lived with them since the trial?' said Steven.

'Not all of the time,' replied Charlotte, looking down at the floor as if Steven had hit a raw nerve. 'I met someone else,' she said. 'Let's just say it didn't work out and I ended up back here.'

'I'm sorry,' said Steven.

'How can I help you?'

'It's about the pornographic material that was found on your ex-husband's computer when he worked at the hospital in Edinburgh,' Steven began.

'God, that all seems a lifetime ago,' said Charlotte. 'He swore he knew nothing at all about it,' she said. 'He told me it must have been a student prank and I believed him. He was a liar, a rapist, a murderer and I believed him. In fact, I believed everything he said right up until the time they found his...inside that poor girl and then the game was over. I realised just what a fool I'd been and I was so angry. God, I was so angry.'

'I'm sure,' said Steven, giving her a moment or two to compose herself. 'I understand you were a legal secretary at the time they found the stuff on your husband's computer?' he said.

Charlotte finished blowing her nose and nodded. 'You have been doing your homework. I worked for a firm called Seymour, Nicholson and Verdi. I was Paul Verdi's secretary.'

'This is going to seem like a very strange question but could any computer material from your office ever have found its way on to your husband's computer?'

'From my office?' exclaimed Charlotte.

'Anything at all,' said Steven. 'A disk, a file transfer, borrowed software, anything.'

Charlotte shook her head and said, 'I don't think so. I just used the office computer for word processing. David used his for all sorts of scientific things. It seemed to be a constant thorn in his side more than a help. Actually...'

'Yes?' prompted Steven, seeing that Charlotte had remembered something.

'There was a time when David thought he'd lost some valuable data and he was acting like a bear with a sore head. I mentioned this to Paul because it was getting me down too and he'd noticed that I seemed preoccupied. When I told him about the missing data he said he'd speak to a friend of his who was a computer expert. A couple of days later he gave me a disk to give to David. It was some kind of utilities program for recovering lost files. *Samson Utilities*, I think it was called.'

'And?'

'It worked. David got back his lost data and stopped behaving like a spoilt schoolboy. I remember he bought a bottle of malt whisky for me to give to Paul for his friend.'

'Do you know this friend's name?' asked Steven.

'Paul never said and I didn't ask.' After a moment's thought, Charlotte suddenly became animated. 'Surely you're not suggesting that this had anything to do with the filth they found on David's computer?' she exclaimed.

'I rather think I am,' admitted Steven.

Charlotte's eyes opened wide and she seemed dumbstruck for a moment but then it was like a volcano erupting. 'But why would anyone want to do that?' she exclaimed. 'And just what is the point of suggesting something like that after all this time and after all that happened? My husband raped and murdered a little girl, for God's sake! Have you nothing better to do with your time?'

Charlotte broke down in tears and her mother returned to usher her out of the conservatory.

A tall, erect man with a white moustache and carrying a cup and saucer in his hand entered the room and introduced himself curtly as James Grant. He was annoyed and Steven did his best at being conciliatory. 'I'm sorry I had to bring back some bad memories for your daughter,' he said. 'But I had to ask her some questions.'

'Bad memories are something my daughter is not short of,' said Grant, accepting Steven's apology and indicating that he should sit back down again. 'Believe me.'

'I understand your daughter has had another unfortunate relationship,' said Steven.

'Unfortunate relationship?' snorted Grant. 'That's a nice way of putting it. Nightmare more like.'

Steven sensed that the man needed to talk.

'Finding out that the man you married, the man whose children you bore is a rapist and a murderer is not something you can ever come to terms with, Dr Dunbar. You really don't need a second bad experience after that.'

Steven nodded. 'I guess not.'

'Lotty became a virtual recluse after the trial. If she put a foot over the doorstep she was hounded by reporters who wanted to know how *she felt*. God, what do these people have instead of a brain? How did they imagine she *felt*?' Grant shook his head. 'They circled round her like preying animals, entirely without any vestige of human decency. "What does it feel like to be married to a rapist, Mrs Little?"…"What do you feel for Julie's family, Mrs Little?"…"What will you tell your children, Mrs Little?" It was a long time before she could be persuaded to go out again socially but eventually the hyenas moved on to new victims and she did. Then she met John Mission. He seemed a nice enough chap and seemed to care for Lotty – even when she told him about having been married to Little. I have to say we all liked him; even the girls took to him right away. When Lotty told us she was going to set up home with him it seemed like things were taking their natural course but Mission had a different agenda.'

Grant took a sip of tea before continuing. 'He told Lotty that he was having trouble selling his property up north and persuaded her to buy a house down here for them, using her own money. Not only that, he persuaded her to put the property in his name so he could use it as collateral for a new loan from the bank. He said it would make it easier for him to move his business down here.'

Steven looked down at the floor and Grant said, 'I know, I

know, I can see what you're thinking but he really did come across as a charming man and Lotty had fallen for him head over heels. Well, I'm sure you know what comes next. Lotty wouldn't say at first but it gradually emerged that he was abusing her. Matters came to a head when she turned up on our doorstep one night with the girls in the car. Her eyes were blackened and her shoulder had been damn nearly dislocated. He'd thrown her and the girls out of the house – her own house.'

'It turned out there was nothing anyone could do. The house was in his name so it was legally his. The police told Lotty that it was a civil matter so they couldn't become involved. All they could suggest was that she contact a battered women's support group. Shortly afterwards Mission sold the house and rode off into the sunset leaving Lotty penniless.'

'I don't know what to say,' said Steven. 'There are some people in this world who take your breath clean away.'

'I'm not a violent man Dr Dunbar but I would cheerfully have throttled that bastard with my bare hands and not have lost a wink of sleep over it. Lotty deserved better after what she'd been through.'

Steven nodded, feeling a little embarrassed at being an outsider listening to family confidences, but it was obvious that Grant was a decent man who cared very much for his daughter. 'I'm very sorry,' he said.

'It's me who should be sorry,' said Grant. 'This is really none of your concern. Please excuse the ramblings of an old man.'

'I'm so sorry I had to upset your daughter by raking up the past,' said Steven.

'You were only doing your job I'm sure,' said Grant graciously. 'I hope she was able to help you.'

'She was,' said Steven, getting up to leave. 'Please thank her for me. I hope I won't have to bother her again.'

A cold wind had sprung up and was gusting in from the North Sea as Steven made his way back to the car park near the beach. It whipped the tops off the waves, sending clouds of spindrift up into the air. Nearer the shore a grey, threatening swell rose and fell around the barnacled support columns of the pier. The clouds were darkening and it looked like rain could not be far away. Steven pulled up his collar and made for the caf he'd visited earlier.

'Not so nice now,' said the caf owner.

Steven agreed and asked for black coffee.

'Find the place you were looking for?'

'Yes, thanks.'

When nothing more was forthcoming, the owner busied himself behind the counter although Steven suspected that he might have been his only customer of the day.

He sat down by the window and looked out at the grey scene while behind him, the owner noisily cleaned the components of the Italian coffee machine. He felt it had been worthwhile coming. It seemed almost certain that the utilities disk that Charlotte Little unwittingly had passed on to her husband had been the source of the pornographic material found on his computer. The fact that it had actually cured the problem on his machine meant that he had not been alerted to anything being amiss at the time.

The plan had been cleverly conceived but he couldn't come up with a reason for Paul Verdi wanting to embarrass his secretary's husband. Apart from that, it hadn't been Verdi who had provided the sophisticated software, necessary for such a scam, it had been his unnamed friend, the 'computer expert'. Could he or she also have been his contact within the forensic lab? Once again, his thinking hit the wall. As far as he knew, no one in Ronald Lee's lab either knew or had any contact with David or Charlotte Little.

Steven walked back to his car and turned his mobile phone back on – he'd switched it off while talking to Charlotte Little. There were two messages on the Voicemail service. One was from Susan Givens saying that she had the new DNA fingerprint; he could pick it up at his convenience or she could mail it to him electronically. He should let her know. The other was from Peter McClintock asking that he call him back as soon as possible. Steven called.

'You're not going to like this,' said McClintock. 'Santini got cold feet over the raid tomorrow. He decided to bring in Tracy Manson for questioning today instead.'

'But that will just alert Verdi to the fact that we know something about the source of the porn film!' protested Steven.

'You know that, I know that, but apparently the great Santini couldn't work it out,' said McClintock.

'Shit for brains,' murmured Steven. 'Did you get anything from her?'

'You were right. It was her who featured in the stuff on Little's computer. She didn't deny it – seemed quite proud of it in fact, like she was some kind of film star. I guess everybody wants to be in show business these days. But we couldn't get her to finger Verdi. She maintains that she had no idea who was behind the video business. She just did what she was told.'

'Believe her?' asked Steven.

'She's a smack-head. You can't believe anything they say.'

Steven's blood ran cold and he didn't speak for a few moments as a nightmare was born inside his head. 'A smack-head?' he repeated slowly. 'Tracy Manson's a heroin addict?'

'Oh Christ, I never thought,' said McClintock, suddenly understanding Steven's concern. 'Look, I know what I just said but she did happen to tell me that she was registered and on a methadone programme so she's not injecting and sharing needles.'

'Doesn't mean to say she didn't in the past,' said Steven.

'No,' agreed McClintock. 'It doesn't.' There was an awkward pause before he said, 'Better get yourself a blood test.' Then he asked, 'Where are you at the moment?'

'Norfolk.' Steven felt as if he was now on autopilot but he went through the motions of telling McClintock what he'd learned. 'You don't suppose that utilities disk might still exist, do you?' he asked.

'Seems unlikely after all this time but I could ask around at

Little's old lab at the hospital,' said McClintock.

'There's one other thing,' said Steven. 'Could you run a DNA fingerprint check for me? I need to compare it with the ones taken from the males in Julie Summers' village at the time of her murder. I'll get it to you as quick as I can.'

'No can do,' said McClintock, stopping Steven in his tracks.

'You can't?'

'They don't exist any more,' said McClintock. 'It's Force policy to destroy all DNA samples from innocent people after a case is closed. It's part of the deal, a social contract if you like.'

'Shit, I should have thought of that,' said Steven, feeling annoyed with himself. 'Maybe you could run it through the criminal database anyway?' he asked. 'Just in case.'

'Sure.'

Steven called Susan Givens and asked her to send the DNA fingerprint she'd come up with to Peter McClintock as an email attachment. He gave her McClintock's email address.

'Everything all right?' Susan asked.

Steven was tempted just to say 'fine' but he admitted, 'I screwed up. The police destroy all DNA fingerprints taken in mass surveys as soon as the case is closed. Sorry.'

'Well, it was a good idea while it lasted,' said Susan. 'Are you sure you still want me to send the file?'

'They'll run it against the known criminal DNA database anyway,' said Steven.

'You sound a bit down,' said Susan.

'Just fed up swimming against the tide,' said Steven.

'Know the feeling,' said Susan. 'You'll get a break soon.'

Steven took his time driving back to Edinburgh. He was angry with himself for having overlooked the DNA problem and he was annoyed with Santini for screwing up the chances of a more successful raid on the saunas but the thing that was uppermost in his mind was the revelation that Tracy Manson was a heroin addict. Needle sharing by drug addicts was a classic way of spreading AIDS.

If Tracy Manson had shared needles in the past, she might

well be HIV positive and if she was…he had had unprotected sex with her. Ironically he might already be under the same death threat as David Little.

He rubbed his forehead nervously. He would have a blood test done as soon as he could arrange it but even if it turned out to be negative he knew he would have to go on having tests for many months before he could be sure that he was in the clear. There would be no quick answer. In the circumstances it was impossible for him not to think of Little and his skeletal appearance, and then his thoughts turned to Paul Verdi. 'Bastard!' he murmured, 'I owe you, mister!'

The prospect of at least six months with the sword of Damocles hanging over his head was not a happy one. The worry was going to be there day and night. It would affect his work, his relationships, his decision-making, and no matter what he did to avoid thinking about it, it would still be there. In his mind's eye he heard the clunk of Little's tooth falling into the metal bowl at least half a dozen times on the drive home.

He was turning over some salad with his fork for the umpteenth time in a motorway service station when he saw a way around the problem. He could confront Tracy Manson about her HIV status. He could simply ask her if she was HIV positive. If the council in Edinburgh operated a tolerant policy towards working girls, it was entirely possible that they might incorporate some element of regular testing. He could ask her when she'd last been tested – maybe even see the result for himself. She would have no reason to lie about something like that. He would seek McClintock's help in getting in touch with her when he got back.

He knew that he should really make contact with John Macmillan to tell him about his meeting with Charlotte Little when he got back but he decided to delay that until McClintock had checked to see if the utilities disk still existed.

Steven had a drink in the hotel bar and was considering an early night when McClintock rang.

'Thought you'd like some good news for once. My

sergeant's just rung me. He's got the disk.'

'The utilities disk? You're kidding.'

'Samson Utilities, a software company that went out of business five years ago but the disk was still there along with Little's old computer and software in a cupboard in the hospital. Apparently no one wanted to take the responsibility of throwing his stuff out so no one ever did.'

'God bless the NHS,' said Steven. 'I don't suppose he's had time to...'

'He has,' interrupted McClintock. 'You were right.'

Steven closed his eyes and gave silent thanks.

'Ryman loaded the disk and ran the set-up file. It ran normally and provided all the functions of the Samson utility program but when it was removed it left something behind on the hard disk, the Tracy Manson pictures.'

'God, it's so nice to be proved right once in a while,' sighed Steven.

'That was a nice piece of police work. Well done.'

'Thanks,' said Steven.

'Incidentally, DS Ryman thought that the great Santini should know about this as soon as possible.'

'So?'

'He loaded it on to Santini's computer so that he'll see it first thing. It's been programmed to run when he turns it on in the morning.'

Steven smiled for the first time that day.

'Santini is having a meeting with the WRVS in his office first thing tomorrow morning to discuss canteen arrangements for visitors to Saughton Prison...'

'Well, that'll be a nice change from his usual screen saver,' said Steven, his grin broadening.

'I'll keep you posted,' said McClintock.

'Peter, I need to contact Tracy Manson,' said Steven, deciding to come right out with it.

'Are you out of your tree?' exclaimed McClintock. 'The Procurator Fiscal hasn't thrown out her complaint against you yet. If you go do something like that you'll be playing right into Verdi's hands.'

'I've got to know if she's HIV positive,' said Steven.

'Jesus,' murmured McClintock. But the way he said it seemed to convey that he knew how Steven must be feeling and could sympathise. 'You can get a blood test, mate, without seeing Tracy Manson.'

'With blood tests you still can't be sure one way or the other for many months,' said Steven. 'I don't want it hanging over me if I can avoid it. She must know if she's positive.'

'I guess you know about these things,' McClintock conceded. 'But confronting the Manson girl is a definite no-no right now.'

'I have to know,' said Steven. 'If you won't give me an address for her I'll have to try the sauna.'

'Christ, man, you'd be giving Verdi's gorillas every excuse to rip your head off. We'll be collecting you in a bucket! Look, sleep on it. As far as I know we're still going ahead with the raid on the saunas tomorrow – for all the bloody good it'll do now that Santini's given them plenty of warning. If Tracy's working at Cuddles we'll bring her in for questioning along with everyone else. I'll call you and fix it for you to have a word with her here while the circus is in progress. Okay?'

'Thanks Peter,' said Steven.

'But wait for my call. Right?'

'Understood,' agreed Steven.

McClintock's call came much earlier that Steven had anticipated. It woke him up at seven thirty in the morning.

'Bad news,' said McClintock. 'Tracy Manson's body was found on Cramond beach this morning. Her neck was broken.'

'Oh Christ,' said Steven.

'Maybe she knew more about Verdi's porn business than she let on yesterday and Verdi decided to make sure she'd stay quiet about it permanently.'

'Or maybe she tried to blackmail him,' said Steven, thinking out loud.

'Maybe,' agreed McClintock. 'But only if she was a few

chips short of a Happy Meal.'

'Has anyone looked over her place?'

'Not as far as I know.'

'I'd like to,' said Steven. 'If she's been keeping something on Verdi as insurance and didn't get the chance to use it, it could be just the lever I need.'

'Maybe a couple of officers should go with you,' said McClintock.

'I'd rather go it alone,' said Steven.

'Fair enough,' sighed McClintock. 'Your idea.' He gave Steven the address of Tracy Manson's flat. 'It's about a mile from the city centre, at Tollcross: it's the street runs up the side of the Kings Theatre if you know where that is?'

Steven said that he did.

'How are you going to get in?'

'I'd rather not tell a policeman that,' said Steven.

'Shit, I didn't ask,' said McClintock.

'Peter?' began Steven.

'I've asked forensics to test her blood,' said McClintock, reading his mind.

The stairs leading up to Tracy Manson's third floor tenement flat were spiral and dark because the bulb was out in the narrow ground floor hallway. Feeling his way to the wooden banister at the foot of the stairs made Steven even more aware of the smell of fried onions and cat pee. The stone treads beneath his feet felt worn and gritty as if they hadn't been swept for some time as he climbed up to the third floor and found the door he was looking for: it was the second along the landing.

Unlike the other doors, which had formal name plates, Tracy Manson's door had a piece of card sellotaped to it with 'Manson' printed on it in blue marker pen. Steven guessed that she rented the place.

He looked at the locks: there were two, a Yale about a third of the way down and a mortise around the halfway mark. The mortise would be a problem if Tracy had actually used it but many people didn't. It was more convenient just to click the door shut behind them on the Yale. He put his right knee against the lower half of the door and pressed. He felt the door move ever so slightly inwards, indicating that the mortise hadn't been used.

He took out his clasp knife and prised the door side panel open a little – just enough for him to slide a slim piece of plastic about the size and thickness of a bookmark through the gap until it reached the tongue of the Yale lock. Three or four attempts at pushing it further and the tongue slid back to release the door. He pressed the side panel back into place with the heels of his hands and stepped inside, closing the door quietly behind him.

He stood for a moment in the darkness as a strong smell of perfume – Tracy Manson's perfume – kindled memories of the dream that wasn't, bringing with them a strange mix of pleasure and fear that made him swallow hard and click on the light to break the spell. He began a thorough search of the flat.

Despite the knowledge that Tracy was dead, he still felt uncomfortable at rifling through her belongings, particularly when he came across an old photograph of her as a young girl on holiday with her family, smiling and looking happy, and when he discovered her collection of cuddly toys on the dressing table in her bedroom, he felt even worse.

In a drawer in the kitchen he found where she kept paperwork, electricity and phone bills, a building society passbook, a methadone script that she wouldn't be using today and a letter from the council saying that communal roof repairs were required. There was also a note from one of the neighbours suggesting that the residents agree on a recently submitted estimate for regular cleaning of the stairs and hallway. Replies were to be submitted to Mrs Grieve (1F1) by Friday.

The small bedroom with its single wardrobe and dressing table yielded nothing but clothes and make-up despite Steven's hopes being raised at the discovery of a small metal box on top of the wardrobe. When he opened it however, it only contained Christmas and birthday cards. None of them was recent. One read, *Sweet Sixteen*, and was inscribed, Love and kisses to our very own princess, Mum and Dad. Steven closed the box and reflected on the raw deal that some people ended up with in life. He noted that Tracy's bed was a single one. The cover had Paddington Bear on it. She obviously hadn't brought her clients here.

He returned to the kitchen and switched on the electric kettle. He didn't think Tracy would grudge him a cup of tea. While he waited for it to boil, he stood on a chair to examine the tops of the kitchen cupboards but again without finding anything.

He was beginning to think that maybe Tracy hadn't kept any 'insurance' here after all. It wasn't the kind of property to boast a wall safe and he couldn't really see her having lifted floorboards – although he did open the cupboard under the kitchen sink where floorboards were often loose but not in this case. He rinsed the grit off his hands under the tap and dropped a tea bag into a mug before adding some boiling water.

While it infused, he ran through a mental check of all the possible places, room by room, where Tracy might have hidden something. In the bathroom he remembered that he'd overlooked the bath panel so he went back and examined the screws securing the plastic panel to its frame. His interest was aroused when he saw that the heads were bright as if they'd recently come into contact with a screwdriver. He brought out his knife and undid them.

At first he thought there was nothing there when he reached in and swept his hand over the rough floorboards but when he stretched behind the bath, his fingers came up against something in the far left-hand corner, something that moved; a container. When he finally managed to extract it, he found that it was a large, tartan shortbread tin. It carried the maker's name on it and the legend, 'Frae Bonnie Scotland' above the smiling face of a boy in a kilt.

Steven opened it and found three videos inside, along with a notebook and some loose sheets of paper with names and numbers on them. 'Eureka,' he murmured, taking the box and its contents through to a flat surface in the kitchen. He had just opened the notebook when he heard men's voices outside on the landing and a key go into the lock on the front door.

Assuming that McClintock had been forced – probably by Santini – to send officers round, he prepared to greet them. The two thickset men who appeared in the kitchen doorway however, did not strike him as policemen. He didn't know them but they knew him.

'Fuck me,' said one.

'Well, well, well,' muttered the other. 'Seems like this bastard didn't get enough last time…he's come back for more.'

Steven felt the hair rise on the back of his neck as he realised that these two were Verdi's men, the bouncers from the sauna. His second thought as he saw the shorter of the two bring out a flick knife was that he had left his own knife lying on the bathroom floor. It was only a Swiss army knife but it would have been better than nothing.

Under normal circumstances he would have felt confident about taking on either of the men in front of him. They were the usual schemie hard men, the sort spawned by run-down council estates all over the country, young and heavily built but relying more on attitude than expertise. Watching Clint Eastwood movies didn't make you Dirty Harry when you came up against those who had trained and fought with the best.

But these weren't normal circumstances: he was a long way short of being fully fit and still hurting badly from his last encounter. There were two of them and the one with the knife was starting to come towards him.

'Verdi says he's a doctor,' said the other one.

'Is that a fact,' hissed the knife-holder. 'Well, ah'm the one who's goin' to be doin' the operatin' today an' ah'm gonnae cut this bastard's balls off.'

Steven's back was already against one of the work surfaces: there was nowhere left for him to go. He searched with the flat of his hands over the surface, feeling for something he could use as a weapon but his eyes never left the knife in the yob's hand. The only thing his fingers touched was a jar of marmalade. He snatched it up and raised it threateningly. The yob stopped then grinned, displaying bad teeth as he weighed the blade lightly in his hand and feinted moves to right and left as if daring Steven to try it.

Steven kept threatening to throw the jar until the yob made the mistake he had been hoping for. In anticipation of having to move his head and shoulders quickly to left or right to avoid the jar, the yob planted both feet firmly on the ground.

That was the mistake.

Instead of aiming the jar at his head or body as the yob was expecting, Steven threw the heavy jar down at the man's feet with all the strength he could muster. It hit him squarely on his right instep before he had time to get out of the way. He screamed out in pain, dropped the knife and started hopping around in a circle, clutching at his foot with both hands. He had barely got out his first intelligible curse when Steven's right foot swung into his crotch and he let out another scream. He fell to the floor where Steven unleashed yet another kick into the side of his head and the noise stopped abruptly.

It was all over so quickly that the other man seemed mesmerised by what had happened but he recovered in time to snatch up the knife that had spun across the floor in his direction.

'Got lucky, ya fucker, did ye?' he murmured as he stepped over his unconscious companion. 'Well, ah've got news fur ye, pal. Lightnin's no gonna strike twice in the wan day. You're a dead man. Ah'm goin tae put yer lights oot just like that silly bitch, Manson.'

'So you killed Tracy Manson?' said Steven, again watching the knife rather than the man.

'Whit's it tae you?'

'I'm putting you under arrest for the murder of Tracy Manson,' said Steven with a calmness that he in no way felt.

'A fuckin' comedian, eh? Just how do ye propose doin' that?'

'Over a cup of tea,' said Steven. He snatched up the mug of tea from the worktop and threw its contents into the advancing man's face. The water in it was no longer boiling hot but it was still hot enough to make him yell out in pain. More importantly, it made him drop the knife. Steven kicked him hard in the stomach and he went down like his companion before him. Steven knelt down and whispered in the man's ear. 'At Hereford, sonny, we were taught to make our own luck.'

Steven stood up again and looked down at the sorry figure, hands held to his face, knees brought up to his chest like a large, ugly foetus.

'Fucking bastard,' the yob gasped.

Inside Steven's head a training sergeant from a time long ago yelled at him. 'This is not a game, Dunbar. When they go down, make sure they stay down!'

Remembering the beating he'd suffered at the hands of these men and the fact that this was the trash who'd murdered Tracy Manson, Steven sent another vicious kick into him, this time into his face. It broke most of his teeth, which scattered across the floor like slimy, red and white buttons. Now, both men lay silent.

'Gratuitous, Dunbar, gratuitous,' Steven murmured as he took out his mobile phone and called McClintock.

While he waited for the police to arrive, he went through the contents of the tin he'd found behind the bath panel and quickly deduced that the making of pornographic films – mainly S&M, judging by the titles – was a much bigger business than he had realised. The notebook contained a list of titles, dates and the addresses of film studios used in the making of them. He gathered that a linked website was used to provide download facilities for the material and attract customers for the mail order of films and videos.

Steven turned his attention to the three videos. They did not have titles on the spine, only girls' names and dates. He put them to one side and sifted through the remaining material to come across a white card, which had three multi-digit numbers on it and a single printed word, 'Nightingale'. He decided that he'd underestimated Tracy Manson. She'd been associated with Verdi for a long time and she'd obviously managed to glean a lot about how the operation was run – smack-head or not. He'd bet money on these being bank account numbers and 'nightingale' a password.

The police arrived in a fanfare of sirens and heavy boots on the stairs. The men on the floor were still unconscious when Steven opened the door and two uniformed men came through. They were followed by McClintock who was still climbing up the last flight and puffing.

'The fags'll be the death of me,' he gasped by way of greeting.

Steven waited for him and ushered him through. One of the uniformed men was radioing for an ambulance; the other was going through the pockets of the men on the floor. McClintock looked down at them and turned to Steven. 'Temper, temper,' he said with the only merest suggestion of a grin.

'This one admitted to the murder of Tracy Manson,' said Steven, touching one of the men with his toe.

Steven handed over the shortbread tin to McClintock saying, 'Frae bonnie Scotland. This is what Tracy mistakenly hoped would put her in a bargaining position. Everything you wanted to know about life, love and the porn business.'

'Didn't you do well,' said McClintock, accepting the tin. 'A fucking tour de force, if you don't mind me saying so.'

'Didn't do me much good though,' said Steven. 'There's nothing about a connection between Verdi and the forensic lab.'

'Maybe an entirely different affair,' said McClintock. 'No reason for Tracy to be involved. Let's see what comes out in the wash when we've had time to unravel this lot.'

'I'll leave you to it then,' said Steven. He left with McClintock holding the tin and all its contents save for the white card with account details. That was in his top pocket. He had a feeling that he should hold on to that for the moment.

As soon as he got into the car – which had attracted a parking ticket and a single expletive from Steven when he saw it – he felt an almost overwhelming sense of tiredness sweep over him. He leaned his head back on the headrest for a few moments, closing his eyes and taking slow deep breaths. The adrenaline that had been pumping through his veins to fuel his fight for life had now dissipated, leaving him monastically calm and free to ponder over what might have been.

When he opened his eyes again he looked at his unmarked hands resting on the wheel and brought them slowly up to his face to run his fingertips lightly down his cheeks. He recognised that he had been incredibly lucky. He had managed to take out two hard men without suffering any further injury himself, not even a scratch. He didn't doubt that the yobs would have killed him. One slip, one missed kick, a jar of marmalade that could have been in a cupboard instead of sitting on the work surface and it could all have turned out so differently. He would be lying dead on the floor of a tenement flat in Edinburgh and Jenny would have been minus a father.

A grey cat came out from underneath the car next to his where it had been seeking warmth and gazed up at him in a frozen, feline stare as if assessing whether he was friend or foe.

'Have a nice day, Puss,' he said.

Steven called Macmillan as soon as he got back to the hotel and told him everything.

'But when all's said and done, none of this has anything to do with the Julie Summers case or David Little for that matter,' said Macmillan, seeing through the smokescreen of achievement that Steven was putting up.

'Verdi's porn business is big,' said Steven.

'And nothing whatever to do with Sci-Med,' said Macmillan.

'True enough,' said Steven, conceding the point.

'Have the police arrested Verdi?'

'Not yet.'

'When they do, you can have one crack at him and then you'll call it a day and this time I mean it. Understood?'

'Understood,' said Steven.

Steven was hungry. He treated himself to a large cooked breakfast, washed down with lots of sweet coffee to restore his depleted blood sugar levels and dispel the fatigue he felt. He saw no point in getting personally involved in the police analysis of the material he'd found in Tracy Manson's flat so he'd wait until he heard back from Peter McClintock. That would take at least a day so he had time on his hands. He'd use it to re-charge his batteries. He'd walk in the fresh air, maybe climb Arthur's Seat – the hill almost in the heart of Edinburgh – and generally seek relief from the sea of squalor he seemed to have been immersed in for the past week or so.

* * *

McClintock called just after four. He sounded strangely subdued. 'Boy, did you come up trumps with these videos,' he said.

'How so?'

'The girls in them were on our missing persons register. We know now what happened to them.'

'They became stars of the silver screen?' said Steven.

McClintock didn't laugh. 'They *died* on the silver screen,' he said. 'They're snuff videos, S&M taken to the limit. All three were tortured to death on film. I'll spare you the details.'

Steven swallowed hard. He'd heard of such things – even films depicting the death of children – but being this close to it made it feel different. All the good of the day was wiped out in an instant. 'Jesus Christ.'

'We've had a busy day, raiding the addresses on the lists in the tin,' said McClintock. 'But we left the saunas alone. They pale into insignificance in the light of what we found in the videos.'

'And Verdi?'

'We've pulled him in but you'll have to wait until tomorrow to see him. The slimy little bastard has done a pretty good job at keeping everything at a distance – but then he's a lawyer. If we're not careful we could end up charging the clowns while the ringmaster walks. Our people are having a go at breaking him before he has too much time to think about things. He was expecting some kind of police action thanks to our illustrious leader pulling in Tracy but he didn't reckon on us getting our hands on Tracy Manson's shortbread tin. He won't be getting much sleep tonight.'

'Good luck,' said Steven. 'How about the goons at Tracy's flat?'

'We've charged both of them with her murder but under advice from their solicitor, they're saying nothing. A shifty little prat in an Armani suit called Tomasso turned up as soon as we brought them in. These bastards carry solicitors' cards in their wallets like the rest of us carry Visas.'

'C'est la vie,' said Steven.

'It's just a pity that Tracy Manson didn't have any information about where the money goes,' said McClintock. 'If the others suspected for a moment that Verdi wasn't in a position to look after them financially I reckon they'd start singing a different song.'

'Mmm,' said Steven, feeling uncomfortable.

'I'll let you know when you can see Verdi,' said McClintock. 'It'll probably be tomorrow afternoon.'

Steven thanked him, feeling relieved that the conversation was over and knowing that he should have told McClintock about the existence of the account numbers but it was an ace he wanted to hold on to himself for the time being. He had plans about forcing Verdi into telling him what he wanted to know.

Steven was to hear from McClintock much sooner than he expected when he called just after 8 p.m.

'We have to meet,' he said.

Steven was about to make a joke about McClintock never appearing to go home but the policeman's tone stopped him.

'All right,' he said. 'The pub in Inverleith?'

'Too near headquarters,' said McClintock. 'Somewhere out of town. Do you know Queensferry?'

'Down by the Forth Bridge?' said Steven.

'That's right. There's a hotel on the water called the Sealscraig. I'll meet you in the bar in an hour.'

'I'll be there,' said Steven. The line went dead before he could say anything else.

He asked at the desk for directions and was told that he should follow road signs for the Forth Road Bridge but take the opening off to the right at the roundabout before it. He did this and found himself descending a steep hill into the village some ten minutes ahead of time. He parked the car by the waterfront and got out to look up at the rail bridge where a small commuter diesel was just about to complete its crossing from Fife. The noise of the train, amplified by the steel girders, stopped abruptly as it reached the permanent way. It was as if some giant hand had lifted it off the track.

Along to his left and lying below and between the rail and the road bridges, he could see the Sealscraig Hotel. On a dark, misty night its yellow lights seemed welcoming and were reflected on the smooth oily surface of the water as he got nearer and entered to start climbing the stairs leading up to the bar.

McClintock was already standing there. He didn't smile although he gave a nod of recognition and ordered another beer.

'Let's sit down,' said McClintock as Steven's beer appeared. The bar was less than a quarter full so it wasn't difficult to find a table where they could speak freely but they still kept their voices down.

'Something's wrong?' said Steven, alarmed at just how worried McClintock seemed to be.

'I wanted to tell you this before I told anyone else,' said McClintock, 'but first, the DNA fingerprint you asked me to check, where did you get it?'

Steven told him how Susan Givens had uncovered it by amplifying up the faint ghost bands present on the gel that convicted David Little. 'She used a computer imaging program to intensify them and then she eliminated the main ones. You've come up with a match, haven't you?' he said, suddenly realising why McClintock had asked the question.

McClintock nodded and looked down at the table.

'Well, c'mon,' Steven prompted. 'Out with it.'

'I think I'd rather it was anyone else on Earth,' said McClintock. 'But it's Hector Combe's DNA.'

'Sweet Jesus Christ,' whispered Steven. 'You're sure?'

'There's no doubt.'

'So he did kill her,' said Steven after taking a moment to come to terms with the enormity of the finding. 'Little *was* stitched up.'

'But Little's semen was in her too,' McClintock reminded him, but the spectre of a huge miscarriage of justice was already in his eyes.

'The lab must have fixed it,' said Steven. 'No one else could have done it. There's no other explanation. They must have altered the evidence to clear Combe and convict Little.'

'But why?'

Steven shook his head. 'God knows but someone in the lab must have cleaned up Julie – that's where the traces of *Virkon* came from – and then contaminated her with David Little's semen before taking new forensic samples.'

'How?' asked McClintock again.

'I don't know how, I don't know who and I don't know why but that's what must have happened. Combe was guilty all along.'

'Christ almighty,' whispered McClintock. 'The press will bury us this time.'

Steven was having his own nightmare. In it, Combe recited, *This little piggy went to market... Snap!*

'What blood group was Combe?' he asked suddenly as an idea came to him.

'I've no idea,' said McClintock. 'But it'll be in the records. What difference does it make?'

'The scrapings under Julie's fingernails must have come from Combe not Little,' said Steven. 'Julie scratched his face just like he told Lawson she did. I have to know what blood group he was.'

'If you say so but what do we do about this in the meantime? I haven't told Santini. I haven't told anyone except you. I didn't even tell the lab where the DNA profile came from.'

'Sit on it for the time being,' said Steven. 'Don't tell a soul.'

'What are you going to do?'

'I'm going to talk to a nurse.'

McClintock drove off, having promised to find out as quickly as he could about Hector Combe's blood group, although still not clear about why. For his part, Steven hurried back to his car and drove directly to the Western General Hospital where he rushed up to the ward where he'd last spoken to Samantha Egan. It was going to be a long shot at this time of night – just before ten – but worth a try.

'I don't suppose Sister Egan is still on duty?' he asked the staff nurse who challenged him when he entered.

The girl shook her head. 'No way,' she said in an Australian accent. 'The night staff took over more than an hour ago.'

Steven screwed up his face. 'A pity,' he said. 'It's important I speak with her.' He showed the girl his ID.

'You might still be lucky,' said the girl. 'I'm pretty sure she'll still be in the hospital. She and some of the other sisters were having a little get-together when they went off duty. One of the gang is leaving so they were planning to break out the Bulgarian red and get stuck into some peanuts.'

Steven smiled and asked, 'Do you know where?'

'I think she said it was in the nursing manager's office. Want me to phone her?'

Steven said not; he'd rather go up there himself. The nurse gave him directions.

The female laughter coming from inside the room stopped when he knocked on the door. After a short delay, a tall woman with a wineglass in her hand opened it. Steven apologised for the intrusion, showed his ID and explained why he was there. The woman turned and said over her shoulder, 'Sam, it appears the police have finally caught up with you.'

Steven was invited into a small sitting room where he apologised again for interrupting and said to a bemused-looking Samantha Egan that he had to speak to her.

'Use my office, Sam,' said the tall woman.

Samantha led Steven through to an adjoining office and closed the door behind them.

'I didn't expect to see you again,' she said as she sat down. 'How can I help this time?'

'This is going to sound very strange,' said Steven. 'But during our last conversation you told me about some kind of mistake you made in Ronald Lee's lab over a blood grouping?'

'Yes, that's largely why I gave up lab work,' said Samantha.

'As I recall, you had been asked to group the blood found in the scrapings taken from under Julie Summers' fingernails?'

'That's right.'

'Can you remember what you *thought* the blood group was?'

'I'm not liable to forget,' said Samantha. 'We are talking about two simple and straightforward tests here. I was devastated when John told me I'd got both the ABO grouping and the Rhesus factor wrong: I just couldn't believe it. But when he repeated the tests in front of me it was obvious that he was right. I realised then that if I could screw up something as simple as a blood grouping, there was no hope at all for me in lab work. I thought the blood in the scrapings was O negative: to my embarrassment, it was A positive.'

'That is exactly what I wanted to know,' said Steven.

'This is all very mysterious,' said Samantha. 'And rather upsetting if I may say so. It was something I really didn't want to be reminded of.'

'I'm sorry,' said Steven. 'But...' His mobile phone went off and he excused himself, walking over to the window to take the call. It was McClintock.

'For what it's worth, Combe was blood group O negative.'

'It's worth a very great deal,' said Steven. He turned back to Samantha. 'You didn't make a mistake,' he said. 'John Merton did.'

'John did?' exclaimed Samantha as if it were the most ridiculous thing she'd ever heard. 'John didn't make mistakes. He was the one who held the lab together.'

'Maybe "mistake" was the wrong word,' said Steven, reluctant to divulge too much. 'But in this case you were right and he...wasn't. The blood was O negative.'

Samantha sighed deeply and bowed her head in silence for a

few moments then she looked up and smiled. She said, 'It's silly but I can't tell you how much this means to me. I know I was only a junior in the lab at the time and my "mistake" was discovered almost immediately but the thought of having made it has been in the back of my mind ever since. To this day I tend not to trust myself. I always check everything twice on the ward.'

'Well, it's a mistake that never was,' said Steven. 'You got the blood group and type absolutely right. I promise you.'

'But how could John have got it...?'

'Tell me about John Merton,' interrupted Steven.

'I don't think I can tell you any more than I did last time. I really didn't know him that well.'

'Everyone I've spoken to has told me that it was really him who ran the lab and covered up as best he could for Dr Lee's shortcomings but no one has ever been able to tell me why. Were they close friends?'

'I don't think so,' said Samantha. 'In fact, I sort of got the impression that John maybe despised Dr Lee a little.'

'What made you think that?'

'Just the way he looked at him sometimes, sort of superior, if you know what I mean. But then, John had a bit of a chip on his shoulder.'

'About what?'

'Sounds awful but I think it was the old working class thing. He was always making jibes about the "establishment" as he called it. The whole country was run by public school twits in his opinion. Maybe he thought his background was holding him back. I don't know but he certainly seemed bitter about something.'

'Was he married?'

'No. The story was that he'd been engaged at one time but the girl had called it off; something else he felt bitter about by all accounts.'

'So he didn't have a girlfriend, or even a boyfriend for that matter?'

'None that I ever saw,' said Samantha. 'But I think it was

definitely girls that John was interested in. I saw the inside door of his locker once. It's a wonder some of these girls didn't catch their death of cold.'

Steven smiled. 'Did you ever visit him at his home?'

'Never,' said Samantha. 'I don't think anyone in the lab was ever invited to John's place. From what he said from time to time I think it must have been full of computers anyway. That seemed to be his big passion in life. He was a bit of a jacket in that respect.'

'Anorak,' Steven corrected with a smile.

'God, yes, I'm always getting that wrong.'

Steven thanked Samantha for her help and apologised again for interrupting the party.

'I'm so glad that you did,' said Samantha. 'You've made my day.'

Mine too, thought Steven as he returned downstairs and started walking back along the corridor. It was now clear that John Merton was the man he was looking for. It was Merton, not Lee or any of the others, who'd been Verdi's contact in the lab. Instead of stopping Lee making mistakes and generally looking after him, as everyone thought, Merton had actually been introducing mistakes, some of which he would subsequently "discover" and blame on Lee, others he would deliberately let through so that Verdi could question the evidence and get his clients off. Lee of course, conveniently got the blame for everything. All he needed now was for Verdi to confirm it.

But it was Merton's role in the Julie Summers case that Steven now concentrated on. Merton had deliberately conned a subordinate in the lab into believing she had made a mistake in typing the blood found under Julie's fingernails. Being very junior, Samantha Egan had accepted it, especially when Merton had apparently repeated the test in front of her but, unknown to her, he must have switched the samples. Group A positive blood wasn't hard to find. Almost half the population had it. It could even have been his own.

If Ronald Lee had succeeded in carrying out the DNA fingerprinting on the scrapings, as had been his intention, he would have come up with Hector Combe's DNA fingerprint. Merton must have persuaded him – as he had Samantha Egan – that he had made some mistake and shown him his version of the test, one that matched the profile of the semen belonging to David Little. As this would have appeared to make more sense in the circumstances, Lee must have believed him and been grateful.

So why had Merton gone to such lengths to fit David Little up for a crime that he did not do and what kind of pathological mind lay behind it? It had to be pathological. No normal person could have done such a thing. Samantha Egan had said that Merton had a chip on his shoulder but this was something else. It was several orders of magnitude different. Merton was a lunatic.

There was still no doubt however, that David Little's semen had been found in Julie's body. How had Merton managed to arrange that? There was no obvious answer. As far as he knew there was no direct link between Merton and Little and only a secondary one between Verdi and Little's wife, Charlotte. Steven decided that there were two people he had to speak to. One was Paul Verdi, now that he knew who his associate was, and the other was David Little. He had to ask Little just who hated him that much and why.

Knowing that he would probably not be able to see Verdi until the afternoon, Steven set out for Barlinnie first thing in the morning. He found Little a bit better in terms of his health than last time. He was lying on his bunk reading but he was not at all pleased to see him.

'I thought I told you to fuck off.'

'You had every right to,' said Steven. 'I gave you false hope when I didn't mean to.'

'Fine; *te absolvo;* now fuck off,' said Little.

'I know that you didn't rape and murder Julie Summers,' said Steven.

Little stared at him, his dark sunken eyes betraying nothing. At length he broke the silence and said, 'Do you know, no one has ever said that to me before. Not even my wife.'

'A man named John Merton framed you. Ring any bells?'

'Merton?' repeated Little. 'I did know a John Merton once but that was many years ago.'

'Could you have given him cause to hate you?' asked Steven.

'We were medical students together,' said Little. 'We were friends. We shared a flat.'

Little stopped talking and appeared to be lost in thought.

'But something happened between you?'

'Neither of us came from a wealthy background so we didn't have much money to play around with,' said Little. 'We lived on cornflakes and beans on toast for the last couple of weeks of every term, then suddenly John wasn't poor any more. He seemed to have money coming out of his ears. He told me that a rich relative had died but he was lying. I found out that he was supplying a foreign pharmaceutical company with human glands. He was stealing them from corpses in the med school,' said Little. 'I tackled him about it and told him that it was a stupid and dangerous thing to do because the corpses hadn't been screened for diseases that could be passed on through the glands he was selling.'

'What did the company want them for?' asked Steven.

'They were extracting growth hormone for sale abroad. The practice was banned in this country because of the possibility of transmitting Creuzfeld Jakob Syndrome but the extract was still being used abroad.'

'So what did you do?' asked Steven.

'He was my friend so I told him that if he packed it in I'd say no more about it. He promised that he would but a few weeks later I found out that he was still doing it – the sports car was a bit of a give-away. We had a fight: I reported him to the Dean and when the dust settled he was thrown out of medical school.'

'He didn't leave you much choice,' said Steven.

'He didn't see it that way,' said Little. 'He didn't seem to see that he was doing anything wrong. He had no conscience at all about it. He blamed me for his expulsion and threatened to kill me. He was engaged at the time to a girl named Melissa Felton, one of the other med students: she left him when she found out what he'd been doing. I think he held me responsible for that too but I never saw him again.'

'He must have gone elsewhere to do a science degree,' said Steven. 'He was working in the police lab at the time of Julie Summers' murder. He manipulated the forensic evidence to fit you up.'

Little tried to take a deep breath to hide the fact that he was being overcome by emotion. Tears started to run down his face.

'But the fact remains that your semen was found in Julie's body,' said Steven. 'Any idea how?'

Little looked at Steven as if the question was ridiculous then he said, 'Oh Christ, we were donors.'

'Sperm donors?' asked Steven.

'First year at med school, one of the research council labs was looking for donors among the students so we went along. We thought it was a hoot. A few minutes with a dirty magazine and a plastic cup and that was it. Easy money. Christ, he must have managed to get my sample from the sperm bank.'

'Not too difficult if you know your way around the university labs I suppose,' said Steven.

'A hoot,' said Little distantly. 'We thought it was a hoot...' More tears started to flow down the hollows of his cheeks.

'Merton was also responsible for the pornography found on your computer,' said Steven. 'Your wife worked for an associate of his. That's how he came to know where you were and what you were doing. It was Merton who supplied the utilities disk to help sort out some problem you'd been having. That's where the porn came from.'

Little shook his head and spread his scrawny arms. 'He said he'd kill me. I just didn't realise that he was deadly serious about it. What's happened to him? Have you arrested him?'

'No, I've only just worked out what happened.'

'The bastard,' whispered Little. 'He took away my

life...slowly...one day at a time...each one worse than the one before. And the police? What are they saying to all this?'

'They don't know yet,' said Steven.

Little looked at him questioningly.

'I only worked out last night who'd set you up and now you've told me why and how. I'll break the news to them when I get back to Edinburgh.'

'You wouldn't like to video it for me?' said Little. 'I don't suppose I'll live long enough to sue the bastards.'

Steven silently agreed.

'Who did kill Julie?' asked Little.

'Hector Combe, the psychopath I told you about, the one who confessed to the crime on his deathbed.'

'The real killer confessed but nobody listened,' said Little.

'I did,' said Steven.

Little turned his head – he'd been looking up at the ceiling. 'Yes, you did and I'm not sure what to say to you. I've had no reason to thank anyone for anything in over eight years. I'm out of the way of such things.'

'No need,' said Steven. 'Try concentrating on positive things. Take your medication and start making plans.'

'Plans?' exclaimed Little. 'Positive things?'

'Even if it's only psyching yourself up to hear apologies from everyone who owes you one.' Steven got up to go. 'I'm going back to set everything in motion.'

Little stopped him with a hand gesture but then couldn't get the words out. He had to settle for two brief nods that clearly said thank you. The tears emphasised the point.

Once back in Edinburgh, Steven went straight to police headquarters and told McClintock everything. 'I'm telling you this because I want you to tell Santini. If it came from me it would look and sound like gloating – and it would be. I don't much care for your boss but to be fair, there was little the police could have done in this instance.'

'Thanks for that,' said McClintock. 'But facts are facts and there has still been a bloody huge miscarriage of justice.'

'Fraid so.'

'Do you still want to talk to Verdi?' asked McClintock.

'Please. Any progress?'

'Not yet. He's still denying everything but we got permission to hold him for another forty-eight hours. He still doesn't know about us having the snuff videos. We're keeping them as our ace in the hole.'

'Mum's the word,' said Steven.

'Give me a moment,' said McClintock. He left the room and came back a couple of minutes later, accompanied by a man in shirtsleeves. 'Sergeant Wills will take you to him,' he said. 'I'm off to tell Santini.'

Despite the intensive questioning he'd been undergoing, Verdi still seemed sharp and alert, thought Steven as he entered the room.

'Shit, this is all I need,' he exclaimed when he saw Steven. 'What the hell do you want?'

'Just a few questions,' said Steven.

'I'll tell you what I told the rest. I don't know anything about Tracy Manson's death or any porn videos.'

'I'm not concerned with Tracy's death; that's a police matter. Same goes for the porn.'

'So what the hell do *you* want?'

'I want you to tell me about your association with John Merton.'

Verdi's eyes narrowed at the name but he said, 'Never heard of him.'

'Yes you have. He deliberately screwed up forensic evidence and then gave you the nod so you could expose the flaws in court and get your clients off – the ones who could afford it that is. Three of them to be precise, all big name criminals and all three acquitted.'

'Don't know what you're talking about.'

'You do, Verdi, but I'm not even interested in them. It's the Julie Summers case I want to know about.'

'Still don't know what you're talking about.'

Steven leaned closer and said, 'You are entirely dependent on your people keeping quiet, aren't you, Verdi? They keep quiet and you'll look after them and their families handsomely. Isn't that the deal?'

Verdi said nothing.

'The trouble with that is that it falls to pieces when you go broke and that's just what's about to happen.'

'What are you talking about?' snapped Verdi.

'The money, Verdi, the money that links you to an international criminal operation involving pornography, maybe even some of the money that the villains paid to you and Merton for getting them off. I know where it is and how to get my hands on it. The police don't but I do.'

'Dream on,' said Verdi as Steven sat back.

Steven took the card out of his pocket and read out the first number.

Verdi winced but kept his composure. 'I take it these are your lottery numbers,' he said. 'Let me tell you, it's a mug's game. You'd be better off buying Premium Bonds.'

Steven read out the second account number and then finally, the third.

Verdi swallowed but didn't say anything.

'Ring a bell?' Steven asked. 'Or should I say, sing a song?'

'What?' croaked Verdi.

'Eleven letters, usually sings in Berkeley Square,' said Steven. 'How am I doing?'

The blood drained from Verdi's face. 'You're serious?' he said. 'The police don't know?'

'They don't,' said Steven. 'I'm the only one.'

'How about a deal?'

'Tell me what I want to know and I'll give you the card back.'

'Not a word to the police?'

'Not a word.'

'All right, I did have something going with John Merton.'

'How did you meet him?'

'We met at a club in the early nineties. Let's say we had a mutual interest in young ladies.'

'And their exploitation,' said Steven.

Verdi ignored the comment. 'John was a computer buff. He convinced me that that was where the real money was to be made. All we needed was a few willing girls and some film equipment. I had a few friends who were in the sauna business so we pooled our resources and made a few videos. John distributed them via the net and they went like shit off a shovel. Then I found out what his day job was and we decided to help each other out there as well.'

'He faked evidence for you?'

'Fucked more like. He messed it up and I brought it to the attention of the court.'

'Tell me about the Julie Summers case. That was different.'

'Yeah, that was different. God help me, I don't know too much about that. None of it was anything to do with me. It was John's thing. He had some bee in his bonnet about the guy who was charged.'

'David Little?'

'That's right. John maintained that he was as guilty as sin and was determined to see him go down for life. The DNA fingerprint evidence against Little was perfect but John said that some of the other stuff was a bit iffy. He asked me not to challenge it so I didn't but that bloody case was just about the end of us.'

'How so?'

'Lee, John's boss, was a piss artist. He didn't suspect anything about what had been going on until the Summers case. John could usually convince him that he must have screwed up but this time he kept on arguing with John about some gel pattern I think he called it. He refused to accept that he'd made a mistake. The drunken old bastard overheard John telling me on the phone about it in one of his sober moments and checked up on the phone number afterwards. He got in touch with Seymour and Nicholson to say that he thought that something "gravely unprofessional" had been going on.'

'The old queens called me in and made noises about calling in the police. I had to point out that they had been sharing handsomely in the money I'd been bringing in to the firm and even if they didn't go down with me, it would be the end of the line for dear old S&N. I put forward the alternative of my resignation from the firm with a bit of a pay-off and they went for it.'

'What about Lee?'

'I had a word with him.'

'What does that mean?'

'I told him that S&N were not going to take the matter any further so there would be no support for him from that direction. If he tried doing something on his own he would be exposed publicly as a drunk who couldn't run a pie stall let alone a forensic lab. On the other hand, if he forgot about the whole thing he would be paid generously for his continuing silence. Guess which option he went for?'

'When did you last hear from him?'

'Funnily, a few weeks ago. He called me to say that some nosy bastard was asking questions about the evidence in the Summers case. I suppose that was you. He was up to high doh about it.'

'So you killed him in case he started talking about it?'

'Christ no, I didn't give a damn about the Summers case. It was nothing to do with me. All I did was not ask a few questions.'

'Did you tell John Merton about Lee's call?'

'As a matter of fact I did.'

'So you're still in touch with him?'

'He runs the website.'

'And finds the customers?'

'No comment.'

'Where can I find him?'

'I haven't seen him in ages.'

'Then how?'

'Through the website. Aren't computers wonderful?'

'So he could be anywhere?'

'You got it. Can I have the card now?'

Steven handed over the card without another word and left the cell.

Chapter Twenty

'How d'you get on?' asked McClintock when Steven entered.

'Real good, how about you?'

'The news went down like a shit sandwich but you couldn't really expect anything else,' said McClintock. 'However, our illustrious leader has come to terms with the situation and has switched his attention to damage limitation. He pointed out that we could do a lot to minimise the harm to the force's reputation if we get a quick result with Verdi and his pals. He's thinking along the lines of, "Edinburgh's finest solve prostitute's murder and smash international porn ring. Oh, and by the way, we locked up the wrong man for eight years."'

Steven nodded and took out a piece of paper from his wallet. He handed it to McClintock. 'This may help.'

'What's this?' asked McClintock, reading out the numbers on it.

'I promised Mr Verdi that I wouldn't say a word about it to the police,' said Steven.

'Christ, these are account numbers!' exclaimed McClintock. 'They couldn't be Ver...'

'My lips are sealed,' said Steven.

'But where...?' began McClintock. 'Shit, they were in the tin, weren't they? Tracy's tin,' he said. 'And you held on to them?'

'I needed an edge,' said Steven.

'You made some sort of a deal with him?'

'He told me what I wanted to know about his arrangement with the forensic lab and I gave him Tracy's card back without saying a word to the police. I didn't say I wouldn't give you a copy of the numbers and let you work it out for yourselves.'

'Remind me not to buy a used car from you, Dunbar.'

'You've started the hunt for Merton?' asked Steven.

'It's under way. We managed to get his old staff photo from departmental records at the university. It's years out of date but better than nothing. It's already been sent out.'

'Maybe I could have a copy?' asked Steven.

'A keepsake?' said McClintock.

'I want to see what evil looks like,' said Steven.

'If only you could tell,' said McClintock. 'It'd sure make the job a whole lot easier.'

Steven picked up the photograph that McClintock slid across his desk and nodded. 'Wouldn't it just,' he said. He was looking at the photograph of a man in his early thirties with nothing to suggest what he might be capable of. He wouldn't have attracted a second glance in a bus queue.

'He's still involved with Verdi,' said Steven. 'But Verdi maintains he doesn't know where he is. He says they communicate through the website that Merton runs as a front for the porn business. He runs his legit business the same way. You might be able to trace him through that but I have my doubts. Merton's no fool when it comes to computers.'

'Shit, he could be in California,' said McClintock, 'or Thailand or anywhere. This just ain't gonna be easy. Maybe I'll have another go at Verdi about him. He must have a base somewhere.'

'Have you thought what you're going to do about Little's wife?' asked Steven. 'Someone's going to have to tell her.'

'I've been pushing it to the back of my mind,' admitted McClintock. 'But you're right. She shouldn't have to read it in the papers. It's funny; I'm not sure if she'll see it as good news or not. I mean, how do we tell her that the husband she divorced and left all these years ago was innocent all along...?'

Steven grimaced and remembered how upset she'd become when he'd brought up the possibility of the porn on Little's computer having been a plant. 'She's going to need some kind of support,' he said.

'Do you think there's any chance your people could deal with this?' asked McClintock. 'I hate to ask but somehow I think the less she sees of the Edinburgh police in the circumstances, the better.'

'I'll have a word with John Macmillan,' said Steven.

'Does she know Little's got AIDS?'

Steven shook his head. 'That's another little surprise to add to the package,' he said.

'Christ, what a fucking mess,' said McClintock, letting his head drop forward on to his chest and rubbing his temples with his fingertips. 'Do you think that bastard Merton has any idea what he did?'

'It's my fear that he does,' said Steven. 'When Little told me how Merton didn't believe that he was really doing anything wrong when he was caught selling corpse glands, I saw the warning signs. No conscience; the sure-fire trademark of the psychopath.'

'Another psycho. My cup overflows,' said McClintock.

'Well, I've got a report to write,' said Steven, getting up to go. 'And then I'll have to start thinking about when I'm going to head south.'

'Will you manage a pint before you go?'

'I'm not sure,' said Steven.

McClintock got up and came over to Steven with his hand held out. 'I can't say it's been a pleasure,' he said, shaking hands with a smile. 'But I've got a lot of respect for you, Dunbar.'

'And vice versa,' said Steven. 'Maybe we'll see each other again.'

'If you're thinking of re-opening any of our old cases, let me know and I'll put in for early retirement on medical grounds,' said McClintock.

'Let me know how you get on with Verdi and his pals.'

'Will do.'

As he left McClintock's office, Steven saw Santini at the end of the corridor. He was coming towards him but the moment he caught sight of him the policeman put his hand to his head – a theatrical gesture, as if he'd just remembered something – turned on his heel and headed off in the other direction.

'Missing you already,' said Steven under his breath.

The good feeling that Steven usually got at the end of an assignment was entirely missing when he'd finished writing up his report. There were just so many wrongs that could not be put right. David Little would be freed but he was a dying man and the contribution that his brilliant mind might have made to medical science had been lost for ever. Even if he were to go into remission and get some respite from the relentless onslaught of AIDS, it would be difficult if not impossible for former friends and colleagues, who had universally shunned him since the time of his arrest, to start behaving as if nothing had happened.

There was also a nightmare in waiting for Charlotte Little and her daughters when it came to meeting Little face to face for the first time in over eight years. Could Charlotte even bring herself to go through with it at all? he wondered. But whether she did or not, Steven could see that society would turn against her when the full story emerged. The overwhelming evidence against Little at the time would be forgotten in an instant and the papers would cast her in the role of the woman who didn't stand by her man. To the tabloids, she and her daughters would be the Railway Children family who'd driven off into the sunset as soon as daddy was arrested. Life was about to deliver Charlotte Little yet another kick in the teeth.

It wasn't as if she'd managed to find happiness in the years after Little went to prison, thought Steven. She'd been forced by the press to live as a recluse for a long time after the trial and God knows what hell her children had had to endure at school when their classmates had found out who they were. Daughters of a child killer? It didn't bear thinking about. Even when Charlotte had got enough confidence back to re-establish a social life, she'd met up with somebody who'd knocked her about and cheated her out of all her money. Jesus! Take a look at life again soon.

Steven wasn't quite sure what to suggest to Sci-Med when it came to informing Charlotte. He was afraid that his original notion of requesting some kind of support for her would translate into a woman PC making tea. A nice cup of tea, the British panacea for all ills. World's coming to an end? Best put the kettle on, love...

The only positive thing that Steven could see in the

situation was the fact that Charlotte had a supportive family behind her. Her mother and father were genuinely nice people who cared deeply for their daughter and had stood by her through thick and thin. It couldn't have been easy for them being associated with a child murderer at the time when the case was all over the papers. He just hoped that they would have the energy to stand by her all over again. Maybe he should warn them in advance?

Steven made a decision. He would not ask Sci-Med to send along strangers to tell Charlotte Little. He would go to Norfolk and tell her himself. At least he appreciated how strong the evidence against her husband had been and understood why she had had no alternative but to believe that her husband was guilty – after all, he himself had been convinced of that at the outset. He hoped that he'd be able to reassure her that she shouldn't blame herself. Telling her that Little had AIDS was however, going to be something else entirely.

Next day, with his final report finished and submitted to Sci-Med and his request for a few days' leave granted, Steven arranged for flowers to be sent to Susan Givens and Samantha Egan, with a note of thanks to each. He handed back the keys of his rented car, checked out of his hotel, and returned to London on an evening BA shuttle. Once there, he went directly to his flat to spend the night before driving up to Norfolk in the morning.

As always, when he opened the door of his flat after being away for a while, he was struck by the still, silent, cold of the place but he quickly headed off maudlin thoughts of times past by switching on the lights and turning on the heating and television to provide warmth and noise as quickly as possible.

There was no food in the fridge or bread in the bin but his trusty stalwarts gin and tonic were available so he downed a couple before heading out to pick up some Chinese food from the Jade Garden. A supermarket trip could wait until he came back from Norfolk. He ate the food in front of the television while he caught up on the news and gave the water heater time to do its job.

The Channel 4 news at seven reported the arrest of a sauna owner in Edinburgh for the murder of a prostitute found dead on the shores of the Firth of Forth. He'd been charged along with two other men who were also thought to have been implicated. The sauna boss was also under investigation over his involvement in the running of an international pornography ring and further charges against him were pending.

'Bingo,' murmured Steven. He was relieved to hear that there was no mention yet of the David Little miscarriage of justice.

Almost as if an adjunct to the news, Steven's phone rang: it was Peter McClintock.

'Congratulations,' said Steven. 'I just saw it on the news.'

'I tried ringing you earlier,' said McClintock. 'You must have been on the plane. Having Verdi's assets frozen did the trick. His two heavies saw things differently when we told them a 100% wage freeze was about to be implemented and their boss was looking for legal aid. They argued a bit but finally one coughed but said the killing was down to Verdi. The other one was keen to agree with that.'

'There was no mention of the snuff videos on the news,' said Steven.

'That's proving problematical,' said McClintock. 'The Fiscal's office has pointed out that actresses die on the screen every day. Getting a jury to believe that it was for real in this case demands that we come up with the bodies and we will. It's just a question of finding the weakest link among the names that Tracy left us. Somebody must know something.'

'I wish you luck,' said Steven.

'I guess you're glad to be out of it,' said McClintock.

'Just one more thing to do,' said Steven. 'I'm going to tell Charlotte Little personally about her husband. I'm going up there tomorrow.'

'You're a good man, Charlie Brown,' said McClintock. 'What made you decide to do that?'

Steven told him.

'Then I wish *you* luck,' said McClintock. 'I'll let you know if there are any developments.'

The battery in Steven's own car, a dark green MGF, had gone flat with standing in the garage unused. The starter motor barely managed to turn over the engine.

'Been lying for a while?' asked one of his neighbours who had been about to drive off when he'd heard the final turn of Steven's starter fade into nothingness. 'These car alarms use up more juice than you'd think. Want to borrow my charger?'

Steven looked at his watch and said, 'If you've got jump leads I'd rather have a start. I've got a way to go so she'll charge herself on the journey.'

'No problem,' said the neighbour. He brought his car alongside Steven's and brought out a set of jump leads from his boot. He connected up the two batteries, trying not to let his smart business suit come into contact with the bodywork as he did so. Steven started his car, blipping the throttle until he was sure that the engine wasn't going to stall.

'I'm obliged to you,' he said.

The neighbour waved away his thanks with a smile as he wiped his hands on a paper towel and got back into his car to set off for work.

Steven thought about the man as he drove across town. It had been a simple, everyday act of kindness but he found himself clinging to it to reassure himself that such things still went on. That he needed to do so was telling him that Verdi's sordid world of vice, pornography and murder had been getting to him more than he had realised, as had thinking about the Littles. There were times when it would be all too easy just to give up on human nature and drift down into the welcoming arms of complete and abject cynicism.

Steven parked by the sea front in Cromer and used his mobile phone. He was relieved when it was James Grant who answered.

'This is going to sound very melodramatic, Mr Grant,' he said. 'But it's Steven Dunbar here and I'd like you to answer one question before you say anything else. Is your daughter in the house at the moment?'

'No, Lotty's out shopping with her mother. They've gone into Norwich.'

'So you're alone and they'll be away for a while?'

'They'll be back around teatime,' said a puzzled–sounding Grant.

'I need to speak to you. I'm in Cromer. Is it all right if I come to the house?'

'I suppose so. I'd rather hoped I'd seen the last of you, Dr Dunbar, if you don't mind me saying so.'

'It's important,' said Steven.

'All right,' said Grant in a resigned tone.

Steven and Grant spoke in the conservatory. Today, a bag of potting compost and several large pots were lying on the floor, as was a trowel and a number of colourful seed packets.

'I was in the middle of doing my early planting,' said Grant.

'Always a nice time of the year,' said Steven. 'What are they?' He could see that Grant was worried: it showed in his face despite the polite small talk they kept up for a few moments. 'I'm afraid I have some disturbing news for you,' he said. 'I thought it best if you heard it first rather than Charlotte.'

Grant's shoulders sagged forward and he shook his head slowly in disbelief as Steven told him of David Little's innocence.

'This just cannot be,' he said. 'Charlotte was told – we all were – that he was guilty beyond all shadow of a doubt. I mean, they found...'

'It must have seemed that way to everyone at the time,' said Steven. 'To be fair to the authorities, there was no other way of construing the evidence.'

'Fair to the authorities?' repeated Grant slowly as if it were the last thing on Earth that he wanted to be.

'I know it's going to be difficult,' said Steven.

'This could prove the last straw for Lotty,' said Grant. 'I know my daughter and she's going to be overwhelmed by guilt. It could well push her into a complete nervous break-down.'

'That's really why I came here to speak to her personally,' said Steven. 'I was convinced that Little was guilty too. I know that your daughter had no option but to believe the evidence presented to her at the time.'

Grant shook his head again as if trying to clear his head of what he hoped might still turn out to be a bad dream. 'But who would do such a thing?' he asked. 'And why?'

'A man with a grudge against your ex-son-in-law,' said Steven. 'His name is John Merton; he was working in the police forensic lab at the time. That's how he had access to Julie Summers' body. The police are trying to find him as we speak but it won't be easy.'

'Will Charlotte have to see David?' asked Grant, his mind wandering to other things.

'That's entirely up to her,' said Steven. 'It's been such a long time. Apart from that, he's very ill.'

'What's wrong with him?'

Steven took a deep breath before saying, 'Well, that's another thing... He has full-blown AIDS.'

Grant's eyes opened wide as if his senses were reeling. His lips quivered as he tried to find words. 'How?' he murmured.

'He was the victim of rape in his early days in prison.'

Grant rose out of his chair and put a hand to his forehead as he turned his back on Steven and shuffled over to look out of the windows. After almost a minute of complete silence he turned round and said, 'I really...I really...I re...'

Steven saw that Grant was about to faint and rushed forward to break his fall, realising that the ceramic tiles on the floor would be less than kind to his head. The contents of Steven's pockets scattered out on the floor as he threw himself forward but he managed to grab hold of Grant's shoulders and lower him the last foot or so to the floor. He loosened Grant's tie and put him in the recovery position while he examined the damage to his own knee, which he'd hit on the unforgiving tiles. It was nothing that a good rub wouldn't heal.

Grant came round and was hugely embarrassed at what he

saw as his 'girlish' behaviour. 'Don't know what came over me,' he said.

Steven helped him to his feet and settled him in a cane arm-chair while he picked up his own belongings from the floor. 'You had a severe shock,' he said.

'That photograph,' said Grant coldly.

In his hand Steven was holding the photograph of John Merton that McClintock had given him. 'This is John Merton,' he said, showing it properly to Grant. 'The man responsible for David Little's arrest and conviction.'

'No it isn't,' said Grant, sounding bemused. 'That man is John Mission.'

For a few moments Steven felt like a man who had just awoken from a nightmare to find that it was all true.

'The photograph was taken some years ago,' he said, hoping that Grant might be mistaken.

'This is John Mission,' said Grant. 'I'm hardly liable to forget him. Damn the man.'

'Then you are telling me that the man who engineered David Little's false conviction and who subsequently treated your daughter so badly are one and the same?' said Steven.

Grant continued to stare at the photograph, his face reflecting the anguish of painful memory.

'His grudge must have extended to your daughter too,' said Steven. 'Merton held Little responsible for having ruined his career and for the fact that the girl he planned to marry left him. Putting Charlotte through hell must have been part of the plan.'

'What kind of man thinks like that?' murmured Grant.

'Merton's a psychopath,' said Steven.

'I don't know how I'm going to tell Lotty all this,' said Grant, looking as if he'd aged ten years in the past half-hour.

'You don't have to; I will,' said Steven. 'Perhaps you could tell your wife while I'm doing it?'

Grant nodded. 'God, I need a drink,' he said. 'Will you join me?'

Steven said not but encouraged Grant to go ahead. He said that he had some calls to make in the light of what he'd just learned. Grant invited him to use the house phone and said that he'd leave him alone until he'd finished. Steven called Sci-Med first and then McClintock in Edinburgh.

'Mission?' exclaimed McClintock. 'Freudian or what?'

'Quite so,' agreed Steven. 'I haven't spoken to Charlotte yet but there's a chance she might be able to give us some clue as to his whereabouts. I'll get back to you if I make progress.'

'In the meantime I'll start the ball rolling with an alert for Mission as well as Merton.'

'Any progress with the video girls?'

'Not yet,' sighed McClintock. 'I'm beginning to think that these particular films weren't made in the local studios. 'There are just too many people pleading ignorance. Even Verdi seems confident we're not going to pin these murders on him.'

'But they were local girls?' said Steven.

'We've established that one of them, a lassie named Sharon Duthie, worked in one of Verdi's saunas at one time and that two other girls were friends of hers. Our thinking at the moment is that Verdi recruited Sharon for a film and she brought in two of her pals but after that the trail goes cold. None of the people that Tracy listed as being in on the making of the films would admit to ever coming across the three girls.'

'Nothing's ever easy,' said Steven.

'I think you should know that the papers are on to the Little situation,' said McClintock. He was transferred to a specialised AIDS unit in a hospital in Edinburgh last night. Word is they'll probably run with the story tomorrow. Little's already got himself a lawyer who's talking seven-figure compensation sums.'

'*Que ser ser ,*' said Steven.

'The civil liberties crowd have been shouting the odds on the phone this morning as have the prison reform lot and half a dozen other groups with axes to grind. You can bet your buns that politicians will be polishing up their outrage as we speak, ready to call for a "full public inquiry". That's all some of these buggers ever seem to do.'

Steven looked at his watch and said, 'Charlotte and her mother should be back in half an hour or so. I'll call you if I find out anything.'

Steven could see James Grant standing out in the garden. He went out to tell him that he'd finished making calls.

'You know,' said Grant, still gazing out towards the sea, 'I have never ever felt so guilty about anything in my entire life. I was absolutely convinced that David Little was guilty. I didn't even consider the possibility that a mistake might have been made. I know what you said about the strength of the evidence against him but I still feel awful.'

'Guilt never sees the circumstances,' said Steven.

'A cross to bear for all of us,' said Grant. 'God forgive us.'

Steven put a hand on Grant's shoulder.

Grant glanced to his right and said, 'That's Lotty's car coming up the hill.'

Steven went back into the conservatory while Grant walked round to the front door to meet his returning wife and daughter. Steven sat and waited while Grant told them of his presence and then stood up when Charlotte appeared in the doorway.

'Not more questions about filth on the computer,' she said, sounding exasperated. 'What does it matter now, anyway?'

'It's not about that,' Steven assured her. 'I think you'd better sit down.'

Steven broke the news to her about Little's innocence to her as gently as he could, constantly stressing that she was in no way to blame for having believed him to be guilty. John Merton, with his forensic expertise, had made sure that there had been no other possible interpretation of the evidence.

Charlotte's face paled with the shock she was feeling.

'I'm afraid there's more,' said Steven. 'Perhaps you'd like a brandy? A glass of water?'

Charlotte shook her head. 'Tell me,' she said, blowing her nose and then crumpling the tissue in her clenched right fist as she straightened her back and looked Steven in the eye.

Steven told her that Little had AIDS and how he'd got it. He watched her fall apart before his eyes.

'Oh my God,' she gasped. 'This is all my fault. I should have believed in him in spite of... I should have known there had been some kind of a mix-up and put up a fight for him. I let him down when he needed me most...'

Steven continued trying to assure her that she had nothing to be ashamed of although he could see that it was a losing battle. He could only hope that at least some of what he was saying was getting through. He took a deep breath and continued, 'The man who did this to David wasn't content with ruining his life,' he said. 'He wanted to do the same to yours. I know this man as John Merton...but you knew him as John Mission.'

Charlotte remained silent for fully half a minute. She seemed stunned, but once she had taken on board what Steven was saying, he could see her take some comfort from the fact that she had to a certain extent shared her ex-husband's suffering.

'He set out to get both of you,' said Steven.

Charlotte hung her head and said quietly, 'It all makes sense now, the accidental meeting, the charming manners, the attentiveness, the sympathy and understanding. I was completely taken in. I thought he was such a...sensitive man.'

'He's a clever, scheming psychopath,' said Steven.

'That would explain the change,' said Charlotte with a rueful shake of the head. 'Once he had cheated me out of my money he treated me like dirt and enjoyed it. He got pleasure from humiliating me. He actually smiled when he was hitting me as if he was enjoying some kind of private joke.'

'The police need your help to find this man,' said Steven.

'I haven't seen him in years,' said Charlotte. 'I can't think what possible help I could be.'

'Maybe not but perhaps we could talk some things through if you feel up to it?' said Steven.

'Of course,' said Charlotte although she seemed far from comfortable with the idea.

'I understand from your father that Mission told you he was some kind of businessman with premises up north.'

'He said he was a computer graphics expert. His company made promotional material for other companies, films, advertising material, websites, that sort of thing.'

'You never visited the company?'

Charlotte shook her head and said, 'Never. He said that there was no point as he was looking for premises down here. He'd be moving as soon as the bank had agreed to the loan.'

'That's what he told you he needed the house for? The one you bought but put in his name?'

Charlotte nodded. 'Fool that I was.'

'Did he ever say where his premises were up north?'

'He said that they were in the middle of the North Yorkshire moors. They needed absolute quiet when they were making films.'

I'll bet, thought Steven. 'Did he ever mention a name? Some place it was near perhaps?'

'Not exactly,' said Charlotte. 'Just that it was in the middle of nowhere but I once heard him talking on the phone in his study. He told whoever he was speaking to that he would see them at The Abbey on Monday.'

'The Abbey? Nothing else?'

''Fraid not.'

'Well, it's a start,' said Steven.

'I'm sorry I couldn't be more help,' said Charlotte.

'You've been wonderful in the circumstances and I'm very grateful to you,' said Steven. 'I'm sorry I had to be the bearer of such shocking news but if it's any comfort, your folks already know.'

'It is,' said Charlotte. 'Thank you for being so thoughtful.'

Steven phoned Sci-Med as soon as he got back to the car.

'You're kidding! There must be a million places all over the country called "The Abbey",' said the duty officer.

'You are looking for one in the middle of the North Yorkshire moors,' said Steven. 'It may be registered as the business address of a firm concerned with making promotional material for other companies. Films and websites and the like.'

'Glossy lies,' murmured the man as he made notes. 'I'll do my best and call you back.'

Steven called McClintock to tell him the state of play.

'Not much to go on,' said McClintock. 'Want me to contact the Yorkshire Police and ask them?'

'Sci-Med's on the case,' said Steven.

Steven drove back to London feeling a sense of relief that Charlotte Little had now been told. She had taken it well although he suspected that all the implications of the news had not yet got through to her. The next few days were going to be extremely unpleasant when the press started to camp out on her doorstep.

It was eleven thirty when the phone rang. The duty man at Sci-Med said, 'It's about your enquiry this afternoon.'

'You're working late,' said Steven, recognising the same voice he had spoken to earlier.

'I like to see things through,' said the man. 'I didn't come up with any place called "The Abbey" in Yorkshire that wasn't a pub or a tea room.'

'It was a tall order,' said Steven. 'But thanks for trying.'

'I did however, come up with a place called Friars Gate Abbey,' said the duty man. It's in the middle of the moors and it's registered to a Belgian company called Cine Bruges. They make PR films.'

'Well done,' murmured Steven approvingly. 'You are a star.'

The man gave Steven details of the location of Friars Gate Abbey and asked if there was anything else he needed.

'Not right now, I'll go up there in the morning and take a look at the place.'

'Do you want us to inform the Yorkshire Police that you'll be on their patch?'

'No need for that,' said Steven. 'I'll contact them directly if the place looks interesting.'

'Thought you might say that,' said the man. 'I've got the number for them in case you need to use it.'

Steven punched the number into his mobile phone memory as the man read it out. 'You think of everything,' he said. 'Who needs a wife when I've got Sci-Med?'

'You don't even have to take me out,' said the duty officer.

Steven was on the road by six in the morning. After some thought he had decided not to go straight to The Abbey. The story of Little's innocence was due to break in the morning papers and if Friars Gate was really Merton's place then a fair amount of activity or even panic might be predicted. His plan now was to reach the general area by lunchtime and approach it on foot.

He had dressed for the task, wearing camouflage gear and lightweight combat boots suitable for fell walking. He had packed a small rucksack containing what he thought he might be likely to need. This included Carl Zeiss binoculars and a Canon camera equipped with a telephoto lens. He was also carrying a hand-held GPS navigation unit that would enable him to establish his exact position on the moors to within a few yards thanks to signals from several satellites. He would use this to navigate and record his approach to the abbey, for which he had the grid reference thanks to a late night session with the on-line Ordnance Survey map of the area. He had also packed bottled water and a few energy bars in case he was there for some time. He made sure that his mobile phone was fully charged before setting out.

From the map he knew that there was only one access road to Friars Gate Abbey. It was a single-track road stretching for some four miles across open moorland. Leaving his vehicle anywhere along the route would be bound to attract attention so he decided to abandon it well before the turn-off from the B road and take the remainder on foot. He didn't have a heavy pack to carry so he was counting on being able to cover the distance in under an hour.

There were times on the way north when it seemed that rain was likely – not a cheering prospect for a trip across open country on foot – but a west wind kept the clouds on the move and the sky was still relatively bright when Steven eventually found a secluded place to leave the car. He hid it behind a clump of fir trees about thirty metres back from the road.

There hadn't been much traffic on the road up to the turn-off but he had passed a couple of large four-wheel-drive vehicles travelling in the other direction. They had caught his attention because they weren't the usual workaday Land Rovers used by farmers. They were Toyota Land Cruisers, fairly new and heavy on polished chrome – the type of vehicle used by the well-heeled to pull themselves out of the suburbs in the morning, or more relevantly, by film and TV crews to move their equipment around. It made him fear that Merton had already been spooked into a move.

Steven checked his location on the GPS and punched in the coordinates for the Abbey. He didn't actually need such sophisticated help at the moment because weather conditions were good but he wanted the machine to remember the route he was taking so that he could retrace it should a mist come down later or if he had to return in darkness.

The terrain wasn't flat – more a wild, undulating plain with low hillocks and rocky gullies and ditches to negotiate. Steven found it hard going but enjoyed the challenge to his fitness. It had been a while since he had been put to the test. With a mile still to go to the Abbey, he finally took a break and a drink of water while he got his breath back.

There was a hillock to his left which he reckoned was about a hundred feet high so he decided to climb it and see if he could see the Abbey. He'd also be able to see the lie of the land ahead and plan his final approach. He crawled up the last ten yards to the crest of the hill on his belly so that he wouldn't suddenly appear on the skyline. It seemed unlikely that anyone at the Abbey would be keeping a lookout but old habits died hard and being over-cautious was always better than taking anything for granted.

Steven found that he had a view of the Abbey. Using the Zeiss glasses he could see that the tower and main building of the Abbey were now ruins but that various out-buildings to the right of the main structure had been restored using similar stone and were obviously in use. He determined that he should make his approach from the left where the ground was hillier and would offer him more cover than the right, which was almost flat for four hundred metres.

Twenty minutes later Steven was in position. He was about a hundred metres from the ruins of the Abbey, lying in a small gully between gorse bushes where he had a clear view of the east side of the buildings that were in use. He had a good view of the single-track approach road so that he was in an ideal position to monitor comings and goings should there be any. There were lights on inside one of the buildings so he kept his glasses trained on the windows.

The room he was looking at appeared to be an office but the two male figures he could see inside seemed to be moving around rather a lot. After a few minutes it became obvious that they were packing things into boxes on the floor as if preparing to move out. Steven was excited at this prospect and what he thought might be the reason behind it although, once again, he had to concede that he might already be too late.

The two men disappeared from sight and after a few minutes Steven heard car doors being slammed and an engine starting up. He didn't see the vehicle until it had come round from behind the building and emerged through an arch to join the track across the moors. It was a white, unlettered Ford van. At this point the driver, a young man in his twenties, paused to wave to someone at the window. Steven's view was obscured by the van until it moved off and then he was able to get a good look at who was standing there. He focused the glasses and had no doubt at all that he was looking at John Merton.

'Well, well, well,' muttered Steven as he reached into his rucksack to bring out his mobile phone. 'Got you!'

He was about to hit the send button on his phone for the Yorkshire Police number he'd been given when he noticed with dismay that there was no signal. Hoping that this was because he was down in a gully, he moved back a few metres and crawled up to higher ground. There was still no signal at all.

Steven cursed but had to admit that this was probably not that surprising. The phone companies didn't spend money erecting masts in the middle of nowhere where there were no customers to use them: he was probably two or three miles from picking up a signal. As he stuffed the phone back in his bag he remembered suggesting once to Sci-Med that they equip their people with satellite phones, which would not be dependent on ground antennae, but budget considerations had won the day. He now had to decide whether to retreat and call in the police or make an arrest himself.

There was no reason to believe that Merton was armed but on the other hand, he could not be sure that he wasn't. He could not even be sure that Merton was the only person in the building, although there had been no sign of anyone else in the last hour. It seemed increasingly likely that the two Land Cruisers that he'd seen earlier had in fact come from the Abbey and had been staff moving out with their gear.

Steven decided against heroics. He owed it to Jenny not to take any unnecessary risks. He would return to his car along the narrow single-track road that he had been reluctant to drive along. This would be quicker than the cross-country route and would also afford him a view of any vehicle using the road. He felt confident that the sound of an approaching engine would alert him in time so he could move off the road and hide until it had passed while getting its number to pass on to the police.

Steven was preparing to move off when he heard a door bang and he dropped down again to train the glasses on the Abbey. Merton was outside and he was moving backwards while he reeled off cable from a drum he was carrying between both hands. He stopped every so often to make some sort of connection on the ground before moving off again. Steven was in no doubt that he was wiring up a series of explosive or incendiary charges before leaving. Why he was doing this could only mean one thing. There was something to hide inside.

Chapter Twenty-Two

Steven knew now that he would have to try and stop Merton. He abandoned his plan to head back to the car and looked for the best way to tackle him. While there was a chance that he was armed it was important that he keep the element of surprise on his side. He couldn't hope to cover the clear ground between him and the ruins while Merton was still in view so he would wait until he had moved out of sight. Steven watched him pause to make two further connections before moving behind the office building he had originally emerged from.

Steven sprinted across the open ground in a crouching run, his heart in his mouth until he found cover in the shadow of the old stone tower where he knelt for a moment to consider his next move. He heard a door bang again and reckoned that Merton must have gone back inside. He peeked out to make sure the coast was clear before making another dash, which, this time, took him up to the end wall of the office building. He saw with relief that there were no windows in the gable end so he was safe again for the time being. There was a dark blue Range Rover sitting there and it was full of black equipment boxes. Steven took a moment to write down the registration number before moving slowly up to the end of the gable. He planned to crawl on his belly along the base of the back wall to reach the door where he would burst in and tackle Merton.

Lying flat on the ground, he used his elbows to push himself just clear of the gable end wall so that he could look along the back wall. All he saw however, was a pair of shoes. They were pointing towards him and about a metre from his face. Steven looked up and saw John Merton, standing there, pointing a gun down at him. Merton used the barrel of the gun to gesture up at the ruins of the tower. Steven looked up and saw the CCTV camera pointing down at him. He cursed himself for having overlooked the possibility.

'Who the fuck are you?' said Merton.

'I'm Steven Dunbar. I'm here to arrest you for offences

connected with the false imprisonment of David Little,' said Steven.

'The fuck you are,' said Merton calmly. 'Well, always nice to put a face to the voice. So you're the guy who got Ronnie Lee shitting his pants, the bozo who's been causing us all the trouble.'

'Put down the gun,' said Steven.

'I'm hardly likely to do that now, am I?' said Merton. 'Let's be adult about this. Get up, turn around and place your hands on the wall.'

Steven did as he was told while Merton searched him for weapons.

'Be sensible, Merton. The police are already on their way.'

'Christ, Dunbar, does Ealing Comedy write your scripts? You'll be telling me next that I won't get away with it. Move!'

Merton prodded the gun into Steven's back and he moved off in the direction that the gun dictated. Merton seemed so calm that he didn't bother coming out with any more clichés.

'It's only right that a good-looking chap like you should join the ladies,' said Merton.

'What's that supposed to mean?' said Steven.

'Just my little joke,' said Merton.

They came to a flight of stone stairs leading down to a heavy cellar door and Merton paused to fumble in his pocket for the key. It was not only obvious to Steven that Merton was going to lock him up in there but that the cellar would almost certainly become his tomb because of the charges that Merton had been laying. When they went off he would either be buried under tons of rubble or burnt alive in a firestorm.

Steven felt like a lamb being led to the slaughter. He told himself that he couldn't just meekly step into his grave but the odds were hopelessly stacked against him. Merton gestured that he go down the steps and he did so but when he reached the bottom he suddenly turned and lunged at him. He managed to reach Merton's arm just as he saw the flash from the muzzle of the gun. It was the last thing he saw before his senses left him.

The sound of the Land Rover's engine revving woke Steven and for a moment he thought the sound was inside his head, such was the headache that welcomed him back to consciousness. He put his hand up gingerly to the left side of his head and through the sticky, matted mess he found there he could feel a groove running from just above his left eyebrow to the top of his forehead. Merton's bullet had not penetrated his skull but it had left its calling card. A few degrees different and Jenny would already have been an orphan.

The fact that Merton was leaving suddenly brought home to Steven where he was and what was about to happen. Panic threatened to take over from pain and its message was clear and simple. If he didn't get out of here, he was going to die. Adrenaline flooded through him but his first scrambled attempt at getting to his feet failed. He lost his balance and fell heavily to the floor again where he remained on all fours, breathing hard and fighting feelings of nausea. He looked up at the one window in the wall above him and saw that there was no glass in it but it was heavily barred.

He pulled himself across the floor, fighting dizziness all the way until he reached the door and could examine it at close quarters. It had to be at least six inches thick and the heavy lock was in good condition. The fact that he could see the outside through the large keyhole when he knelt in front of it told him that the key had not been left in the lock.

Steven rested his cheek against the door for a moment, knowing that even if he had the strength to put his shoulder to it, the most likely outcome would be a broken collarbone. He turned and looked at his surroundings in the light that was coming in through the barred window. He had no idea what the original use for the cellar had been when monks had been at the Abbey but in more recent times it had been used for storing gardening tools and equipment. Most of it looked as if it hadn't been used in many years. The tools were rusty and covered in cobwebs and the writing on several of the bags of what he supposed was fertiliser or weedkiller had almost faded away to nothing.

There was an old wooden bench with an ancient paraffin primus stove sitting on it along with bits and pieces for making tea – a heavy black kettle that would have been at home in a Victorian kitchen, a rusty tea caddy, a couple of tarnished spoons and a half-full sugar bag that had once been white but was now parchment yellow.

A muffled explosion outside made him stop breathing in anticipation but there was no after-blast and no sound of crashing masonry. Merton had set incendiary devices rather than explosives. As if to confirm this, a searing wave of heat came in through the window and made him screw up his eyes. When it abated he continued examining his surroundings. The ceiling was solid stone. The floor was covered in stone flagging and there were three extra stones propped up against the wall under the window, not that being able to stand on them and get up to the barred window would be much help.

Steven revisited his earlier fear that this cellar would be his tomb and found little comfort in being proved right. He did however, see the irony of a British tomb having tea-making equipment in it whereas an Egyptian one would have provided a more expansive spread for the journey into the afterlife. Another explosion and the sound of fire taking hold told him that his own journey must be imminent.

Although his stomach was knotted with fear, Steven took out the notebook that he'd noted down the registration number of Merton's car in and tore out a clean page in order to write a last note to Jenny. By the orange glow that was coming in from outside, he addressed the note to Miss Jenny Dunbar at Sue and Peter's address in Glenvane. In it he told her that he loved her very much and hoped that in time she would forgive him for not being there for her but he felt sure that she would grow up into a young lady that her Daddy and Mummy would be very proud of.

With tears mingling with the sweat and blood on his face, Steven looked around for something to put the note in, something that would protect it from the fire and allow it to survive to be found one day by someone who would deliver it. His eyes fell on the tea caddy and he lurched across the floor to empty out the tea, which had long ago turned to dust. He put the note inside and replaced the lid but then realised that the tin was so flimsy that it probably wouldn't be up to the job. Supporting himself with a hand against the wall, he moved unsteadily around the cellar looking for some safe place to put it. The temperature seemed to be rising by the second. He stumbled when the floor beneath him seemed to give way, then found that he was standing on bare earth. The flagstones under the window weren't extra stones. They were part of the floor that had been lifted.

A fantasy of being able to tunnel his way out quickly gave way to cold reality. Even though there was an old spade in the corner, he would have to dig down at least six feet and then out for three before coming up for six again but at least he could bury the tin in the earth here. He knelt down and started scooping earth away with his bare hands as sweat dripped from his face into the hole. To his surprise he found that the earth was quite soft and he made good progress until he hit something that at first he thought was a flexible pipe. He gripped it and pulled hard until it seemed to come away at one end. It wasn't a pipe. It was soft and it had a hand on the end of it.

Steven recoiled in horror as he realised that he was in the process of unearthing a body lying in a shallow grave. Some of the flesh had come away in his hand when he had pulled the arm and he scraped his palm against the wall in an effort to free himself from the horror of it. Although badly decaying, he could see that the hand was a woman's. It was small and slim and still had two rings on it. He realised now what Merton had meant by 'joining the ladies'. This must be where the bodies of the snuff film girls had been buried.

Steven pushed the arm back down into the hole in the earth, feeling more of the rotting flesh peel away as he did so and having to fight the bones of the girl's hand, which seemed to have other ideas about being buried again. Finally he placed the tea caddy in the hole and scooped earth on top. He tamped the surface down with his knees and then crawled to the opposite corner of the room where he threw up until his stomach was empty. The flow of sweat from his brow was stinging the open wound in his head and the pain inside it was reaching crescendo pitch as he retched and blinked back tears of anger, fear and frustration.

Another wave of heat followed in the wake of yet another explosion and the air inside the cellar momentarily became too hot to breathe. Steven looked to the side to avoid the bright orange glare at the window and his gaze fell on the old sacks. The bright light had made the contents label on one of them just legible: it contained sodium chlorate.

Three thoughts came to him in rapid succession. One, sodium chlorate was a very effective weedkiller; two, it was a very strong oxidising agent that made any fire infinitely worse by feeding the flames pure oxygen and three, it could be explosive when mixed with certain other compounds. One of these compounds was sugar...

Steven's heart missed a beat as he looked at the bag sitting on the bench. He might well be deluding himself but he believed that he had the makings of an elementary bomb. He grabbed at the sugar bag and found that the contents had congealed into a solid lump. He slammed it repeatedly down on the bench to break the lump and then ground the smaller lumps feverishly with the heel of his hand until it looked more like granular sugar. He had to keep clearing the sweat from his eyes, trying at the same time to avoid it falling into the sugar. When he had generated a respectable pile, he tore at the sodium chlorate sack to get at its contents, praying that it was old enough to have avoided the modern requirement for a fire retardant to be added to it.

What he needed now was some kind of hollow pipe in which to confine the explosive mix, otherwise it would just flare up and he would have constructed an incendiary device. Talk about coals to Newcastle... He also needed to decide what he was going to do with his bomb. The walls and door were so thick that any blast big enough to breach them would almost certainly kill him...but that might be preferable to being burnt alive, he concluded. He would at least go down fighting.

Steven could not find any hollow pipe or tubing. He was almost at his wits' end, when he saw the possibility that a hollow-tined garden fork held. The tines on the end were in effect hollow metal tubes although they were very small compared to what he had in mind. But he suddenly saw that being that size meant that he could insert one of them into the keyhole on the door!

The temperature in the cellar was now almost unbearable but he set to work with a vengeance, twisting and bending one of the tines until it finally gave way. He closed off one end of it by hammering it flat with the edge of the old spade and then bending it over the edge of the bench to form a seal. He mixed sodium chlorate and sugar in an approximate 2:1 ratio and packed it tightly into the tube by pushing it down with the blunt end of his biro pen until it was full.

He had to take more care with the sealing of this end. He couldn't hammer it for fear of creating a spark, which could easily result in his arm being blown off. He put the tube on the floor and used his right foot to press the blade of the spade down on its end, slowly directing all his weight down on to it until it closed.

There was one more thing to do. He had to create a small hole in the side of the tube in order to ignite the device. He didn't have his rucksack with him in the cellar – Merton must have taken that away – but he hadn't bothered to empty his pockets so he still had his Swiss army knife. He used the spike to work a small hole in the side of the tube, nearer to one end than the other so that he could still see it once it was in position in the keyhole. He moved the spike very slowly when he felt it was just about to penetrate the metal and suddenly it was through.

It was done. He was holding his one chance at life in the hollow if his hand but there was little time to ponder that. He knelt down in front of the door and slid the tube into the keyhole, turning it so that he could just see the hole in its side. What he needed now was a spark and that was easier said than done, despite the world outside the door being full of crackling fire and flame. He needed a spark right next to the tiny hole in the side of the tube.

Steven took off his shirt and ripped it into shreds. He fashioned some of the pieces into a long cord-like strand, which would reach from the keyhole down to the floor, and then rubbed sodium chlorate into it before pushing one end lightly into the keyhole. He laid a trail of sodium chlorate, starting where the cord touched the floor and stretching across the floor into the far corner of the cellar. He knelt down and repeatedly struck the blade of the spade against the stone flagging until the rust and corrosion on the end of it was ground away to expose bright metal. The blows now created a small shower of sparks every time that metal hit stone.

On the third strike Steven's fears that the sodium chlorate must have had fire retardant added to it after all disappeared in a blinding flash as the chlorate ignited and the flame raced across the floor and up into the keyhole. The blast that followed threw Steven against the wall and deafened him momentarily but when the smoke cleared he could see that the door was swinging free. Its lock had been blown clean off.

The blast had also created a small gap in the fire outside but Steven knew that this would only be a momentary respite. He dragged himself across the floor as quickly as he could, his head pounding and coughing as the smoke invaded his lungs, but the pain and discomfort was as nothing when viewed against the fact that he was now free. He dragged himself up the steps and tried getting to his feet to run but was only partially successful. He had to be satisfied with a combination of running, stumbling, crawling and finally rolling across the grass in front of the old tower until he was far enough away from the fire to feel safe.

As he looked back, a great belch of flame and smoke spewed out from the cellar where he'd been imprisoned as the flames reached the sacks of sodium chlorate. As he thought about what might have been, Steven was forced to look up as something caught his eye. The great east wall of the old ruined tower was moving. As if in slow motion, it leaned more and more to the right, until finally it gave way and crashed down on to the roof of the cellar, burying it completely under hundreds of tons of rubble.

The buildings used by Cine Bruges had already been reduced to roofless stone shells containing little more than smoking piles of ash but Merton's scorched earth plan to destroy all evidence would be of no avail, thought Steven, because he had survived and he knew where the bodies were buried. It would take a bulldozer and many men with shovels some days to recover them but it could and would be done. Forensic science would see to it that a man who had abused it so badly would be brought to justice by it.

With a heavy heart, Steven looked at the road stretching over the moors and knew that he had more than four miles to go before he could alert anyone. In his present physical condition this represented as big a challenge as he'd ever faced. He'd be covering a great deal of the ground on his hands and knees because of the dizziness that still plagued him whenever he tried to stand up.

'Well, my son...' he murmured as he reached the start of the single-track road, 'as Chairman Mao once said...a journey of ten thousand miles...begins with but a single step.' He had barely taken ten when it started to rain.

At first he found the rain refreshing. It felt cool after the heat of the fire and the water helped wash the mess of blood, sweat and earth from his face. He was very thirsty so he drank rainwater from pools that formed in holes in the road as the rain persisted. It tasted of mud but that didn't matter.

After fifteen minutes however, he began to feel cold and started shivering. Four miles was beginning to seem like a journey to the ends of the earth. He hadn't felt this bad physically since his early training days with the paras in the Welsh mountains when, having completed a particularly arduous exercise and reaching the end – as he had thought – an NCO had simply said, 'Very good, Dunbar, let's do it all again, shall we?'

Steven looked at his watch. He had trouble focusing but when he finally managed he saw that nearly an hour had gone by and he had covered less than a mile. He sank down on all fours and stared at the ground while rainwater dripped off his nose and chin. He was in trouble. The basic survival gear he had been carrying had all been in his rucksack and God knows what had happened to that.

He was concussed, soaked through and very cold. Night was falling and the temperature with it. He was close to complete exhaustion but still had a long way to go. He concentrated hard on one single thought. He had to keep moving. If he gave in and lost consciousness it was odds on he would never wake up. He would have escaped fire to die of hypothermia.

As time went by he tried to aid progress by singing dirty songs at the top of his voice. He had never been very good at remembering song lyrics so the lines tended to get mixed up – if not made up – as he went along. He was making a rhymeless mess of 'The Ball of Kirriemuir', when he saw two lights coming towards him. At first he peered through the rain at them on all fours, not sure if he was hallucinating, but then he heard the engine. He stood up unsteadily in the middle of the road waving his arms above his head and making largely unintelligible noises until the police Land Rover came to a halt.

'Not very well equipped for walking on the moors, are we sir?'

Steven managed a silly grin before passing out.

Later, in hospital, he discovered that the pilot of a light aircraft had reported seeing a large fire on the moors and the police had been sent to investigate. The officers had summoned a rescue helicopter which had taken Steven to hospital and possibly saved his life by avoiding any delay. He in turn was able to furnish the police with the registration number of Merton's car and Merton was stopped and arrested at Dover some four hours later. Steven was discharged from hospital two days later and returned to London, none the worse for his ordeal, the local police having recovered his car for him. He called John Macmillan as soon as he got back.

'You know, Dunbar, you're the reason our health service is in such a perilous state. You're never out of hospital. You're a tremendous drain on our resources, you know.'

'I'll try to be more careful in future,' said Steven. He liked John Macmillan but, at times, he found his sense of humour about as amusing as a heart attack.

'Seriously, you did a fine job.'

'Thanks,' said Steven.

'I've warned Miss Roberts you'll probably be wanting a few days off and quite right too.'

'Two weeks,' said Steven flatly. 'I'm having two weeks off.'

'Well, if you feel you must,' said Macmillan.

Steven rang off. He called his sister-in-law in Dumfriesshire and asked if it would be all right for him to come up and stay for a bit. 'I need to get away.'

'Mission accomplished?' asked Sue.

'All over,' said Steven.

POSTSCRIPT

The bodies of all three girls featured in the snuff videos were recovered from the ruins of Friars Gate Abbey some ten days later and both Merton and Verdi were charged with their murder. Several other people were charged with being accomplice to the crimes. Merton was also charged with the murder of Ronald Lee.

Charlotte Grant and her daughters visited David Little in hospital in Edinburgh and were reconciled. Charlotte continued to visit Little until he died some three months later from AIDS-related meningitis. It was Little's wish that any money arising from his compensation claim against Lothian and Borders Police go to her and their daughters.

The HIV test on Tracy Manson's blood proved negative.